SAVED

The Saved Series

LORHAINNE ECKHART

www.LorhainneEckhart.com

All rights reserved. No part of this book may be reproduced in any form by any electronic or mechanical means including photocopying, recording, or information storage and retrieval without permission in writing from the author.

Saved Copyright © 2013 Lorhainne Ekelund
Originally titled The Captain's Lady Copyright © 2008 Lorhainne Ekelund, All Rights Reserved
Saved Paperback Copyright © 2017 Lorhainne Ekelund
Editor: Talia Leduc

All rights reserved.
ISBN-13: 978-1978406360
ISBN-10: 1978406363

Give feedback on the book at:
lorhainneeckhart@hotmail.com

Twitter: @LEckhart
Facebook: AuthorLorhainneEckhart

Printed in the U.S.A

"A Passionate Tale of Love during the Iraq War."

—*"Eckhart knocks one out of the park with this great story."*

RT Book Reviews

—*"Taken! Okay you had me at the first page"*

Katy M.

—*"God Bless our Military Men! It takes a horrible, but real tragedy and shows how love can be a true healer. We need more men like the Captain!!"*

Reviewer, Spring Hale

"Growing up I had dreams that one day I'd fall in love, get married and start a family. Then one night I was taken. But I survived, I escaped and I was saved. Eric didn't see me as damaged. He didn't see my baby as a monster. He protected me, he kept me safe ... he saved me."

The Saved Series

SAVED: "Growing up I had dreams that one day I'd fall in love, get married and start a family. Then one night I was taken. But I survived, I escaped and I was saved. Eric didn't see me as damaged. He didn't see my baby as a monster. He protected me, he kept me safe ... he saved me."

In VANISHED, Abby has married the man of her dreams. He rescued her, and he's the father of her child. Everything should be perfect, but she begins to relive her nightmare from when she was taken... and one night she disappears, leaving her children alone in the dead of night, her husband on a military ship halfway around the world.

But when Eric arrives home and the search begins, there are two disturbing questions: Was someone in the house? And how is it possible for Abby to simply vanish?

In CAPTURED, Captain Eric Hamilton is now settled on base after giving up his first love, the sea, for his wife, Abby, and their children. He watches day in and day out as his friends are deployed, burning with an empty feeling as if life is passing him by—that is, until his friend Lieutenant Commander Joe Reed is captured while deployed in Iraq.

While his family is at home, helpless, Joe's life hangs in the balance, and Eric is forced to make a decision he swore he would never make again: Should he leave Abby and their children to go halfway around the world in search of a friend who may be dead?

Prologue

THURSDAY JUNE 19, 2004

The Northern Arabian Gulf

There was a point right at the break of dawn when darkness parted swiftly, much like a curtain drawn open making way for the coming day. On a typical morning, this was welcoming, a sign of a new journey to look forward to, but for Abby, today could very well be the last day of the rest of her life. She knew it, she felt it deep in her bones, but she also had hope.

As she watched the bright orange and yellow reflection at the edge of the water, she wondered if maybe today would be different—maybe today she had a chance, maybe today she'd finally make it. She'd come this far against all the odds, so she needed to hang on just a little longer. She rested her head against the stiff side of the rubber dinghy and shivered under the dark abaya, damp and sticky from her sweat. It was so humid, the air thick and heavy, that she struggled to breathe as she stared at the miles and miles of open water, still with nothing in sight. She probed her tongue gently to the side of her chapped, swollen lips. She was so thirsty she'd do anything for a cup of cool water. It was painful, horrible, being so thirsty, because that was all she could think of. Staring at miles of open water only tempted her. How long could she go without water before her body started breaking down? The dew clinging to the side of the dinghy glittered like a handful of diamonds, and, like a starved woman, she licked it with her tongue and gagged from the saltiness. She dropped her head to the side again.

She was so tired. She'd lived in fear for so long that it had become her constant companion, keeping her on her toes, awake in an instant, as if her soul knew it wasn't safe to sleep. As always, she felt it slice out of nowhere, the buzz that ripped through her, keeping her body and mind on the edge of sanity. She couldn't rest, even though she needed to. Abby peeked over the side, her eyes burning into the shadows, and she squinted, wondering if she was seeing things. Was he coming for her? Was that a boat on the horizon? She swiped her palms hard across her eyes and looked again, and for a minute she stopped breathing, moving, but she couldn't still the thudding of her heart. It had a mind of its own and pounded the walls of her chest so hard she thought her ribs would crack. She waited and blinked again.

"It's just water. Come on, get a grip." It hurt to speak, but she needed to believe it. Those brave words weren't convincing her at all, though, because it was only a matter of time—and time was not on her side—until he found her. She knew he'd search to the ends of the earth to find her. He never let go of what was his, ever.

Abby had no idea where she was, as she was floating with no paddle. Being at the complete mercy of the waves meant just one more thing she had no control of. Each minute the sun rose higher, she could feel the heat climb.

Out here it was so intense, rising as though someone had switched on a furnace, slowly building until it scraped her lungs as she struggled for each breath from air that was so thick and humid that she'd swear a knife would have trouble slicing through it. Out of nowhere, a sharp gust of wind blew from the northwest, rocking the dinghy up and over the waves, and for a moment the breeze was unexpected and welcome. Then the dinghy bounced faster, higher, moving through the water and crashing down as the water slapped the sides, awakening her again to the reminder that she wasn't safe. Any minute, he could appear on the horizon, and there was nowhere to hide. Maybe that was why she didn't think as she dropped down and curled onto her side. A burning jab poked her ribs, shooting shards of fire through her, and she bit on her lip, drawing blood as she fought not to scream. "Don't move, stay still and you'll be fine," she whispered to herself and panted out huffs of air. Even though there was no one to hear her breathing, she was still afraid.

The skill she had survived on, always being on guard, wouldn't let her stay still, so she peeked up again, her shoulders taut and wound so tightly her head was starting to throb. She couldn't think about tomorrow, only now, this moment, because her future wasn't anything tangible—it was a speck of ashes that could disintegrate in an instant. She stroked her dry, chapped hands over her rounded belly and blinked back tears. Their future right now wasn't looking like a mother and child's should. It should have been a magical time when Abby dreamed of holding her tiny baby, whispering her love while planning their future. But what possible future could her child have?

If it was a boy, maybe. For a girl, there was no hope. Not here. Not now. "One day at a time, Abby." She stripped off the dark abaya and took in the pale blue cotton of her loose dress. The front was splattered with blood, and she couldn't remember if it was hers. If it wasn't... she might very well come to wish she were dead. Her body seemed to follow her mind, as it started shaking and couldn't stop. It had too much adrenaline, and she recognized that her fight or flight instinct had been all that was keeping her running for so long now. As she stared up at the blue sky, she wondered about the inevitable and whether she'd have the strength to jump in the water when the time came. Could she do it, allow the weight of the abaya to pull her under? Drowning herself would be better than the alternative, if she had the courage to do it, to end her life and her baby's, too.

"How will I ever survive this?" She ran her tongue over the swell of her bottom lip. It was split, and she tasted dried blood. "Ugh." She touched it with her fingers, and, pulling them back, she stared at the fresh blood. She pressed her fist to her mouth. "Shh," she whispered, but she was so tired she didn't think she could stay awake much longer. She had to stay awake, though, and keep watch, even though she didn't have a clue what she'd do if she spotted his boat. Her eyes ached, and she'd swear sand coated the whites of her eyes. When she shut them, the back of her lids scraped her eyes like broken glass. Closing them seemed almost worse, but her lids were becoming so heavy it hurt to keep them open, so she gave herself a minute, and then another, until warmth and a bright light surrounded her, and for one moment she felt peace. She breathed softly again, and again, until there was nothing more.

Chapter One

Alarms sounded and buzzed over and over, louder and louder. Footsteps pounded up the stairwells and ladders as emergency lights flashed in the passageways. The five-hundred-foot guided missile destroyer cut a wide path through the waters of the Northern Arabian Gulf, and the roar of the engines against the power of the water slapping and vibrating against the steel hull had his every instinct buzzing and ready to react in an instant. The speed of this ship could let them easily overtake their enemy. Captain Eric Hamilton braced his hand on the wall as he ducked his head, making his way onto the bridge of his ship, the USS Larsen. Hamilton took everything in as he moved, and his crew snapped to attention. He shouted, he commanded and ordered, and he didn't ever consider whether he'd hurt someone's feelings. This was the US Navy—he didn't coddle his crew. He expected loyalty, and his crew would do what he expected or they'd find themselves on the wrong side of a man whom many feared. Oddly, knowing how he was seen by his crew didn't bother him at all.

By the time he crossed the bridge, the hair on the back of his neck was poking up like sharp wires that sent a chill through him, a warning that kept him on his toes. It was a warning that had saved his butt time and again, a warning he lived by, and he swore he'd die before ever ignoring it. The crew were on edge, alert. He could always pick up the change in their voices. They shouted above the alarm that continued to buzz over and over, their eyes wide. With an instinctive reaction at the snap of his fingers, his crew jumped as one to respond. Eric could feel the adrenaline pumping from all of them. Everyone was at their stations. Even though the humidity was at an all-time high this early in the day, he knew the beads of sweat trailing down his back and soaking his shirt were from the unknown that they were racing into. This damn war around them kept him pumped and his adrenaline surging like a shot of high caffeine. He lived for it and couldn't imagine any other way. To him, this was normal. He loved this, life and death, power in his hands and under his command.

By the time he reached the windows spanning the width of the bridge, binoculars had been thrust into his hand. Up until now, he hadn't said one word, as his officers knew their parts and their roles.

"Captain, there's a raft just off the starboard side. Can't tell from here whether there's anyone or anything on it." Lieutenant Commander Joe Reed approached from behind. The man was Eric's good friend and the current XO, executive officer, on this deployment.

He didn't need to turn as he raised the binoculars and zeroed in on a black dinghy that appeared empty at first sight as it rocked up and over the waves. For a minute, he felt sick, and his pulse pounded harder and faster still when the thought of the USS Cole bombing popped into his head. No, it couldn't be that again. He wouldn't let it happen.

He glanced at Joe beside him. "What the hell are we walking into?"

Joe shook his head. He was never one to talk out of turn or to guess. Joe was Eric's right-hand man and more often than not was the voice of reason among him and the crew—and just about everyone else.

Eric raised the binoculars again and stared at the black dinghy. He didn't know what he expected.

"We have no reports of a ship in distress in the area, Captain," announced the communications officer.

Eric squinted, thinking. "What about fishing boats?" he snapped.

"No, sir, no reports."

Looking once more at his first officer, he dreaded what he needed to do. "Send out a rescue team to check it out," he barked as he handed the binoculars off to one of the crew members and strode off the bridge, digging into each step, heading directly to the ship's launch. The crew hurried around him, feet pounding the deck. All of them knew their roles, what was expected, and there was no hesitation. Joe jogged up beside him, and they watched as the small rigid hull of the rescue boat, with its team aboard, splashed into the water and sped off toward the dinghy.

His heartbeat was slamming now inside his chest, so hard and loud that he glanced at Joe, wondering whether he could hear the thump that roared in his ears. Beads of sweat ran down his brow, his back, under his arms, and his short-sleeved tan shirt was sticking to his back.

At times, he hated not knowing, because he had to think quickly and respond just as fast. His work was a love-hate relationship, a marriage really, the only one he'd ever have and could never live without.

"So what do you think?" Joe leaned on the rail, staring after the team, and then raised a pair of binoculars to his eyes.

"I don't know, dammit. Wish I did. I don't like sending them out like this. Maybe I should have gone."

"Not your job, Captain. You stay with the ship. Let the men do what they need to. They're trained for this; you're not."

Eric knew Joe was right, but he'd never admit it. He didn't like being told what to do by anyone, including Joe. This attitude was a challenge in the Navy and had gotten Eric into more hot water than he could measure. "Maybe so, but I'm still the captain here," he stated, mainly because he would always have the last word, and he reached over and snatched the binoculars from Joe.

"You're right, Captain, you are, which is why you need to be leading the crew on the ship."

This time, Eric just glared at Joe. Joe should have stepped back, apologized, but when Eric turned away, he also knew Joe was the only one who never reacted in fear to him, the only one who could get away with speaking to him that way. He raised the binoculars again and studied, helpless from this distance, as the three-man team approached, then secured the dinghy. If something went wrong, there was nothing he could do from here. This part he really hated, as he waited with unease squeezing his gut tighter and tension knotting its way across his shoulders until they were so tight his neck began to throb.

The radio Joe held crackled: "There's someone in here, a woman, and she's in pretty bad shape."

Eric didn't know what to think, but he also knew that with the hostile situation in the area, this could be anything. He took the radio from Joe. "If it's a body, don't touch it. Could be booby trapped. Check for wires or anything unusual."

The line clicked with static. "Captain, she's still breathing. Don't see anything on her," the deep voice hissed. Eric nodded to Joe and handed him the radio.

"Bring her back. Secure the dinghy," Joe ordered.

Eric watched the scene as two crewmen lifted a body. He knew the other crewmen were searching for wires or traps, anything unusual. Then they moved her into the small, rigid rescue boat.

"Someone get Lieutenant Saunders on deck," Eric shouted to a crew member. At this moment, he was grateful Lieutenant Larry Saunders, the senior medical officer from the Vincent Carrier, was still aboard and had scheduled this week for training with the onboard hospital corpsmen. "Bring her up!"

Crewmen shouted and worked as another team went down to secure the dinghy. The crew hovered, hands reached out, and the team lowered a woman to the deck. Eric watched and studied, but he couldn't believe what he was seeing. She was soaked and wearing a heavy blue sack-like dress. She was barefoot, and she was an absolute mess. A blanket was draped over her.

"Move back. Let me through!" Lieutenant Saunders was a solid man, about average height. He was much shorter than Eric, who was well over six feet. Larry pushed through all the testosterone, crowding around the young woman. "I need some room here," he said loudly as he squatted down beside her.

"Everyone who doesn't need to be here, move back to your stations," Joe shouted at the crew, who were pushing and crowding around the woman.

Eric moved closer and stood just behind Larry, studying her face. She appeared young, and her eyes were closed, but it was the bruises on her face, her lip swollen and split, with dried blood crusting over it, that made him angry.

She tossed her head to the side. "Ohhh," she mumbled. Her eyelids strained as she struggled to open them.

"Easy, take it easy." Larry rested his hand on her shoulder as she moved her head to the side, blinking, her eyes staring up at the sky and then locking on to Eric. For a minute, she blinked and lifted her arm. When she tried to move, she screamed.

"Don't move. I need a stretcher in here!" Larry shouted.

Eric watched her and her wide eyes, which appeared confused and panicked, as if she couldn't make sense of anything.

"W-where am I?" Her voice was dry and raspy, and then she coughed.

"Get her some water," Eric said to a sailor. He squatted beside her as the doctor moved away. Eric brushed his hand over her shoulder when she stared at him with wild-eyed fear from the most amazing baby blue eyes he'd ever seen. "It's going to be okay."

"Are you an angel?" she said.

What the hell? That was not what he expected. Before he could answer, a cocky voice called out from the group of sailors behind him, "Oh, that's one he's definitely not been called before." Several others chuckled, and Eric was tempted to kick some ass, though he couldn't quite figure out which one of them had said it.

He draped his other arm over his knee and swiped a hand over his jaw, feeling the bristled hair that he still needed to shave. "I'm Captain Hamilton with the US Navy. You're aboard my ship, the USS Larsen. We recovered your dinghy off the starboard bow. Can you tell us where you came from, what you're doing out here?"

She squinted eyes that appeared so fragile. "The US Navy, the United States Navy?" she asked in a way that was almost pleading as tears spilled and traced a path down the sides of her face. She swiped at them and then her nose. "Really, am I safe?"

Eric glanced over his shoulder at Joe, who was also watching her. It was obvious he didn't know what to make of her, either. Her hand was shaking, so Eric took it in his to try to calm her down, and she held on tight in a way that surprised him for someone in such bad shape. "What's your name, honey?"

"Abby. My name is Abby," she said, her voice dry and raspy.

"Abby, you're safe and under the protection of the US Navy."

"Captain, please." Lieutenant Saunders moved to her other side. "Abby, take a drink of water." He lifted her head, pressed the cup to her lips. She tried to guzzle it, but Larry pulled it away before she downed it all. "Slowwww now. Nice and easy, or you'll be sick."

"How long was I out there?" She sounded breathless.

"I was hoping you could tell me," Eric said, as she kept seeking him out, her eyes on him. She shook her head, and creases appeared between her brows. She was obviously thinking. Eric watched her eyes, studying her to see if this was a trick, a game.

"I don't know. I couldn't stay awake." Her voice shook, and she struggled to pull away, to sit up.

"Whoa, don't move." Eric held her shoulders down. "No, just lie still, Abby."

"Abby, I need to get you down and take a look at you, make sure you're okay," Larry said. Two crewmen set a litter beside the captain, and he moved back and watched as they lifted Abby and the blanket fell away. He heard the outburst behind him, but that was nothing compared to his own shock as he stared at the swollen belly of a very pregnant woman.

"Where are you taking me?" Her eyes widened with fear as the two sailors adjusted straps to secure her to the litter. She was starting to fight them, and she was very afraid.

Eric moved in and put his face close to hers. "Abby, I need you to look at me. Calm down, you're safe. Right now, we're strapping you to the litter to move you to sickbay. I need you to tell me you understand. We're *not* going to hurt you."

She searched his eyes with hers, which appeared so vulnerable and innocent, yet at the same time, it was as if she'd seen everything horrible in the world. She grabbed his shirt and fisted her hand in the damp cotton. He didn't try to pry her hand away. He covered it with his and held it against him, pressing his other hand over her forehead and smoothing back her hair.

"Take a breath. Slow down. Let it out slowly. Come on. That's it, good girl," he said. She shivered and then glanced at the doctor on the other side. "Keep your eyes on me, Abby."

She was absolutely petrified, like a woman on the edge, and for the first time he felt as if he needed to talk her down. She stared at him, watched him, blinked, and breathed out hard again and again until he felt her hand relax on him.

"Good girl. Okay, let's move her," he said as he stood up, slipping her hand from his shirt and nodding to the crewmen. They lifted her, and she started to sob. "Abby, I'm right behind you." Eric tried to get her to look at him and smiled to calm her so she didn't become hysterical. She was obviously afraid of something. Eric touched her foot so she would know he was there and walked beside the stretcher until they reached the hatch.

"Everyone, back to your stations. Show's over," Joe ordered the remaining crew.

"What do you make of this, Doc?"

"Don't know. I think someone worked her over. By the looks of her dehydration and being pregnant… well, let me have a look, but just know we're not equipped for this, not here."

"Got it, Doc." Eric fell in beside the doctor behind the stretcher, boots clanging on the metal floor of the passageway.

"Watch your side," one of the crewmen shouted to the other as they turned and lifted the stretcher through the hatch and into sickbay.

Eric gestured for the doctor to hang back so Abby couldn't hear. "Just say the word, and we fly her off."

Larry paused and studied the captain for a second. His freckled face and round cheeks showed his worry, and he inclined his head, then stepped into sickbay. "Put her on the table," he ordered as Abby was unstrapped and moved. The two young sailors stared at Abby, who was lying helpless.

"That'll be all." Eric dismissed them so they wouldn't linger anymore.

"Lieutenant Lynn, we need some help here," Larry said.

Todd Lynn brushed past the sailors as he stepped into sickbay. He was another tall, good-looking sailor, with a million-dollar smile all the ladies swooned for when he walked into a room. "What happened to her?" he asked.

"She was found in a dinghy like this. Let's get these wet clothes off her."

Lynn used a pair of scissors to cut off the clothes and dumped them in a heap on the floor, covering her with a sheet. Eric didn't turn away, although watching her naked before a sheet was draped over her had rocked him. She was staring at him again, as if she was reaching out for his hands.

They checked her blood pressure, and the doctor was talking to her. "Where does it hurt, Abby? She's got heavy bruising around her ribs. Let's roll her on her side."

"Here. It hurts here." She touched her chest and moaned when they turned her.

"I know it hurts, Abby." The doctor placed the stethoscope in his ears and listened as he leaned down. "Take a deep breath, Abby. Hold it." She scrunched her face. Larry pulled the stethoscope off and looped it around his neck. "Sounds rough. What's the BP?"

"One-fifty over eighty-five. Got some bruising here, too, around her kidneys." Eric walked around and saw the purplish bruising on her back. "Some older bruising here, too."

"I'm going to check your ribs here." Larry slid his hand under her breast and probed.

"Ohhh!" she cried out.

"I know, Abby." Larry lifted his chin and glanced at the captain. "Bruised for sure. Hasn't punctured the lungs, though. The ribs may be cracked. Abby, how far along are you in your pregnancy?"

Abby was still on her side, but she turned her head and watched Eric. "I'm not sure. I think I have another three weeks."

"Okay, on your back again."

They rolled her, and the lieutenant placed a towel over

her breast and pulled the sheet down. The doctor probed her swollen belly. "When was the last time you felt the baby move, Abby?"

She shook her head. She scrunched her eyes and searched out Eric again. "I don't know. It's been a while. Is my baby okay?"

"Right now I just want you to stay calm. I'm checking everything out, and in a minute we're going to listen to the baby's heart."

Larry raised his head and gave the captain a look. Eric knew he was worried and wanted to make sure the lady stayed calm, so he stepped around the doctor and stood beside Abby.

"Let the doc finish his exam before you panic, okay? Just relax."

She reached for his hand. Hers was so tiny and frail, and his big one all but swallowed it. She turned her head into his hand, brushing the side of it. He tried to picture her without the bruises, and to him she was stunning, innocent, but what the hell was she doing in the middle of a war zone?

"Abby, I'm going to listen to the baby's heartbeat. This may be a little cold." The doctor placed the stethoscope in a few spots on her belly and listened, then stared at his watch as if counting. "The baby sounds good. That's a good thing, Abby." He draped the stethoscope around his neck and patted her arm.

She started crying, and she wouldn't let go of Eric's hand. "I'm sorry." She suddenly looked so embarrassed as she dropped her eyes and then started to pull her hand away, helplessly wiping her tears and her nose.

"Abby, here's a Kleenex." Lynn handed her a couple, and she took them and blew her nose.

"Captain, can I have a word?" the doc asked as he tucked the stethoscope back into a secured drawer.

Eric watched Abby as she lay there, looking so lost and vulnerable, her eyes puffy and red from tears. At the same time, she was doing everything she could to hide her humiliation. He'd seen rock bottom many times, and he recognized when someone was there.

"Abby, I'll be right back. I need to have a word with the doc." He settled his hand on her bare shoulder and didn't miss the way she reached out to him with her eyes but then blinked away as if ashamed. Just from that touch, he sensed her fear, her need, and a shadow of something that had her pulling away. "Lieutenant, check her vitals again in a few minutes and see if you can get some juice into her."

"Yes, sir."

"So, Doc, tell me: What's the verdict?"

Larry squeezed the back of his neck, wincing. "She's extremely dehydrated, and I suspect her body is breaking down protein, which is a problem for the baby. However, once we get her hydrated and some food into her, we should see an improvement." He crossed his arms and glanced at Abby and the lieutenant, who was checking her vitals again, and rubbed his jaw before crossing his arms, turning away. "I am concerned about the bruised ribs. She's tender, but I don't think they're broken or cracked. Her right ankle is slightly swollen, and from the looks of things, I would say there's a mild sprain. It's definitely not broken."

Eric was a tall man, so he could easily watch Abby as Lieutenant Saunders described her injuries. He just couldn't reconcile in his mind how someone could beat a woman—how could someone drive their fists into a pregnant woman? But he'd seen so much ugliness that he'd given up trying to understand the monsters that lurked inside so many, leading them to do the most despicably evil things.

"Whoever did this didn't just slap her around; they used their fists on her," Saunders said. "She was beaten pretty bad, and it doesn't appear to be the first time, either. The baby appears to be okay. Heartbeat's strong. It looks like her face got the worst of it."

A dark purple bruise outlined her cheek and slightly swollen left eye, the same collage of colors as her jaw. Her lips were dry and cracked, the right side of her lower lip swollen with dried blood. Eric had to force himself to look away as he felt a rage building inside him. *Just let me find who did this and give me five minutes alone with the bastard. I'll make him pay.*

Eric was far from a saint. He'd been called the devil himself by some, and he loved a good fight. He'd been in so many, driving his fists into lowlife scum, but it went against everything he believed in to hit a woman. Any man that would stoop so low was not a man, in his book. Men were supposed to love and protect women, not use them as punching bags. He had seen it so many times, drunken sailors assaulting their girlfriends, and, as he thought about it, he still remembered the last time he'd tried to step in, back in homeport, while stationed in San Diego.

One night, he had been at the local pub with a few friends. They'd met for a night of pool to catch up and shoot the shit when a young, arrogant sailor started arguing with a young girl and then slapped her across the face. One minute, Eric was holding his pool cue. The next, he'd snapped it in half across that sailor, yanked him by the collar, and pounded his face with two sharp jabs until he'd fallen to the floor, blood trickling from his mouth. Eric still couldn't believe how that girl had reacted. She'd screamed and dropped to her knees, hovering over that useless prick and pleading with Eric to leave him alone because it was her fault—she'd provoked him.

The sailor had pushed her away, and Eric's friends grabbed his arms and said, "Let's go."

Eric had jerked away and jabbed his finger in the girl's face, shouting, "Get yourself together! What's wrong with you, letting some guy knock you around? Don't you have any self-respect?" He then leaned down at the sailor, who tried to get up until he met the monster who stared back at him, and Eric became aware of the sailor's reaction to him: His eyes widened, and fear or perhaps recognition of who Eric was obviously cut through his drunkenness. "If I ever catch you hitting another woman again, I will take you out back and kick the crap out of you... you piece of shit!"

He didn't know why thinking back on that incident bothered him so, but he also couldn't shake it off. As he stared at Abby, he didn't like one bit of where his thoughts were going. Would she defend whoever did this to her, too? "I need to talk to her, find out what the hell she was doing in the middle of a war zone dressed as she was, in the shape she's in," Eric snapped.

The doctor shook his head. "Captain, let me get her stabilized, calmed down, rehydrated, get some food into her. I know you need to speak with her."

"When?"

"Couple of hours."

Eric walked around the doctor. Abby's eyes were drooping.

"Captain, we need to get her moved to one of the beds." Lieutenant Lynn glanced at the doc, waiting for his okay. "Abby, they're going to move you." Eric touched her arm, which was resting on the table beside her.

She turned her face up to Eric and then started to get up.

"I'll be back in a few hours to check on you," Eric said.

"You want to talk to me, don't you?" she asked bravely, but the tremble in her voice betrayed the strength she was trying to exude. He had to wonder, really, who and what she was.

"I do. But don't worry about that now. The doc and lieutenant here are going to get you settled." He watched her, and she said nothing, staring at him unforgivingly until she dropped her gaze.

"Okay," she said. The response seemed so unreal and artificial, as if she had said it because he expected it.

Eric turned to leave, but something stopped him, making him turn and watch. What was he looking for? He didn't know what it was, but there was something about her that bothered him, something that wasn't right.

"Abby, we're going to help you sit up. Let's take it slow, and then we'll get you settled in a bunk," Larry said.

Eric listened to the doctor as he and the lieutenant helped her sit, and she glanced over at him in the doorway as if she knew he was standing there watching her. There was a sharp connection between them in that second that had his heart thudding as if the earth had just opened up and something was reaching up to pull him under. Despite every dark, murderous, ugly thing he'd seen and been part of and tasted over the years, this situation absolutely rocked him.

It was he who turned away, he who shut the door and stood in the empty passageway and breathed to clear his head and shift his thoughts to where they needed to be: here, commanding this ship and meeting with Joe, the one man he could trust to do some serious digging and unravel the mystery surrounding this woman's dramatic arrival.

Chapter Two

There was something about that first step through the steel gray of the hatch and onto the deck, at least for Eric. His body was jolted by the power and sway beneath his feet, seeing the open water, feeling the spray from the sea. The scent of the humid salty air sharpened his mind as the destroyer once again resumed patrol in the Gulf. He realized everything moved on, continued, as there was no time to sit and absorb what had happened. It was life, and he dealt with it. He did what he had to do and moved on. He based his entire existence of walking, sleeping, and running his ship on that motto, except this time he'd been shaken by the sight of Abby and plagued by her haunting blue eyes. They seemed to reach inside him as though he'd been plugged into a socket, and it rattled him. He should have just walked away, let the doctor deal with her, and then gotten her off this ship. His ship. He didn't want or need any distractions. Drama was all around them, and they didn't need any more, because something this close to home was a distraction none of them could afford.

Two uniformed crewmen were at the boat launch. One

was kneeling, running his hands over the dark rubber, while the other was complaining and swearing over the shit job they'd been assigned. Normally, Eric would have kicked their asses and reprimanded them, but he found himself just watching. They had no idea he was even standing there. It was amazing sometimes, the difference in the crew, how they responded when he wasn't around.

The pounding of feet behind Eric had him turning to Joe, who strode confidently toward him.

"Captain," he said in his deep voice, and the two sailors jumped. The tall, lanky one flushed. "You two find anything?" Joe asked the sailors as he gripped his hands behind his back.

"No, nothing on here, nothing in it," the sailor still on his knees muttered.

"Pack it up, then," Joe ordered. "You three, back to your stations," he shouted at the midshipmen who lingered aft of the launch. Joe was a tall man, with light brown hair, and, as he'd heard whispered by many of the female crew, there was something attractive about his boyish smile, restrained charm, and the way he genuinely cared about everyone. The fact was that half the female crew were panting after him and ogling him when he wasn't looking. Eric knew Joe had the women dropping all around him, but Joe wasn't the flirt some men were in the Navy. He always made it known he was happily married to his first love. Maybe that was why women still pursued him, because of his loyalty.

Eric had known Joe for years—he was the only person Eric would trust with his life. "So what did you find out?" Eric asked as he stared back out at the miles of open water.

"Not much. There's been no report of any boats in the area: fishing, downed ship, nothing," Joe said as he shook his head. "It's as if she just appeared out of nowhere, which is damn odd considering where we are. You talk to her yet?"

Eric pressed his lips together and shook his head. "No. Later."

"How is she?"

"Pretty banged up. Someone did a number on her, bruised ribs, dehydrated. Doc's getting some food into her now. I'll go back in a couple of hours."

"What about the baby?"

Eric squeezed the back of his neck with his hand. He'd never thought of having kids, because he'd need a woman for that. And with his track record... it would be a one-way road to heartbreak. He wasn't going there. But being faced with a young pregnant woman on his ship was doing all kinds of things to his peace of mind and taking him places he didn't want to go. He certainly didn't want to admit to anyone how much it bothered him. "Doc said its heartbeat is strong. He doesn't want her getting worked up, wants her to rest for a few hours."

Joe squinted and shook his head. "Captain, do you want me to get a hold of Intel, make some inquiries about her?"

Even in the humidity, Eric felt a bone-deep chill creep up his spine. Just the mention of Intel brought a wave of uneasiness that sat like a lead ball in his stomach. At times, they were the scum of the earth, feeding you what they wanted you to know, sharing only what was needed. The last time they intercepted a boatload of guns, one of his crew had been shot. Apparently, whoever had been getting the Intel wanted it to happen, but they had conveniently forgotten to inform him. He hated their games and how they operated. He stared down at the swell of waters below and then glanced aft to view the wake of the ship before squeezing the rail with his large hand. "Make it un-official,

Joe. Anti-official. I want to talk to Abby first and get a better sense of the situation. There's something about this that just isn't right."

Joe stood right beside him. He had heard before that they looked so much alike, that could have been brothers, although Eric was a little taller and not as nice. He'd been accused by his commanding officers of being too damn hard to read. Personally, he considered that a compliment. Obviously, so had others in the Navy, the ones that mattered, because he'd been promoted faster in rank than others his age. Being a success in the Navy was his biggest and only accomplishment at thirty-five. For Eric, it was his entire life, his only reason to live, and this gave him peace when out on deployment. On land, he became depressed. He often wondered if this was because he had no one waiting for him on shore.

So why was he so distracted by Abby? He shook his head and muttered out loud, "Damn, you know she was worked over pretty good. Blond, blue-eyed pretty young lady. Did you notice?"

Joe crossed his arms and shot a piercing look at a few curious crewmen who were passing by and listening in on what they were saying. "You two got nothing to do? 'Cause I'll find you something!" he shouted at them. They started, came to attention, and then scurried away through the hatch. "Yeah, I noticed. What are you thinking?"

"Look at where we are. I'm hoping I'm wrong...." Eric stopped mid-sentence, as he didn't want to put into words what happened to women in these parts.

"Yeah, but if you're not, find out from her, and then we'll need to contact the embassy."

Eric turned around and leaned his back against the rail. More and more crew lingered and appeared on deck. "Let's finish this in my office," he said. He didn't wait for

Joe to respond, knowing his friend would follow his lead. Joe closed the cabin door behind them as Eric took a seat behind his polished dark wood desk. The leather chair swooshed when he leaned back, and he rubbed the scratchy bristles of his cheeks and groaned. He still needed to shave. He looked a mess, and he was one to always be neat and tidy, something he insisted from everyone aboard his ship. Even their uniforms had to look shipshape.

His cabin was large and spacious, with dark carpeting and a separate sleeping room. Across from his desk on the other side of the room were a sofa and chair where they held their daily department head meetings. The furnishings resembled those that could be found in the office of a CEO of a large corporation. The ship was new, and all the amenities were first rate. It was deceiving: every time he walked into this cabin, he could almost believe he was entering a five-star hotel, until he looked up and was rudely jolted back to reality by the gray pipes and cables weaving their way above his head. He had laughed the first time he saw them.

Joe slid out the upholstered chair on the other side of the desk.

Eric wanted to kick himself for being this rattled. "So what are we going to do about her?" he said, only realizing after the fact that he had spoken out loud.

"Can you fly her off to the Vincent Carrier? Or maybe to Bahrain?"

Eric dropped his feet to the ground hard and leaned forward, resting his arms on his extremely neat desk. "You know what? Right now, she stays here. We'll decide where she goes after I talk to her and the doctor," he snapped a little too sharply.

"What's really bothering you about this? Eric, I've known you a long time, and I woulda thought you'd transfer her off or have me make the arrangements. You've never given a woman a second glance." Joe was one to cut through the bullshit, and he was right: Eric was not one to become emotionally attached.

"Shit, Joe, I'm not a monster, but evidently whoever did this to her is."

"You're right, but we don't know the whole story."

Eric didn't expect that from Joe. He stared at his friend, wondering just what the hell was up with him.

"You should let me talk to her, Captain. Let me handle this." Joe was really pushing it.

Eric thought about it, but there was something different about Abby. Something had happened, and he didn't feel right letting anyone else talk to her. "No." He jabbed a finger at Joe. "What I want you to do is notify command, let them know where we found Abby. Tell them that as soon as we have more details, we'll fill them in. Then get in touch with some of your contacts in Bahrain, unofficially, of course. I want to know what boats were in the area. Have them pull up satellite, and find out any information about this girl, if anyone saw her aboard the boat and with whom. You and I both know what she most likely escaped from, but I want all the cold, hard facts, because right at this point, we really don't know anything." Raising his steely hand, palm forward, he stopped Joe from leaving his chair. "One more thing." He gestured toward the door. "Make sure the crew keeps away from her. I don't want some curious young sailor wandering down there, so post a guard outside the door of sickbay. Make it clear to the crew that she's off limits."

"As you say, Captain. How soon are you planning on getting her off this ship?"

This time, Eric wouldn't look at his XO but swiveled

his chair around and stared out the port window. "That'll be all."

Joe hesitated and gave a chuckle that was something between a groan and irritation as he slid back his chair and stood. For a moment, Eric could feel his gaze burning into him as if he wasn't finished and had something more to say. "I've know you for a lot of years, Eric, and you're a damn hard man for anyone to read, except me. I know you better than you think I do." Then he left, leaving the door open behind him.

Eric wondered for a moment what he meant by that. Sometimes, it bothered him that he shared everything with Joe. As pointed out by a staff shrink, he didn't like to share anything about himself: his abandonment issues, his lack of commitment. This was a window into his soul that any enemy could use to overpower him, get in his head and fuck with him. Even friends with loose lips said and shared things without thinking, and Eric swore he didn't want anyone getting that close to him again. But as his thoughts swept over to Abby, a vulnerable picture of her all alone, a flow of questions surrounding her arrival consumed him.

Where did you come from? Who are you? What happened to you? Who did this to you? They were dark and ugly, the thoughts that crept in, from the possibility of terrorist links, to a trap, to this girl being tortured and abused willingly just to fool them. But that last part didn't feel right. Eric knew deep down that his first thought had to be to his crew and ship's safety, and his responsibilities wouldn't let him dismiss the thought that this whole thing could be a trick. The enemy did absolutely despicable things and wasn't above using a pregnant woman.

Eric picked up the pile of reports awaiting his approval on the side of his desk. He flipped impatiently through the pages of information. Sighing in frustration, he threw them down while silently wanting to kick his own ass for this distraction, because Eric didn't allow distractions to ever interfere with his duties. He lived and breathed this ship and the Navy. He did what he needed to do and pushed away everything and anything that pulled him from his duties. He often frowned on the married sailors who'd get a letter or email from home and lose it over something they couldn't deal with from this distance, yet here he was, doing the same thing. He shook his head, disgusted with himself and swearing under his breath. He tossed the papers in his drawer, pushed away from the desk, and marched out determined to have his little chat with Abby right away.

Chapter Three
─────────────

A tall guard was posted outside sickbay. If there was one thing about Joe, it was that he followed through on everything asked of him without hesitation. Eric nodded to the guard as he opened the door and stepped in, closing it behind him. His hand was still pressed against the steel door when he caught sight of her. For a moment, he found it difficult to breathe as he gazed over her lying on her side, propped with pillows nestled in one of the bunks. A sheet had been draped over her, but her slim bare legs were sticking out, her right palm resting easily on the mattress. White tape covered the entire surface of her small hand, which held the plastic tube of an IV in place. Her eyes were closed, and she was an absolute picture of innocence and peace. A picture of life-to-be. He hated to wake her and found that watching her this way stirred something in him. He felt something jam his throat until it felt oddly uncomfortable. He'd closed himself off for years, and he'd been able to control his caring for anyone at a snap of his fingers. He could shut it down and move on, and he'd had to do that. It was too painful to care, to want, and then have it all ripped away from him and told he was worthless.

He didn't know what made him look over, but he spied Gail Carruthers, second-class hospital corpsman, on duty. There was something about her that set his teeth on edge. There were those he tolerated and could put out of his mind, but her, she seemed to know which of his buttons to push, and it was as if she went out of her way to stomp on each one. In fact, she was doing it again now. She wasn't acknowledging him and his authority as captain. She stared at him as if he wasn't there. What the hell? He took a step toward her and was about to strip her down and yell at her, reminding her of her position, when he glanced at Abby again and paused mid-step. He couldn't and didn't want to upset her. "Where's Lieutenant Saunders?" he growled at the short, mousy-looking corpsman.

"He went down to the wardroom. He'll be back at twelve hundred," she replied, as if he was just another sailor and no one of importance.

The captain blinked again and gripped his hands behind his back, and it took a minute to register in his head that she hadn't addressed him as required. Why, this arrogant chit was about to get the dressing down she so deserved! He stared down on her, watching her feeling the fires of hell burning inside him, and he knew he had to be shooting sparks from his eyes. He felt his face burn and cheek twitch as he contained what he really wanted to do-throttle her! He knew he was close to the edge, and any sailor who had pushed him to this point would have wished to be anywhere other than forced to stand in front of him, sweating and pissing his pants.

But this woman didn't seem to care. She stared at him, then glanced away as if he was keeping her from something important, as if he were an insect. His mind was spinning as he tried to remember who she was and what the hell she was doing on his ship. He growled inside, but it was a rustle from Abby that had him hesitate and stifle the urge to toss this corpsman in the brig until she learned some respect. "How's Abby?" He gestured toward Abby with a subtle tilt of his head.

"Her vitals are stable, sir." Carruthers had one of those obnoxious screechy voices, and she spoke a little too loudly, considering where she was.

Abby moaned and rustled again. What the hell was the matter with this corpsman? He gestured to Abby and stung Gail with a look that implied she should know better. Then, in a clipped tone, he said, "That will be all, Carruthers." He was proud of himself for the restraint he'd shown, but instead of this woman getting the hell out, which would have been the smartest thing to do, she stood there as if confused.

Of course, that was the final straw. "Get the hell out of here!" he shouted, jabbing his finger toward the door. This time, he got the reaction he expected. She fled out the door, and he had to hold himself back from wanting to race after her and unleash the monster inside of him, putting the fear of God into her, after he noticed Abby was watching him.

He stopped everything as warmth shimmered in her startling blue eyes for him. She was a mess, an absolutely gorgeous mess. Her long hair was so dirty and tangled, but it was lovely to him. "Hi, how are you feeling?" He approached her, and her smile was so subtle and warm and blinding that it was doing all kinds of horrible things to him. He felt as if he'd just been lit up, as if fireworks were going off inside him, and he felt flustered, which pissed him off. Get it together, man! He wanted to shout at himself. He stared at her as she tried to pull the sheet over her leg.

"Better. Thank you... for everything." Her face tinged pink, and he could feel the instant his eyebrows raised. When had he ever faced a woman who blushed? He watched as she pressed her hand to the bed and started to sit up before wincing. She pressed her hand to her ribs and sucked in a breath.

Eric placed his hand on her shoulder over the faded hospital gown she now wore. "No, don't move," he said in a near whisper. "I didn't mean to wake you..."

Voices outside the door had him turning just as it popped open, and Lieutenant Larry Saunders stepped in, carrying a food tray. He hesitated. Eric was quite aware he was early, and the doctor was most likely surprised. The guard didn't hesitate or linger, pulling the door closed behind the doc.

"Captain." Larry placed the tray on the silver counter along the wall. Eric watched the doc take a sweeping glance around the sick bay. Larry frowned. "I seem to be missing a corpsman," he said in a low voice.

"Actually, Doc, I dismissed your corpsman." Eric felt the reins of his temper fray again as he thought about Carruthers and how it had seemed she was challenging him.

Larry only nodded and then faced Abby. "I see you're awake. I brought you some lunch. Eat. It's not Sunday champagne brunch at the Ritz, but it's edible." Larry strode beside the bed and slid his hand under her elbow and shoulder, supporting her while she sat up, sliding her legs over the side of the bed. "Captain, could you slide that table over here?" he asked, gesturing to the small brown table behind him. Eric slid it over in front of Abby, and Larry set the tray upon it.

"It smells good; I didn't realize how hungry I was," Abby said. This time, her voice sounded smooth and silky, but he could hear the traces of weariness in her tone. She glanced shyly up at the captain and, with shaky hands, tucked long locks of hair behind her ears. She tried to run her fingers through the knots in her tangled hair, pulling hard enough he thought she'd rip her hair out. She was so nervous of him.

"Eat your lunch, Abby. After you're done, I'm sure the doc here can get someone to scrounge up a brush for your hair, maybe a shower, too, so you can get cleaned up."

She glanced shyly again before immediately lowering her gaze as if she should know better. "Thank you, sir. That would be nice." She unrolled the napkin that surrounded the utensils and seemed to hesitate, as if she needed his permission to continue.

"Abby, you're a guest here. Please eat."

She nodded, her hands clasped together, and then lifted a spoon to her lips and sipped the dark broth.

"Doc, can I have a word please?" Eric asked. He didn't wait for a response as he crossed the room, just out of earshot, then crossed his arms and faced the doc. "Your corpsman is a problem you need to deal with."

"May I ask what she did, sir?"

"She's insubordinate. Refused to address me as her captain. I wonder if she has a lick of common sense in that brain of hers. Just what the hell is she doing here on my ship?"

The doc flinched and raised his eyebrow. "Sir, I will speak with her. But she's told me a few times that you make her nervous. She's quite uncomfortable around you. She, like most of the women on this ship, knows your views on women, sir." Larry was quick to add the last bit, then cleared his throat as if he'd said too much.

"My views on women? Would you care to elaborate, Lieutenant?" Eric spoke in a low voice, but he wondered if Abby had heard, as she seemed to visibly start, and her eyes flicked up to him for a brief second before dropping her gaze again. She continued spooning soup into her mouth.

"Oh, how you believe women don't belong here in the Navy but at home waiting for their husbands. How the man should be the head of the household, and a woman should do right to figure out her place, stop trying to fit into a pair of men's pants, pretending she's got a penis. You know, that Old World view that's gotten you into hot water time and again. What was it you said to that lieutenant that got you reprimanded from the colonel?"

Eric wanted to knock that smug look off Larry's face, because he remembered all too well, and so did Larry, what he'd said to that tight-ass game-playing bitch who he'd slept with a few times. She had been good in bed, with long, slim legs, but she'd wanted him and his position to launch her own career, and the first chance she got, she'd hopped into bed with the commander of the Neilson but forgot to mention it to Eric. Yeah, he'd called her out, almost spat in her face on base and in front of a few officers that women had only one role to play, and it was best done on their backs: having children, looking after them, and keeping their husbands' slippers warmed, leaving all the decision to the men so as not to clutter up their heads. She'd slapped his face, leaving her imprint, and he'd been ordered to apologize.

"Just deal with her, or I will," Eric snapped.

"Yes, Captain."

Eric gestured over the doc's shoulder. "How is she?"

"Actually, she's doing pretty good, considering what she's been through. Her blood pressure's stable. We've managed to get her rehydrated. Considering her advanced state of pregnancy, with those bruised ribs, she has to be extremely uncomfortable every time the baby kicks. Unfortunately, it'll cause her discomfort for a while yet."

Eric heard everything the doctor said, but he watched Abby as Larry spoke.

"Captain?" Larry cleared his throat.

"Anything else, Doc? Can she be moved?"

"She needs to rest for the next few days, stay off her ankle. You can't put her on a chopper yet. She's too far along, but she could be moved by boat stateside to the base hospital in Bahrain. She was worked over pretty good, Captain, so she needs to be monitored for a while yet."

"Before we move her, I want to talk to her. I'd like to have a word with her now."

"I just want to check her vitals, and then I'll let you speak with her."

"I'd like to speak with her alone, too, Doc."

Larry paused mid-step and gave a sharp nod. "Yes, Captain, but I feel I need to warn you. Best to take care and not get her worked up." Larry walked over to the steel counter along the wall beside the exam table. Unlatching a secured drawer, he pulled out a stethoscope, and he stepped closer when Eric gestured.

"The last thing I want to do is upset her. But I do need to talk to her. Please make sure Carruthers stays gone."

Larry nodded. Abby finished her lunch and set the spoon and bowl on the tray. She remained seated, dangling her feet. She appeared distracted as she rubbed her lower back.

"Abby, I want to check your vitals again. Did you get enough to eat?"

She nervously tucked her hair behind her ears. "Yes, thank you. It was more than enough." She smiled pleasantly, and Eric couldn't help thinking it was something she did because she thought it was expected. It had to be, because he could see, just watching her, how tightly wound she was. Anyone else in her condition would have been complaining and seeking comfort. She seemed to be holding all of it inside, but there would come a point that she'd snap.

Larry looped the stethoscope around his neck and then pulled the table back to help her slide around into bed. She tried to lie down, but he held her arm. "No, I need you to sit up this time." He gestured to the locker against the sidewall facing the door. "Captain, can you grab me a couple of extra pillows from in there?"

"Sure, Doc." Eric pulled out two pillows from the locker filled with bedding and other supplies. "Is this enough?"

"Yes, thanks." Larry positioned them behind her back for support.

Eric lingered by the door and then leaned against the counter as the doc listened to her heart and lungs, taking her blood pressure and temperature again and scribbling notes in a chart.

"I think we can probably remove this, too, Abby." Larry slid out the IV and covered the back of her hand with a bandage. "You're doing great, Abby, but I want you to get some rest, too."

Eric watched the warm smile Larry gave her. What it did was set his blood boiling to the point that he felt his temper simmering just below the surface. He wanted to grab the doc by the shirt collar and send him on his way. Just what the hell was the matter with him? He felt his muscles bunch his back, his shoulders, as they strained his shirt. "Hey, Doc, you want to wrap it up and move on out?"

The way the doctor glanced at him, he must have realized something, as he stashed his equipment in the secured drawers and strode to the door. "If you need me, sir, I'll be in the mess hall."

Eric said nothing as he crossed his arms and remained in his stance, the one he'd developed as he fought. Larry swallowed and then left, the door closing with a sharp click. When Eric faced Abby, he saw a woman who wasn't about to shrivel up and cry but who was watching and waiting for his move, a woman who would take what was handed to her and would most likely deal with it without one whimper or complaint. This rattled him completely and without question.

Chapter Four

Eric grabbed one of the steel-back chairs and slid it over beside the bed, lowering his large frame, all solid muscle, into the chair. He knew his size intimidated many, but he also knew he was many a woman's fantasy, as he'd been propositioned more times than he could count. The last thing he wanted to do to Abby was appear threatening in any way. He leaned forward and inclined his head, staring at doe-like eyes that were bluer than some of the cleanest blue seas in the tropical south. "Abby, it's time you tell me what happened."

Her face instantly paled, and again she lowered her head. Her tiny hands fisted into the thin white blanket tossed across her lap.

"It's okay, Abby. Whatever happened, you *can* tell me. Please trust me." He reached out and slid his hand over hers until she relaxed. She glanced at the door, and he wondered for a moment if she wanted to race out of there. What she did surprised him. She blinked a couple of times and pursed her lips, hardening her young face, and he watched and waited for her response.

"I'm from Seattle. I…" She stopped and cleared her throat roughly. "I was traveling Europe. I went to a nightclub in Paris, and on the way back to my hotel, two men grabbed me and I was sold to an Arab man. I escaped from his boat, and then you found me."

He was stunned by the lack of emotion in her voice, because there was no way a woman could be okay and so matter of fact after surviving that. He knew all too well that women didn't just reappear in Europe. The human trafficking ring was massive, high-powered, and the women who were bought and sold disappeared forever.

"Abby, I don't know what to say."

"Don't say anything. It is what it is. When can I go home?"

He was stunned. He had expected tears, a woman on the edge, as he slid his eyes over her rounded belly. He also expected that the sick, perverted man who'd bought her was also the father of her unborn child. He shuddered to think of how it had happened. "Do you have family in Seattle we can contact?"

She seemed to hesitate for a moment, as she stared hard at his hand, which still covered hers, until he pulled it away. Maybe his touch repulsed her—possibly all men repulsed her. When she answered finally, she looked at him with something haunting lurking like a shadow in her eyes. "No, not anymore."

There was definitely something there, but he didn't want to push too hard. He also had to realize she may have been suffering from Stockholm syndrome. This could have been some ploy to get her aboard his ship. "I need you to run through a few details, Abby, but first I need your full name."

"Abigail Carlton, Abby for short," she said.

He nodded and crossed his arms. "Tell me, how long

ago was it that you were taken from Paris? How long ago was it that you were sold?"

"It's been three hundred and twenty-two days since I was taken," she said matter-of-factly.

He'd seen prisoners of war and marines, sailors who'd been captured by the enemy and then released, and they had been a mess, so much so that many hadn't hesitated to put guns to their heads. Abby seemed so calm when she spoke, but it was her hand that gave her away, trembling so hard she grasped it with her other hand to stop the shaking and held it so hard he was sure she would leave a bruise.

"I know this is really hard, Abby. Can you tell me about the day you were taken, about who took you?" He wanted to reach out and put his hand over hers, but he worried that with what she'd been through, she may not welcome his touch. He could see her thinking and holding her jaw rigid as her eyes filled with tears, turning the whites of her eyes red. She cleared her throat roughly.

"I… I." She stumbled, and her voice cracked. A few seconds passed before she could continue. "I had arrived the day before in Paris. I decided to stop in at a nightclub close to the hotel. I had a drink, danced, and left a few hours later. When I walked out, I didn't know I'd been followed. At least, I think I was—it happened so fast. A car pulled up and squealed its tires. I was grabbed from behind by some man and forced into the car.

"I don't know where I was taken, but a hood was put over my head, and I was kept tied up with other women. It was five days of listening to that strange, unfamiliar language, Arabic. I know that now. Then I was told that I was a gift to a great man. Is that what you want to know, or do you want to know what he did to me? I'd never been with anyone, and he knew it. Apparently that increased my value. He owned me and could do anything to me."

"Who was he, this man who bought you?" Eric asked her, studying her face, wondering how she could keep talking without falling apart the way women always did. Hell, most of them cried over a hangnail.

She cleared her throat again. "Seyed Hossein was his name. It is his name… if he's still alive. He was cruel, and I was nothing but something for him to play with."

"How did you get away, Abby?"

This time, she looked directly at him. Tears popped up and streamed down the side of her face, not in a free-fall but a trickle. She didn't fall apart, speaking plainly. "Seyed came to the room where I was kept and said he was taking me out. I put on the abaya and veil I had been given, making sure I did everything right. I didn't want to make him angry, and he angered easily. We left, and I was in the backseat of a car that drove to a marina, and I followed him onto a boat."

"Do you know the name of the boat?" he asked as she brushed her hand roughly over her cheek and wiped away the tears.

She shook her head. "I don't know. It was dark out, and I was sent down below and sat on a narrow bunk. I was told not to move."

"That's okay. What happened next, Abby?"

"Seyed and the man who drove were arguing about something. I don't know what because I couldn't understand them. They were angry, though. Then I heard the engine start up, and the boat began to move." Abby's face took an edge as if she was trying to hide her discomfort. She pressed her fingers into her lower back and then leaned to the side, resting on one arm.

"You all right? Your back sore?"

"Yes, sorry. I didn't want to —"

He cut her off before she could finish, absolutely

furious because she was trying to hide all her pain. "For God's sake, Abby, if you're hurting, you've got to say something." Eric stood beside her and held his hand out. "May I?"

She gazed up, a bit startled, and then nodded. "Okay."

Eric sat beside her on the bed and rested one hand on her shoulder, sliding his other across her lower back and massaging the stiffness. "How does that feel?" he asked. She wouldn't look at him, but he could feel the tension in her muscles wound tightly, as if they were made of stiff wire that would snap before it would bend. He grabbed the extra pillows on her bed and plumped them higher. "Here, lean back against these. Hopefully that will feel better."

Abby slid back on the bed and rested against the stacked pillows. He saw her hesitate a second as though waiting for his permission to move.

"Abby, lie down, relax."

She nodded, her eyes cast downward, and leaned into the pillows. Then she turned on her side. "Is it all right if I lie this way?"

He couldn't believe she was asking him this. He felt his throat thicken for whatever had happened to her to break her down so. "Abby, I know I've said this, but you're safe here. You don't need to keep asking to be comfortable. You need to tell us if something hurts. *Okay?*"

She lifted her chin to look at him, but she was so uneasy, and she blushed a bright pink before nodding and then staring at her fidgeting hands. Eric still stood over her, and she lay there in front of him as if she expected him to stay there, but he couldn't do that to her, so he sat back down and leaned back, tilting his head to look at her face, a face that, once free of bruises, he had no doubt would be absolutely stunning.

"Abby, do you want to continue?"

"I suppose you want to know all the details." She didn't wait for him to respond; she just kept talking. "The boat was moving. I don't know for how long, as I was so tired I must have fallen asleep. I remember him shaking me awake, telling me to come up on deck. I followed him up in the darkness, seeing only a handful of stars in the sky. For some reason, at the time, I thought it must have been cloudy. Then I remember looking around for the other man, but he wasn't there. I was alone with Seyed, and even after everything I'd been through, there was something about being alone with him on a boat in the middle of nowhere that absolutely terrified me. Even in the darkness, I sensed this look in his eyes that sent an icy chill up my spine, as if someone was dumping icy water on me. It was horrible."

"So how did you get away?"

"I didn't plan it. It just sort of happened. I remember I couldn't breathe, and I did it without thinking. I removed the veil and abaya. It was so windy that my hair was all of sudden free and whipping around my face. I had to hold my hair back, but it was the most amazing feeling. I don't even remember looking at him. I just remember him yelling, and I was so scared because he was furious and shouting in Arabic. I didn't understand him, but I knew he was angry because I had taken off the veil. I didn't have time to put it back on. He grabbed me by the hair and struck me, knocking me down. I hit the deck so hard it knocked the wind out of me.

"He kept hitting me." Abby rested her hand over her bruised cheek. "He grabbed me by the front of my dress and lifted me and hit me again and again. He punched me so hard in my ribs that he knocked the breath out of me. I don't remember how I did it, but somehow I hit him with this long metal tubing I picked up off the deck, and I was standing over him...." Her eyes took on a faraway look, and she gasped for her next breath. The color faded from her cheeks. "He didn't move; he just lay there. There was some blood on the side of his head. Funny, for that time, it felt as if I was watching the whole thing happen to someone else. I don't even remember hitting him. When I looked down at him, I felt nothing. Does that make me a monster?"

He was stunned by her question. "Abby, when someone is trying to hurt you, you fight back with everything you've got. You don't ever let someone beat you."

"What if I killed him? Am I now a murderer?"

He watched her. It was as though she was trying to figure out how come to terms with something horrible and not understanding how to do it. "It makes you human, and you had every right. That's not murder, Abby; that's doing what you need to do to protect yourself."

She nodded again, her eyes meeting his. "I don't know how long I stood there, but when the pipe slipped out of my hand, it was the sound of it hitting the deck that knocked me out of my stupor. That was when I saw a dinghy tied to the back of the boat. I climbed into it, untied it, and drifted from the sailboat, praying it would move faster before he woke up, if he woke up. And then I prayed that I killed him. Isn't that horrible? Will I burn in hell for that?"

He couldn't let her keep thinking this way. Maybe that was why he reached out and cupped her chin with his large hand. "Look at me, Abby." He knew he sounded angry, but he couldn't help it, and he watched as she cautiously drew her eyes up to him. "He's the one who'll burn in hell. You deserve a medal. You did what you had to, and I want you to remember something: When someone tries to hurt you, you fight back with everything you've got. I'm proud of you for having the guts to defend yourself. You have no idea the number of women who don't fight back when a man knocks them around, and they aren't living the horrors that you were."

"So what happens now? What happens to me?"

He let go of her face. "Nothing for the next few days. You'll stay right here, under my protection. You said your home was in Seattle, and you have no family."

"I sold everything to travel Europe after my grandmother died. I put everything I didn't want to get rid of in storage. I wanted to figure out what to do next with my life."

"Okay, just one more thing, Abby. Why did he take you on the boat? What was he doing? Where were you going?"

"He owned me. He ordered me around. He didn't tell me what was happening. I don't know where we were going or what he was doing."

There was one thing Eric knew. This Seyed hadn't just been out for a midnight cruise. He was up to something, and, depending on who he was, Intel and the CIA would know all about him. This could give them an idea of whether there was some hidden danger or possible threat against one of the ships in the area. But why take Abby? What was her role to be? Eric wondered for a moment if there was more she wasn't saying, and he started to ask, but something held him back. "Abby, after you got away, do you remember how long you were out there on the dinghy?"

Abby frowned. Lines crinkled between her brows as she struggled to remember, shadows flashing across her eyes. "I think I saw the sun come up twice." Shaking her head in confusion, she added, "But I don't remember when you found me."

He decided to go ahead with the question that burned

in his throat. "Do you remember seeing any other boats out there, anything at all?"

"Not when I was on the boat. It was dark. On the dinghy, nothing. I just knew if he found me, he'd kill me." She said this as if it would be expected. She yawned and quickly stifled it. "I'm so sorry."

He did his best to hold on to his irritation, but he couldn't control the twitch in his cheek, and the last thing he wanted to do was set her on edge any more than she already was. Besides, he now realized he needed to do some checking into his own homework and then come back and talk again. "Abby, you're tired. I'll come back later. I'll send the doc back in, but get some rest."

"Sir, would you mind terribly if I used the bathroom?"

It was the first time ever that his mind blanked out, and he was at an absolute loss for words. He wondered for a moment if she'd been lying there in agony, needing to use the bathroom but stoically waiting for him to finish. He really didn't know what it was going to take to get her to relax, to speak up. Instead of saying anything, he leaned down and scooped her up in his arms, carrying her to the bathroom across the room. She didn't shriek when he opened the door with one hand, and her face was bright red when he deposited her beside the toilet. "Do you need any help?"

She wouldn't look at him. She opened her mouth to speak and closed it just as quickly, shaking her head instead.

He turned in the doorway, and he was disturbed by how she was visibly trembling. "Call me when you're done. I'll carry you back to bed." He stood outside the bathroom door and listened to the toilet flushing and the water running. He heard her stifle a cry. "Abby, are you all right?" He pounded on the door.

"Yes, I'm fine." The reply was strained.

"Can I come in? Are you done?"

"Yes, of course you can come in."

When he opened the door, the first thing he saw was her leaning against the sink, pale and shaking. "What's wrong?" He reached her side in two quick strides.

"I forgot about my ankle and put too much weight on it. I'm sorry. I didn't mean to make any noise."

"Abby, stop it," he barked. Her head jerked up, her deep blue eyes wide as those of a deer in headlights. He'd scared her, and that was the last thing he wanted to do. He scooped her up and carried her back to bed. "How do I make you understand you're safe here? Stop making yourself so damn uncomfortable because you're afraid to disturb anyone. Whatever happened to you, don't be scared *here*." He deposited her back on the bed and helped her settle in.

"Thank you, Captain," was all she said, but he could feel her stiffen even though he was no longer touching her.

"I'll be back later to see how you're doing." He didn't know why he did it when he reached down and smoothed back the stray wisps of hair that dangled in her face. "Remember what I said, Abby: You're safe here. If you're hungry, you say something. If you're scared, tell me. If you're hurting, you have to speak up. No one is going to hurt you here. I don't know how to make you believe it."

She was staring at him now, but for the life of him he couldn't figure out what was going on in her head. He let out a sigh because there was nothing more he could do here. His hand was on the door, and he was about to yank it open when she said, "Captain, could you do me a favor?" He turned around and faced her and was nearly undone by her eyes, swimming with a sheen of tears.

"Could you keep telling me I'm safe? I think if I hear

you tell me over and over, I'll start to believe it. I think I will."

The way she said it clogged Eric's throat to the point that he didn't think he could speak, so he looked up at the pipes that made up the ceiling until he knew his voice wouldn't crack. "I will, Abby, until you believe it. I swear it." Then he left, allowing the guard posted outside the door to shut it behind him.

Chapter Five

Larry Saunders made a point of avoiding conflict, but when facing a problem that could escalate into something bigger, he firmly believed in sitting down face to face to work it out. He was a diplomat, and he loved playing the role of peacemaker, searching for the good that existed in everyone. He truly believed that sometimes, with some people, he just had to dig deep to find it.

After asking several crewmen about Gail Carruthers' whereabouts, he was told to try the mess. Several of the enlisted moved over to let him pass. It never failed to amaze him that the majority of the personnel aboard looked like kids. This should not have been surprising, as so many of them were under twenty. He wondered about the captain and the officers dealing with these kids. At times, it was so much like high school.

Walking into the mess, he took a minute of searching over the heads of all the crew crowding the cafeteria-style seating before he spied Gail, seated with the other female enlisted. As he approached, he noticed their heads gathered close together and the serious conversation they were engaged in. One of the girls noticed him, and her eyes widened. She whispered something to the rest, and they all turned when he approached. Six women, all junior crew members whom he didn't recognize, gathered their trays when he stopped at the table. They then promptly stood and acknowledged him, saying, "Lieutenant." All except Gail.

"Carry on," he said.

"Yes, sir," each of them replied. All except Gail. She sat there as if she carried a dark cloud over her head. He didn't miss her oversight. It was a deliberate slap, obviously, and if this was what she had done with the captain, she should have been thanking him for not having her court-martialed. He took the seat across from her, and she gripped her tray and started to get up.

"Sit down; we need to have a chat," he said, holding his narrow hand up as he waved her back down. "And you will address me as your commanding officer, sailor."

Larry had a sudden feeling that she was going to ignore him. Then he saw her face tighten, and she slowly returned to her seat. When she finally looked over at him, he was a little taken back by the hostility blazing in those dull brown eyes.

"Tell me, please, what that was all about," he said, squinting in fury as he tilted his head towards the women hurrying to leave the mess hall.

The abrupt turn of her head scattered the unruly curls in her hair as she watched the retreating women with a defiant tilt in her chin. "Nothing, sir. I was just having lunch with my fellow crew members."

"Bullshit. I don't know what's going on with you, but when you enlist in the Navy, there are rules you follow, and I am not about to let some chit start an upheaval on this ship. Do I make myself clear?"

She flushed and looked away, and Larry was finding himself leaning towards the captain's way of thinking. Right now, he was finding it downright impossible to see anything likable about this girl. He wondered too for a second whether he could get away with giving her a good swift kick in the backside. Sometimes, someone with that kind of arrogant chip on the shoulder could only understand one thing.

"I want to know right now what happened with the captain in sickbay," Larry said.

A coolness manifested from Gail as she tensed, sitting up straight as if someone had pulled her by the scruff of the neck. She appeared to clamp her mouth shut, as if unwilling to part with one bit of her story.

"At ease, Carruthers. Please, let's speak freely."

She raised her bushy eyebrows and then frowned. "All right, sir. The captain obviously doesn't like me, and he makes no bones about it. I was just doing my job when he walked in and started questioning me about the patient. I told him how she was doing, and then, for no reason at all, he got mad and told me to get out. I did nothing wrong, sir. He makes a habit of treating us women on this ship as if we're nothing." Tears appeared in her dull brown eyes as her chin began to wobble.

Resisting the urge to put her on report, he said, "You've had other problems on this ship. I understand when you were on the Vincent, as well, there was some conflict between you and your commanding officer."

"He didn't like me, sir, is all."

Larry was trying to remember the details of why she requested the transfer. She may have trouble with men, period. Perhaps it was time to move her again. "Are you looking for another transfer, Carruthers? Is that what this is about?" He slipped out of the seat and watched her, frowning, as she refused to look at him or rise and acknowledge his leaving. "Stand up, Carruthers."

This time, she did.

"You are very well aware that when an officer enters, you are to acknowledge. Are you not, Carruthers?"

"Yes, sir, I understand."

"Good. See to it you remember in the future, as this is the only warning you'll get from me. Your attitude needs to change. You sound like a whiny high school kid with a chip on her shoulder, and you better figure out right quick where you are, because this is the last time we're going to have this kind of chat. Another officer is not going to be as forgiving as I am." Larry didn't wait for her response. He left, running his hand over the coarse hair at the side of his head as he swiftly stepped out into the passageway, realizing that before he returned to the Vincent, he'd need to see that Carruthers was posted elsewhere, anywhere but on this ship.

Chapter Six

The rest of the day, Eric continued putting out one fire after another. He hadn't finished his reports, and because he hadn't followed up with the chief concerning the mess, the refrigeration system had broken down, and the meat, namely the beef for dinner, had gone bad. Most couldn't be salvaged. On a typical day, this would have been handled, but the problem was that all this had happened during Abby's dramatic arrival, so dinner was changed to something resembling rations, and of course everyone on board complained.

By the time the captain walked through the door of sickbay later that same evening, the first thing he was aware of was Abby, who refused to look at him or have anything to do with him. It wasn't so much that she was pouting. It was as though she had resigned herself to some unknown fate. This wasn't the same young woman he'd left earlier, with whom he'd felt a glimmer of connection. This woman was doing her damnedest to blend into the wall.

The doctor was standing at the counter, shuffling papers and scribbling notes before popping the pen back in his pocket. He glanced at Eric and then over at Abby when Eric approached. "Ah, yeah. Well, I was going to ask you what happened when you showed up, as she's been like this since I got back."

The captain stared over at Abby, who lay on her side in bed, her chin pulled down, her hand resting on the blanket. She didn't glance up at all. "Did someone come in here and say something to her, Doc, before you got back?"

"No. I asked the guard at the door when I couldn't get more of a 'Yes, sir' and 'No, sir' out of her. I presumed something happened during your talk with her, after what she's been through. This is something resembling shell-shock. Listen, if you want to talk to her, I need to go check on some supplies."

As Eric, approached the bed, Abby never looked up, but he could tell just by watching her that she was wound tighter than a top. He was sure she'd jump if he touched her. Had he missed something? "Hey, Abby. How are you feeling?"

"Fine, sir." She kept her head lowered.

For the life of him, Eric couldn't figure out why she was two steps back from where he'd left her. Had he, in fact, triggered something? Eric grabbed a chair and sat down beside the bed. He was tall, but with the height of the bed, he could look into her face. What he saw bothered him like nothing before. Her face was blank, showing nothing. The only thing that gave away the fact that something was wrong and that she was upset, scared, was how tightly she gripped the blanket over her legs.

Eric didn't try and reach out to her because he knew she'd most likely recoil from his touch. "You know, Abby, I told you that you were safe here. I don't know how to make you believe it. Did... did something happen?"

Her eyes glassed over, and he saw how tightly she held

her face, fighting against shedding one tear. She opened her mouth and let out a sigh, but her breath caught, betraying her.

"Abby, can you look at me, please?" He said it in a way that was kind, but he also needed her to do it. Her eyes flickered up to his and lowered, and she looked at him again as if she had to convince herself it was okay. Eric turned his head and softened his gaze. "It's okay, Abby. Tell me what this is. You're upset. Is it from something that happened to you from our talk?"

"I'm safe, you say. But how is this any different? I'm still a prisoner."

He didn't know how to address that with her. For the life of him, he couldn't figure out how she'd ever jump to that conclusion. Frowning, he said, "I have no idea where you'd ever get an idea you were a prisoner, Abby. We're the US Navy. You're under our protection. I'll personally see that you get home."

This time, she frowned, furrowing her brows before glancing at the door and right back to him. "Why is there a guard at the door, then, if I'm not a prisoner?"

He really wanted to chuckle, and he did for a second under his breath before he shook his head and glanced at the door. "No, Abby, I guess I can see why you'd come to that conclusion, but I posted that guard there to keep everyone out and away from you. Your dramatic arrival caused quite a stir with the crew. I have no doubt that without that guard there, you'd have just about every sailor sneaking in to catch a glimpse of you and talk to you. You're quite the exotic passenger."

Her face flushed in embarrassment. "Oh."

"You know, Abby, it actually never even occurred to me that you would interpret it that way, and for the distress it obviously caused you, I am truly sorry."

She pressed her white hand to her bruised cheek to hide her deep blush, but it wasn't working. "I'm sorry for jumping to that conclusion. But how was I to know? You said nothing to me." As soon as the words were out of her mouth, he saw her backpedal as if she shouldn't have said what she did.

He really wanted to say *that a girl show some backbone*, that she shouldn't dare pull back, but he was also the captain. "Abby, this is my ship. I am the captain, and I don't discuss a decision I make with anyone. I'm never questioned by my crew."

"But I'm not a member of your crew, so how does that apply to me?"

She actually stumped him, and he looked at her, hoping she was finally coming out of her shell. "Maybe so, but you are under my protection, so the same goes for you. But just so there are no more misunderstandings, ask me. When I decide something on this ship, however, you won't be privy to it."

Her face softened a bit, and for a second, Eric wanted to reach out and touch her. But he couldn't do that, not to her, so he slid back his chair and stood up, squeezing his fists so he wouldn't be tempted to do something stupid. There was something that passed between them, when she looked up at him again, and for a moment he couldn't breathe, so he said not a word as he gave her a curt nod and crossed to the door, yanking it open. He stood in the doorway, watching her watching him with something in her eyes that, from any other woman, would have had him running for the hills.

Chapter Seven

The enlisted female bunkroom that Gail Carruthers occupied contained eighteen bunks, all filled on this deployment. She lingered in the closed confinement of her rack as four of the women who shared the bunkroom with her gathered by the TV to watch a reality show they were able to pick up.

"He really pisses me off," Gail said. "He needs to have someone knock him off his high horse. I don't know who he thinks he is, but he treated me that way because I'm a woman."

The four women relaxing around the television stilled, then looked at each other in a wary sort of way, as if there were eyes and ears listening everywhere.

Petty Officer Jennifer Hampton was a pretty girl from Ohio with long dark hair, slender and curvy. She moved closer to Gail. "Would you keep your voice down?" She leaned against the bunk and reached out, swatting Gail's leg. "I agree with you, as do most of us girls on this ship. He's a bastard when it comes to women, but you need to watch your step, girl. He's the captain, and you need to be careful of what comes out of your mouth."

Gail shrugged and rolled off the rack. "Not if we go together and file a discrimination suit against him."

The silence was so sharp that if someone was listening, they'd most likely wonder what the hell was going on in there.

"You're crazy, girl. What's wrong with you, coming up with something stupid like that?" Petty Officer Mary-Jo Johnson murmured as she pushed herself out of a chair.

"No, really, please listen. I heard that there is a lady commander out there who is next in line to command a ship like this one. If we can get rid of this asshole, then we don't have to worry about being passed over for promotion just because we're the wrong sex."

Two of the other enlisted women shared a glance and appeared to be considering the idea.

"We all know he's made his position clear regarding women. He's never hesitated to spell it out. You all know I'm right. He believes we were born to stay at home and wait for our husbands, holding their slippers in our hands, bearing their kids, wiping snotty noses and waiting hand and foot on them like bloody slaves. It's like something out of the dark ages!" Gail gestured with her hands as if leading this group of women. But dark-haired Mary-Jo continued to frown and stand as if on guard, arms crossed… as if perhaps just waiting to take Gail down.

The three other women, who ranged from blond and pretty to tall, lanky, and dark, shared a look that would have caused some worry to anyone watching. Gail had to suppress a smile, wanting to high-five herself for the quick thinking. The captain's one mistake was her advantage: He had voiced objections to the presence of women in the

Navy, but even worse was his damning statement that they lowered the integrity of the service.

She jumped when Mary-Jo stepped in front of her, nose to nose with a hard take-no-shit look, as if she was considering pounding the crap out of her. "Okay, girl, you got a point about the captain. He *does* have a problem with us women, and he has said some stuff that has right pissed me off, too. But you don't forget he's the captain, and if he says jump, we ask how high. This ain't Wall Street, and he's not just some boss. So I wonder whatcha think you're gonna do about it?"

Swallowing, Gail cringed inside, wanting nothing more than to take a step back, but she was trapped with her back to the bunk as she stared into eyes so dark she wondered if the woman had ever had a happy thought. She stifled the urge to cower, her heart pounding, very aware of Mary-Jo's strength and the fact that the woman would go down fighting to the death before ever backing down. She didn't run and hide from anyone. Gail could always think herself out of a situation, and she counted on that, praying it wouldn't fail her now with this woman who scared the crap out of her and was breathing down her neck. She had to find a way to win her over. Mary-Jo was the one person on this ship who was impossible to read, and Gail definitely did not ever want to piss her off.

"Ladies, I got a plan, and I'll be counting on your help. You know we have to stick together. Women in the Navy have to remain united or we'll never get ahead, and you know we'll continue to get passed over for promotion here under Captain Hamilton's command," Gail said.

Mary-Jo held up both hands, and Gail wondered if she was going to grab her and shake her, but instead she took a step back and jabbed a finger in Gail's face. "You can just stop right there, girl. I'm not interested in any dirty business or getting involved in any scheme of yours to hurt the captain. You can count me out. I had enough of these games with my sister back home. I'm certainly not gonna stoop to doin' somethin' that's gonna start trouble, especially when it's not based on any *facts*." Mary-Jo stared with a hard look at each one of the women in the room—a look that had Gail trembling under her skin. Then she almost growled at Gail before shaking her head and turning without another word and walking into the head.

Gail was breathing hard, pressed against the bunk as she listed to the squeak of the faucet and the water spilling through the pipes. Then the faucet squeaked off. A moment later, Mary-Jo returned to the bunkroom. She didn't look any calmer.

"Humph. You just remember what I said, and if I was you, Miss Gail, I would drop it and start doin' the job you're supposed to do and keep your nose out of the captain's business."

The angrier Mary-Jo got, the more pronounced her southern accent became. It wasn't something Gail had seen often, but she had heard it once or twice whenever some young sailor had made a backhanded comment. Mary-Jo swept her gaze past each of them, clenching her fists, and suddenly smacked Gail on the back of the head. "What's wrong with you, trying to cause trouble? And what's wrong with you girls, sittin' here listening to this? Shame on you." She gave each of them a final dark glare before heading for the door of the bunkroom. "If you even think about causing trouble and I hear about it, I'll go straight to the Cap'n. I won't stand by and take it, and I won't do it sneaky like the coward you are. I will be in your face and wipe the floor with you." She leaned in to Gail's face, and for a moment Gail thought she'd spit on her, but then she turned and left the bunkroom.

The remaining women gazed at each other before one of them said, "She's right. Just let it go."

But no, there was something inside Gail that hated being humiliated or having one of her ideas squashed by some darky piece of trash. The way the other women were turned away from her now, after she knew she'd almost convinced them—no, she'd find a way. She had to. After all, Captain Eric Hamilton had pissed off the wrong woman and needed to be taught a lesson. Instead of sulking away, she plopped into one of the chairs by the TV, earning a pitying glance from Jennifer, who had her long brown hair pinned up. She absolutely loathed that feeling, when someone turned the tables on her, and at this moment she hated all of them for making her feel this low.

Chapter Eight

Eric sat behind his big desk, considering the officers in the room. Joe was still sitting in the chair by the sofa, where they had just held their daily department head meeting. The meetings were, as a rule, held in the morning, but with the sudden arrival of Abby and the ensuing commotion, they'd rescheduled it for 1900. He acknowledged each officer as they passed by his desk. "Captain," each said before leaving. Eric downed the last of his bitter coffee in one gulp and reread the orders clutched in his hand: Undetermined extension of existing orders to remain in the Persian Gulf, conducting operations in support of multinational forces in Iraq and maritime security operations in the Gulf in order to set conditions for security and stability in the region.

"Stability in the region, that really sums everything up," Eric said. He didn't look at Joe, but he could feel his friend watching him.

When the USS Larsen pulled out of their homeport six months earlier as part of the battle group now stationed in the gulf under Operation Iraqi Freedom, emotions had been high. The thrill of being back on the open sea was the biggest adrenaline rush he had ever experienced. He lived and breathed the Navy. It was a part of him. Among the crew, just about each one of them had it in their blood. Most had left behind wives, children, and families; some had even become new fathers while out at sea. But that was what happened when you chose a life in the military. Your spouse had to look after the home front, and if something happened at home, there wasn't a damn thing a sailor could do. Many didn't get the messages until whatever the trouble was had been resolved.

When Eric announced the orders of their extended stay, he'd seen the disappointment in the eyes of his officers. They were ready to go home, to see their families. Johnson, a redheaded, blue-eyed officer, had a young wife pregnant with their first, and she was due to deliver when he was supposed to be home. That was all anyone had heard from him the last few weeks, that he was going to be in the delivery room when his baby was born. When Eric looked into the distress on Johnson's face, even though the officer had tried to hide it, well, he felt lower than dirt, and he apologized to him. He felt guilty and horrible, because when he read the order, he'd been happy beyond words. He had no ties to shore, only a cheap rented apartment in Portsmouth, furnished second-hand. He had no emotional ties, and he never gave a second thought to the shore. No, this was Eric's true home, his lady love, the sea, the only place he truly felt alive.

He sighed and placed the orders back in the folder. Then he dropped it neatly to the side of his desk. An order was an order, and he wasn't about to coddle his crew. They all needed to suck it up, especially with the new task force that had just been created because of the escalating tension and increase in danger in the area. The task force was scheduled for dispatch later in the week.

Eric had been hesitant about bringing up the subject of Abby, but he knew there was no way around it. He had to say something to his men. They knew she was here, so all he'd said was that they wouldn't be moving her, and, for the time being, she would remain in sickbay, off limits to the crew. Of course, he wasn't surprised by the response and the way they looked at each other as if wondering why she was still here. This included Joe, but Joe, being his right hand, steered the discussion in a different direction. Eric knew all too well that behind closed doors, alone, he'd be hearing from him. Before the meeting, Eric had spoken with Vice Admiral James, who was the commander of the US Navy and Marine Forces in the Gulf. They addressed the fact that the Brits were still very much in the area. In fact, they'd spotted one of the British Class Sheffield Destroyers on the horizon to the north.

The fact was that Eric was stalling, and that was something he didn't do. He was, though, concerned with how the admiral would react toward Abby and the reason she was remaining on board. When he brought up the matter, he'd met a heart-pounding silence in which he could hear a pen clicking on the other end of the line, but then the admiral had said, "I will leave it to your better judgment." Eric didn't know when he'd decided to keep Abby on board. He'd just known, for some reason, and because of what had happened to her, that he wanted her to stay under his protection right now.

Eric didn't glance up until the door clicked closed behind the last officer. That left him alone with Joe. "Sorry about the extension. I know you miss Mary-Margaret and the kids."

Joe tightened his mouth and glanced away. "Thanks, Eric. Yeah, I miss them."

Eric watched his friend struggling with his emotions before he cleared his throat roughly.

"So what did the admiral have to say about Abby?" Joe asked.

This was the part he didn't want to address, because Joe was like a dog with a bone sometimes and read him very well. So he turned away and jabbed his fingers through his short dark hair. "He said he'd leave when and if she's moved up to me."

"What do you mean if she's moved?"

"Abby was quite upset about the guard. You know, she thought she was a prisoner. She misunderstood my intentions."

Joe was still watching him, still waiting for Eric to answer him, and Eric knew that hard look from those deep blue eyes. It was one Joe gave Eric when he knew he was blowing him off. Any other time, Joe would keep digging until he answered, but Eric didn't want to talk to anyone, even Joe, about why he felt the need to keep Abby here for now.

Instead, he said, "I'm looking for some information—any information—on this Seyed Hossein, the guy who 'bought' Abby, who did this to her."

"Turns out there's not much available," Joe answered. "Not even a hundred percent sure the guy exists." He picked up the files, then sat across from Eric. He tossed the file on the desk and added, "You know that the French police report that every year, at least several *thousand* girls are reported missing from Paris? The police believe these girls have been abducted for prostitution in Arab countries. What's really sick is that even Intel has information that there are auctions in Africa where these abducted white women are sold to Arab customers, and blond women like Abby are like platinum."

Eric touched his forehead, trying to still the boiling rage that was ripping through him. He couldn't stomach what he was picturing, and Abby had lived it.

"These women disappear, never to be seen again. For what it's worth, Abby is one of the lucky ones." Joe held up a manila file folder. "I believe this Hossein is responsible." He slid the file across the desk to Eric.

His stomach burned, and the bile threatened to climb up and close his throat. He had to swallow hard a couple times before he could speak. "They can be quite the sick, perverted bastards, can't they?" He leaned back as the leather hissed, propping his feet up on the desk.

Joe cleared his throat. "I'm not sure I should mention this, but I overheard some talk on board of how Abby might be some sort of terrorist."

Eric slammed his feet on the ground, standing up so fast he sent the chair crashing into the wall. He braced his arms on the desk and leaned down, feeling the predator in him clawing to be set free, and he wondered, by the look on Joe's face, whether his friend thought he'd tear this ship apart.

"Whoa, calm down and don't head out that door to kill anyone just yet. I did put an end to the rumors."

"Who started them?"

Joe gave him a look as if Eric should know better. "Kind of hard to tell, you know, especially on a ship where the crew lives for whatever tale someone can tell. If I didn't know better, I'd think you were a little taken with this girl."

"Look, I'm concerned about her. I mean, how many of these girls who are taken are ever found?" He shrugged because he felt something for her, but he was sure it was because he had found her. He had saved her. "Joe, I think we should get Intel on to this Seyed Hossein. My gut tells me there is more to this guy and situation than we know about. I mean, why does he have her on a boat in the middle of the night out here, alone?"

Sitting down, he squeezed the back of his neck. His mind was going faster with ideas and reasons, and he liked none of them. There was a feeling he got whenever something didn't click, didn't settle, because he knew there was more, and that was the feeling he had about this elusive Seyed Hossein. He still couldn't figure out what Abby's role was to be, because he knew deep in his bones that she hadn't been along for a pleasure cruise. Guys like Seyed were dangerous animals. Nothing they did was without an agenda. He'd have to talk to Abby again. He hated upsetting her, making her relive this horrible thing over and over, but it couldn't be helped.

"Captain, did you hear me?"

Eric blinked a couple times. "Sorry, was just thinking."

"I said there are a number of boats, particularly fishing boats, sailboats, that have been reported as suspicious. Their activities are being monitored."

"Really. That's quite interesting. So anything about Seyed and one of these boats?"

"Apparently two nights ago a sailboat that was overdue was returned under rather suspicious circumstances at a sports club on Kish Island. The club manager, who was on duty at the time, filed a report of a missing dinghy. The lone occupant was noted as being rather disgruntled and uncooperative, saying the dinghy had been lost at sea, and he wasn't willing to elaborate on the details."

"That sounds like our guy, does it not?"

"The details are sketchy, but I think you're right. I don't have to remind you that this information is unofficial, and it came from a friend of mine at Intel," Joe said.

Eric shook his head and laughed. "So who exactly is this friend of yours?"

The wide smile flashed a row of perfect white teeth. "Do you remember Edwin Harley?"

Eric frowned, trying to remember where he had heard that name before.

"Edwin is with the Marines, a major. He's been doing some recon work with the Special Forces for the last eighteen months. We grew up together; his dad and mine are good friends. Remember Christmas dinner six years ago at my house? He was there with that young bombshell wife, Carlie."

A sudden shiver ripped up his spine as he swallowed a groan. "God, how could I forget? Shit, she was all over me when I came out of the bathroom. Her husband in the next room, unbelievable." He leveled Joe with a sheepish look. "I couldn't help feeling sorry for that poor guy. I couldn't even look him in the eye. A woman like that, gives you a bad taste."

"Yeah, well, as my wife said, she always did go after all the hunks—she just didn't like the same ones all the time. Anyway, she's gone now. Took off with some guy to LA."

Eric closed his eyes for just a second and then shared a pitying look with Joe for the guy's misfortune. "When did you talk to him?"

"I put a call in to him after Abby showed up on board. I thought we could use his contacts."

For some reason, Eric felt the thread holding his temper unravel, and Joe must have seen something in his face.

"I told him this was unofficial as well as confidential. He clearly understood that we didn't have a conversation."

"Just be careful what you say, Joe."

"I always am."

Joe had more friends and contacts in the military than Eric had ever seen. But then again, Joe was a Navy brat coming from a military family. He was charming, tall, with a dimpled smile and looks that kind of snuck up on you and sucker punched you, as he'd heard from the women when they didn't think he was listening. The men all wanted him around because he was fun, dependable, reliable and, to Eric, the best friend he could ask for.

Eric remembered well how Joe always included him in family gatherings, Christmas and holidays, always dragging him along even when Eric said no. When Joe married his wife, Mary-Margaret, a short, cute, bubbly woman, she had never once judged Eric. She accepted all of him, including his chauvinistic views of women, and she was always teasing him and trying to fix him up with one of her friends, telling him that he was so damn good looking, so strong, with a body that every woman dreamed of. It was a shame to waste, and he grimaced every time she tried to take charge of his love life and fix him up on one blind date after another. But he loved her as Joe's wife and didn't have the heart to tell her to stop. She was a treasure, and on more than one occasion, Eric had told Joe how lucky he was. He envied Joe for having found Mary-Margaret, a woman fiercely devoted to her family, and it showed with the close, loving relationship she and Joe still shared after eleven years of marriage and three kids.

"Listen, is there anything else you were able to get out of Edwin?"

Joe frowned. "Not much else, I'm afraid. He's going to do some checking, see if he can track this guy, find out what he's up to. He asked to be kept apprised of any other information that you get out of Abby, anything else she may remember. She may know something more of what this guy was really up to." Joe crossed his legs before continuing. "As you know, we won't be privy to whatever information he may have, but he will unofficially find out and let me know."

"Thanks, Joe. But for now let's just keep this between you and me. I need to decide the best way to handle this."

Joe didn't sit around and wait for Eric to dismiss him. He took his leave, carrying on with his duties. Eric remained in his chair long after Joe left. He was treading on shaky ground keeping Abby on board, but for some reason he couldn't explain, he wanted to keep her close. He really didn't want to over analyze it, because he didn't get involved with women. He didn't want to care for them, and protect them, and plan futures with them. Not him, a child who'd been abandoned in an alley when he was a kid by his own junkie of a mother. He'd never had a loving, honest relationship with any woman.

He swiped his weary eyes and glanced at his watch: 2200. No wonder he was tired. He stuffed the file Joe had left in his top drawer and eased to his feet, stuffing the keys in his pants pocket. He headed off to bed, making a mental note to speak with Abby first thing in the morning.

Chapter Nine

"Taylor, any trouble, anyone trying to sneak in?" the captain asked the guard posted outside sickbay.

"No, sir. The doc just returned. Just Carruthers inside with the patient," the young sailor replied.

Eric pushed open the door, and the first thing he saw was an empty bed. The doc was rummaging through the cabinets.

"Where is she?" Eric asked.

"Bathroom." Larry gestured across the room just as the door swung open and a very pregnant Abby hobbled out with a crutch under one arm. Her hair was brushed, her face a colorful palette as the bruises healed. She was beautiful under all that in a simple sort of way.

She stopped and stared off to the side at a set of lockers, then frowned. Eric stepped closer to see what had put that frown on her face, and he spotted Gail Carruthers shoving a clipboard in a locker. Her cheeks were pink, and she turned her back on Abby.

When Eric glanced back at Abby, she was watching him with startled eyes, a heavenly blue that reached across the room and hit him in the gut. This time, she didn't lower her eyes, but he could tell she was taking all her courage not to hide herself. Her hand was trembling as she tucked her long bed hair behind her ears and then tried to smooth it down a second time.

His heart was pounding hard in his chest as he stepped across the room to her. Then he heard the sharp clang of the door closing, and he glanced over, realizing Carruthers had left.

"How are you this morning? Did you sleep well?" he asked.

She was so tiny that the top of her head barely reached his shoulder, so she had to look way up at him, and that was when her crutch started to wobble. Eric slid his arm around her back at the same time as he pulled the crutch from her. He was nearly undone, feeling the swell of her belly and the baby inside her.

She nodded, and this time she did glance away, but he could feel how he was affecting her as he helped her back to bed. Her heart was pounding, and she was trembling underneath his touch. He wondered for a moment if she feared him, and that thought brought an ache inside of him. He didn't want her to fear him.

"Abby, don't be scared of me. I'd never hurt you."

She stopped moving and slowly brought her head up, looking at him as her face flushed. "But I'm not scared of you. I know you wouldn't hurt me."

Eric was stunned until her meaning finally sank in, and then she touched his arm and held on to his wrist as he helped her onto the bed. That one simple touch was setting off all kinds of sparks, as if he'd just been plugged into a socket. No woman had ever affected him as Abby did. He was sure there had to be something wrong with him, because he didn't welcome this feeling at all. He pulled his arm away after she was settled in bed, and he nearly jumped from the footsteps behind him.

"So, how are you feeling this morning, Abby?" asked the doctor as he appeared beside the captain.

"I'm good."

The doctor slid the blood pressure cuff around her arm. Eric stepped back and watched him pump it up. Abby didn't look at Eric again. She watched the doctor and what he was doing.

"Your blood pressure is still a little high. How did you sleep? Bad dreams, anything upset you?" He ripped off the cuff.

"I'm fine. I actually slept really good. When I woke up, I was confused, is all. I couldn't remember where I was."

The doctor draped the stethoscope around his neck.

"I didn't dream, though, which is odd. I don't ever remember sleeping that deeply."

The doctor reached for her chart on the counter and scribbled something. "Abby, I actually gave you a mild sedative last night with the vitamins."

Eric watched her face pale, and she placed a protective hand numbly over the baby, nestled securely inside her womb. She gazed down at her baby and said nothing, but Eric could feel all kinds of confusion and worry pulsing off her in waves and knew she wouldn't say one word to the doctor about what was bothering her.

"Doc? Is it safe for her to be taking sleeping pills when she's pregnant?" Eric asked.

"Yes, yes, perfectly safe. It's more important for the baby that Abby has a good night's sleep. After yesterday and what she's been through, she needs rest."

Abby tilted her head and looked up at Eric with softness, and something else passed else between them. She was grateful. She was reaching out to him as if he was her lifeline. Then she nodded.

Larry motioned for her to lie down. "I need to check the baby. Can you lie flat on your back?"

The hospital gown she wore slid up her slender, pale legs, and she slid to lie down. She blushed furiously and gripped the gown to try to pull it down. Eric reached for a blanket and covered her legs, while Larry supported her arm and helped her lie flat. She struggled for breath, and Eric could see the discomfort in her face, in her eyes.

Larry pulled the blanket up then raised her gown, exposing her swollen belly. "I know it's uncomfortable, Abby. I'll be quick." He pressed her belly with his fingers around the baby. "Any tenderness?"

"No."

"Have you felt the baby moving this morning?"

This time, she smiled, and it was subtle and easy, even with her swollen lip. "Yes. A little while ago, the baby stuck its foot in my back."

Larry pulled down her gown and helped her sit up. "That's good." He grabbed a couple of pillows at the foot of the bed and set them behind her back. "A few more days in bed, Abby, then I'll let you get up and move around a bit. Until then, you stay put and only get up to go the bathroom. Got it?"

"Yes, but do you think I could maybe have a shower and wash my hair?" she asked in such an unsure voice that Eric wondered whether she thought the doc would say no.

"She can have a shower, right, Doc?" Eric asked.

"Absolutely. I'll get Carruthers to help her." He glanced behind him. "Well, she was here when I came in."

"Please don't bother her. I don't need any help. I can shower myself. I just need to know how it turns on and—"

"Larry, don't bother with Gail. I'll have Petey get one

of the other female crewmen in here to help her," Eric interrupted. Abby seemed relieved and gave him another look that had him wondering if something had happened between her and Gail.

Eric grabbed the phone behind him, and when Petey answered, Eric asked him to arrange for a female crew member to come down and help Abby shower and to get her whatever personal effects she needed.

"That would be fine, Captain," came the reply.

"Are you done examining Abby, Doc?" Eric asked after he had closed the line.

The doctor stuffed supplies and his equipment back in the drawers. "Yes, that's all for now. I'll be back a little later to check on you," he said to Abby. "If you'll excuse me, Captain." Larry left, pulling the door closed, leaving Eric alone with Abby.

Eric leaned against the counter beside the bed, crossing his arms and once again watching her, trying to figure out what it would take to break through that thick shell she had built up around herself. Under it all, he could see an innocence that a monster had done his best to destroy. But it was still there. Even though she appeared so fragile, there was something about her that was rock solid. She had the strength to walk through hell and keep right on going.

He blinked when he realized he was staring at her and making her uncomfortable. "Sorry, Abby. Do you think you're up to having a talk?"

"A talk? About what, Captain?" She stumbled over her words and appeared wide-eyed, almost afraid.

He grabbed a chair and pulled it over to face her. He sat so that he was at eye level with her. "I know you've been through hell, but we need to talk again about what happened."

Her face tightened, and she seemed distressed. She

blinked hard, as if fighting off tears. "You don't believe me?" she whispered.

Eric wondered why she immediately jumped to that conclusion, but he also didn't miss the distress in her voice, along with her deeply wounded spirit. He reached out and touched the back of her slender hand, rubbing his thumb over her knuckles until she relaxed. "Abby, I do believe you. Of course I do. I just need more details. Stop jumping to conclusions."

Several minutes passed before either said a word. Then she slowly looked up at him, as if she was deciding whether she could trust him. "All right," she said. "Where do you want me to start?"

"Abby, this time I'm going to walk you through it. Can you just go along with me?"

Before she could say anything else, a knock sounded at the door.

"Enter," Eric said in his loud, commanding voice. He pulled away from her and stood up. The door opened briskly, admitting a young black female officer.

"Petty Officer Mary-Jo Johnson, as requested, sir." The words were strong and confident as she saluted the captain.

Waving her hand down, the captain stood beside the bed, directing Mary-Jo's attention to Abby. "Johnson, this is Abby. Did you receive instructions that you are to assist her to the shower?"

"Yes sir, Captain." Not easing her stance, she stood with her arms at her sides while holding a bundle under her left arm.

"Abby, go have your shower. We'll talk when you're done."

Mary-Jo set the bundle on the side counter. "Does she need help getting to the shower, sir?" Petty Officer Mary-Jo was somewhat cute, with a chubby round face, big dark eyes, and thick tight curls cropped short.

"She has a crutch, but you need to help her." The captain gestured to the bag Mary-Jo set on the counter.

"Essentials, sir: soap, shampoo, clothes, everything she'll need," Mary-Jo replied while opening the bag for the captain to inspect.

"Looks like you're in good hands, Abby."

Mary-Jo smiled at Abby. "I had to guess your size, so if nothin' fits, we'll scrounge up somethin' that will," she said.

Eric watched Abby as she gazed with longing at the simple bag, then over at Mary-Jo, unable to hide her humble appreciation. "Thank you" was all she said to the petty officer.

Mary-Jo cleared her throat and motioned to the door of the bathroom with her hand. "Shall we?"

Eric grabbed the crutch and helped Abby up, positioning the crutch under her arm.

"Thanks again for your help," Abby said again, first to Eric, then Mary-Jo.

"It's no problem, really, ma'am," Mary-Jo replied.

"Notify me when she's done. Contact my ensign if you need anything." Eric strode to the door and yanked it open.

"Yes, sir, Captain."

He stopped and turned to the young petty officer who was now supporting Abby's arm, helping her to the bathroom. She was kind, efficient—he liked her. As he closed the door behind him, he realized he was starting to soften, and he wondered if this was all because of Abby.

Chapter Ten

Abby was running a brush through her still damp hair, sitting on her bed, wearing a pair of tan dungarees and a large white t-shirt that hung loosely over her belly. On her feet, she wore a pair of black thongs. Eric studied her for a moment from the door, and her eyes became immediately alert to him. When she glanced over his shoulder to where Joe was standing, she sat a little straighter, her hand paused with the brush.

Eric let the door close behind them. "How was the shower?"

Her blue eyes held an edge of nervousness, and she shyly glanced Joe's way again. "It was great. Thank you. I feel so much better."

Eric stopped in front of her. "Abby, I'd like you to meet Lieutenant Commander Joe Reed. He's my first officer, otherwise referred to as the XO. He's the man who runs the ship. He knows everything that goes on everywhere."

She looked over at Joe, who respectfully stood a few feet away. Joe did his best to ease her stress. Any fool could see how uneasy she was, but then Eric realized she'd never seen Joe before.

"I brought my XO along to document any details you may remember," he explained.

Abby stiffened and lowered the brush in her lap. She started squeezing the handle until her fingers turned white. She wasn't looking at anyone. She'd reverted to that subservient role of keeping her eyes cast downward. Eric exchanged a knowing look with Joe, who seemed to know and to be aware of her unease.

"If you would rather not have me here, I do understand, Abby," Joe began.

She appeared to swallow as she slowly lifted her chin, glancing at Eric first and then hesitantly at Joe. "No, it's fine, Lieutenant," she said. This time, when she glanced back at Eric, he could tell that she trusted him but was also begging him not to hurt her. This was absolutely terrifying, because at one time that would have been all he wanted in a woman. However, having a woman in this situation was absolutely maddening, because everything about her, him, and the shadow surrounding her made everything about this impossible. Eric sat in a chair beside the bed, making sure to keep a respectable distance this time.

Abby took a deep breath. "Where do you want me to start?"

"I want you to go back to when you first saw the other guy who was with you and Seyed on the boat and picture him. Close your eyes," Eric said in his deep voice.

She hesitated before closing her eyes, but then winced and pressed her hand to her lower back.

Eric reached for a couple of pillows. "Here, settle back on these. Try and relax."

She had such a pretty smile, and it reminded him so

much of a child's. But she wasn't a child, because children were innocent, or they were supposed to be, anyway.

"Close your eyes again, and I want you to picture him and describe this guy in every detail. Start with what he looked like," Eric said.

"He had dark hair curling a bit just past his ears." She had her eyes closed, and he could tell she was thinking as she gestured with her hand. "He didn't have a beard, but he had facial hair, as though he hadn't shaved for a few days." She started to open her eyes.

"No, Abby, keep your eyes closed. Don't open them until I tell you. What color were his eyes? Did he have any scars, marks on his face, anything that would stand out? How old do you think he was, young? Was he fat or thin?"

"He had dark eyes, his face was slender, and he was older. Not old, but maybe in his thirties, I think. He had this bump on his nose—it really stood out. I remember he was also dressed differently. He had a dark jacket on, slacks, and that was all I could tell. It was dark."

"When you first got on the boat, before you were taken down below, was there anyone around? What did you see? Was it a marina? How many boats were there?"

She opened her eyes and gave him a look of confusion. "It happened so fast. I didn't see anything, or anyone."

"Come on, Abby. Close your eyes."

Reluctantly, she did.

"Tell me where you are as you're walking to the boat. Tell me what you see."

"It's so dark. I'm in the backseat, and Seyed grabs me, pulls me out. I walk behind them. I see buildings, and we're at a marina. We walk on a boardwalk. There are many boats there, but I don't see anyone. Wait—there was a whistle. I didn't dare look up, but the other man in front of Seyed did this bird whistle back. I don't know where it came from except it was over a ways from my left. Then I was on the boat and taken below. I fell asleep not long after, I was so tired." She opened her eyes. "I'm sorry I can't remember more."

He couldn't help himself. He took her hand. "Are you kidding me? You were actually very helpful."

Joe moved forward and stood at the foot of the bed. "I'm going to get right on this." He held up the notes and gave her a wink to break the mounting tension. "Thank you, Abby. You gave us more than you know." Joe hesitated beside Eric and gave him a pointed glance, and Eric wondered for a minute whether his feelings were showing. "I'll talk to you later," said Joe, and then he left.

"I didn't think I told you anything more than I did yesterday."

Eric slid the chair back against the wall. "You did good, Abby." He smiled down on her but kept his hands to himself. Each time he touched her was doing all kinds of wild things to his control. He couldn't be the arrogant self-possessed man everyone knew on that ship, who barked orders, who demanded. With her, he needed to listen, and something about her made him care about everyone more.

She shivered and wrapped her arms across her bosom.

"Are you okay?" He slid his hand over her shoulder and down her arm. She didn't pull away, and he wondered for a minute if she actually leaned into his touch or if he was just imagining it.

"Yes, I'm fine. I just don't like having to think about him. Eric, I mean, Captain, do you think I'll have to see him again?"

This time, Eric sat on the edge of the bed beside her and slid his arm across her shoulder. "Where would you ever get the idea you'd have to see him again? The man's a criminal. He *bought* you —"

"But this is his child," she interrupted him. "Do you really believe he'll just let me go? I've seen the monster he is. He'll hunt to the ends of the earth for me, for this child, and then he'll kill me."

"Abby, he will not get your child. You are going back to the US, where you'll be safe."

The look she gave him told him loud and clear she didn't believe him. "Seyed and his people have quite a reach in the US, too, you know. I've seen and heard things I wish I never had. Please don't make promises you can't keep."

Eric was stunned by her cool. There was something inside of him that wanted to scoop her up and make those promises, then hide her somewhere where nothing bad could ever touch her again. But he didn't, because he couldn't, so instead he moved away. "I'll come back and see you later," he said. He didn't wait for her to respond. He strode to the door, running his fingers through his hair, and turned the door handle. He glanced over his shoulder and met her gaze, and he started to promise her something, anything, but stopped, because that wouldn't be fair, not to her. So he gave her a stiff smile, one he knew never reached his eyes, and left.

Several hours later, Joe knocked on Eric's cabin door. He closed the door behind him. "Captain, I filled Edwin in on our talk with Abby. She's very nice, by the way. A real trooper for what she's been through." Joe didn't wait for him to respond, which was good, because he was still feeling like crap because his promises to keep her safe meant squat as soon as she left this ship. She knew it, and he knew it.

"Eric, are you listening?" Joe asked.

"Yeah, sorry, so what did Edwin say?"

"They suspect the guy that Abby described was most likely part of the ring responsible for some of the sabotage that happened on one of the British destroyers last month. Edwin confirmed that he also believes it was Seyed who arrived on Kish Island, and right now, they're tracking his whereabouts. He said he couldn't reveal anything else right now, but he did say they suspect that whatever was planned, there was most likely another boat out there, and the plan changed when Abby clubbed this guy over the head and then disappeared on the dinghy."

As Eric listened, a sick feeling stirred in his gut.

Joe said, "The CIA may try to get a hold of Abby to talk to her."

Eric vaulted out of his chair, sending it flying, and leaned over the desk, bracing both hands in front of him and glaring icily at Joe. "No way in hell are they going to talk to her, get their hands on her, or come anywhere near her."

His heart was pounding so hard he couldn't hear anything over it. He was shaking. He was so angry, and he wanted to slam his fist into something, anything, because the CIA knowing anything about Abby being here was about the worst thing possible. They'd use and break her spirit for their own means. They didn't give a crap who she was. "They'll have to go through me if they want her!"

Joe closed his eyes and looked away briefly before speaking. "Eric, get a grip. You and I know damn well that if the CIA wants her, they'll find a way to get her. Right now, Edwin was giving me the heads up."

"How does the CIA know she's here to begin with? Did Edwin tell them? I thought you told me he wouldn't repeat whatever you said," Eric shouted.

"It wasn't Edwin, but someone did. Could be anyone, Eric, you know that. It went out on the wire when we found her. Command knows, the admiral—she's the whole talk on this ship, with the fact that she's still here."

Eric threw his hands in the air in answer.

"You know it could mean your career if you interfered," Joe said. "How far are you willing to go for her?"

In reply, Eric fixed a dark, penetrating look on him. He was furious the CIA knew anything about Abby, and he pumped his fists a couple times, imagining pounding the crap out of whoever had filled them in on the matter.

Joe sighed. "Look, Eric, hopefully it won't go there, but you need to be prepared. Just what do you think you can do to protect her, anyway? It's not like you're married to her."

Eric glared at Joe. "Stop it, would you? This is about a young woman who never asked for any of this to happen to her. She was kidnapped and sold like an animal, and you know what this animal did to her. She's now pregnant with his kid, and she was beaten so badly...." He stopped, unable to finish.

"I know that, Eric. I was there when she was brought aboard."

"I will do what I need to do to protect her. Do you know what she said to me after you left?"

Joe simply shook his head.

"She said I can't protect her, because when she goes back to the US, Seyed will still get her, and when he gets his hands on her, he'll take the baby and kill her." He shook his head. "As long as she's here, though, on my ship, no one can get her. This Seyed Hossein—tell me Edwin at least gave you something on him? His whereabouts would be nice."

"He narrowed it down to some activity with sailboats

in the Gulf a week ago. From what we understand, they were going out at night, possibly targeting military ships in the area. Unfortunately, Edwin's information is sketchy. He assured me they will track this guy and find out what's going on."

Troubled by the sudden iciness in the air, Eric paced the room.

Joe rose from his chair. "Eric, I understand how you feel, but how long do you think you can keep her here?" He didn't wait for Eric to answer. He must have seen that his stubborn friend had made up his mind and there was no reasoning with him, because the next thing Eric knew, Joe had pulled open the door and left.

Eric dropped back in his leather chair and groaned. Not since he was a kid forced into the system had he remembered feeling so helpless. In that moment, he made the decision that he would do whatever was needed to protect her. For just a second, he allowed his thoughts to wander to the reason for this protective instinct. As commanding officer, he had taken her under his protection. "Yeah, right." He spat the words out, shook his head, and cursed aloud at such a ridiculous argument.

Pulling open the top drawer of the desk, he reached in and took out his medals. He looked down at them and tried to rekindle those powerful feelings of satisfaction, glory, and pride from when he had earned them on a mission years ago in the South China Sea. Try as he might, he couldn't remember that feeling of excitement. He'd been lonely for so long he hadn't even realized it, and for the first time all this glory meant nothing without someone special to share it with. Sighing, he returned the medals to the drawer and then closed it. He left the cabin, slamming the door after him, making a decision to do the one thing that had always worked before. He would bury himself in work: his first love, the sea.

Heading up to the bridge, Eric made a mental note to do a surprise inspection at all the stations. His crew were really going to love him for this.

Chapter Eleven

"Captain!" someone yelled again. The pounding on his cabin door brought Eric from his bed and ripped him from the sound sleep he'd finally fallen into. He yanked open the door to young Petey, his corpsman, who looked barely old enough to enlist.

"What the hell?" Eric barked. He shoved his arms in his shirt and buckled the pants he had shoved on when he jumped from bed, quickly lacing his black boots.

"Captain, Doc said to get you. Abby's in labor."

"What do you mean, she's in labor? I thought it was too early." He tucked his tan shirt in his pants as he headed out the door, buttoning it as he walked at a hurried clip, Petey on his heels.

"I don't know what happened, except the guard heard her screaming. Scared the shit out of him, he thought someone was killing her. He got the doc, and he said to get you."

Eric made it in record time to sickbay. The guard jumped to attention and opened the door for him. Both the doc and Lynn were beside Abby, the lights blazing overhead. "What's going on? Petey said she's in labor."

"Deep breath in… blow it out. That's it, Abby. Now relax," said the doc as he pulled back the blanket covering her.

Eric was right beside her as the doctor grabbed latex gloves and shoved his hands in.

"She's having contractions," Larry said. "I need to check if she's dilating."

Lieutenant Lynn wrapped a black cuff around her arm and checked her blood pressure. "One-eighty over sixty," he said to the doc as he scribbled her vitals into a chart.

"Deep breath in, Abby. That's it. Don't hold your breath.… Let it out slowly. Abby, I need you to relax and take a deep breath. I need to examine you. I want you to tell me as soon as you feel another contraction coming on, okay? Come on, legs up."

Eric moved to stand by her head as the doc spread her legs, resting his one hand on her knee.

"You're going to feel some pressure, Abby."

Abby sucked in a breath, and her hands went helplessly to her chest, reaching for anything to grab.

Eric took her warm hand in his large, calloused one. "It's all right, Abby."

The doc pulled his hand out and ripped off his gloves, dumping them in the receptacle behind him. "The cervix has thinned, but she's only dilated about one centimeter. Let's just wait and see how it goes for the next little bit."

"Am I in labor? I was dreaming. It was awful." She was breathless as she spoke.

"Abby, you were having a nightmare, thrashing about pretty good," Larry said. "The poor guard heard you screaming and thought someone was in here trying to hurt you. You want to tell me about it?"

Eric saw the fear light up her eyes as if she was facing the fires of hell. She shut her eyes, and a lone tear slipped out. She didn't let go of Eric's hand. In fact, she squeezed harder, and then she shook her head and stifled a frantic hiccup. She groaned and rolled to her side, clutching her belly, gasping for breath.

"Another contraction, Abby. Come on, don't hold your breath."

"It hurrrts," she moaned.

Eric could feel her starting to panic. He rubbed her shoulder and back with his other hand. "Look at me. Don't hold your breath. Let it go.... Breathe in. Come on, that's it. Good girl. Now let it out slowly."

She locked eyes with Eric, and he could feel how she needed him, someone to be here with her. He also knew that whatever she dreamed had put the fear of God into her.

As soon as the contraction passed, she took a deep breath.

"Captain, can I speak with you?" the doctor asked in a low voice.

Eric stood and let go of her hand. "Abby, I'll be right back."

When they emerged into the hall, Eric turned toward Larry. "Doc, what happened here? I thought the baby wasn't due for a while." His voice was sharp, and he knew he sounded annoyed.

Larry shook his head. "The guard heard her scream and yell. When he came in, she was thrashing around. One hell of a bad dream, I'd say. It's obvious the stress of it put her in early labor. I just examined her. The contractions are strong. It's too early, so we have to get the contractions to stop. Best-case scenario is if they stop on their own. Keep her in bed, and help her relax. If they don't stop, I need to give her some terbutaline. The only problem is side effects. The drug can increase the heart rate of both Abby and the baby, but right now it's a moot point, as we don't have it on board. We'd have to have it sent over from the hospital on base in Bahrain."

Abby groaned again and sounded as if she was almost whimpering. Eric could see the beads of sweat on her forehead, and she doubled over, clutching her belly and gritting her teeth. He could see her trying to breathe. Lieutenant Lynn was talking to her.

"That was five minutes since the last one," Todd said to the doctor as he approached. Eric took Abby's hand again, and she held on.

"Isn't it too early for me to have my baby?" Her voice trembled.

The doctor stood on the other side of the bed and leaned down so she could see him. "Listen to me. It's early, but we're going to try to stop it. First, though—and this is important—I need you to relax. It looks like your nightmare brought on early labor. Right now, chances are really good that we can get it to stop. You haven't dilated past the point of no return yet. If you continue past five centimeters or your water breaks, there will be nothing I can do to stop labor, so I need you to calm down, take some deep breaths, and try not to move. Lieutenant Lynn is going to check your vitals again while I talk to the captain."

Eric smiled gently, and gave her hand a reassuring squeeze. "Listen to the doc. I'll be right back."

The doc stood in front of Eric with his back to Abby when he said, "By the time Todd and I got here, we heard her screaming, pleading, and crying. She was having a hell of a nightmare. This is something I've seen from soldiers with PTSD, and I'm talking pretty bad cases. When I woke her, her blood pressure was through the roof. She was trembling, and her eyes were wild with fear, something I can honestly say I've never seen before. She was so scared that I'm pretty sure it took her a minute to remember where she was. She was soaking wet, she was perspiring so much. This is the kind of stress that put her in early labor. I don't know if we can get the contractions to stop."

Eric ran his hands over his face. "When will you know?"

Shaking his head, the doctor let out a deep breath. "We're going to have to play that by ear. Her water hasn't broken, so that's a good sign. We need to get her blood pressure down, keep her feet elevated, keep her calm, and I want to get some fluids into her. I will hook her up to an IV."

Eric glanced over his shoulder at Abby, meeting her eyes as the lieutenant moved aside to document the vitals in the chart at the counter beside the bed.

"I'll be staying here to keep an eye on her, so I'll be sure to let you know of any change or if she progresses further."

"Actually, doc, if you don't mind, I'll stay," Eric said.

"All right. It could be a long night."

"I'm up, so what can I do?" the captain asked.

"Help her relax from whatever that nightmare was that scared her so much. Help get her mind off it. I need to examine her again, see if she's dilated any further."

Eric nodded and followed the doc back over to Abby.

"Her blood pressure is down. Her last contraction was eight minutes ago," said the lieutenant when they approached.

Abby was propped up with several pillows on her side, drinking some apple juice. She finished and held up the empty cup, handing it back to the lieutenant.

Eric noticed how Abby's hand immediately flew to her

belly when a contraction started. But this time she didn't fight it. She reached for Eric's hand as he helped her ride it out.

"Just relax. Almost over, Abby."

"It wasn't as bad this time," she said wearily.

"I need to examine you again and see if your cervix has dilated any more. Try and make yourself as comfortable as possible." The doctor pulled back the blanket again.

"Okay," she mumbled.

"Over on your back, Abby." The doctor pulled out the pillows and helped her lie flat. This time, she blushed a deep crimson as he lifted her gown and once again propped up her knees. She turned her head to the side, and Eric could almost feel her acute embarrassment, so he touched her face, the side of her head, with his long work-roughened hands.

"Okay, so far so good. You haven't dilated any further. As long as your contractions continue fading, I'm hopeful this little guy won't be making an appearance tonight." He pulled her gown back down and covered her once again with the blanket, ripping off the latex gloves and disposing of them. "Check her vitals again in thirty minutes," he said to the lieutenant.

"Yes, sir," Todd responded.

Chapter Twelve

The bright yellow and orange of the sun was just skimming the horizon when Eric finally returned to his cabin. He was tired, probably because he'd tossed and turned for hours before finally drifting off right before Petey pounded on the door, waking him. He had stayed with Abby and talked to her, telling her stories of when he had enlisted and first met Joe, what it was like during his first deployment on an aircraft carrier as a lowly sailor. That was when he had fallen in love with the sea, visiting port after port and miles of open water. Abby had watched him with joy reflecting in her eyes.

She had listened to him with her whole heart. As she relaxed, she had held his hand for hours as her contractions faded, and at dawn, she fell asleep. Eric had watched her and felt such overwhelming peace. No matter how much he fought it, he realized he was beginning to care a lot for her. Abby was amazing, and he wanted nothing bad to ever touch her again. She wasn't like other women he had dated. She didn't appear to have a selfish bone in her body or a mind that worked overtime, scheming and planning or plotting for her own means. This scared the hell out of him. He was alone for a reason. He wasn't made like Joe, to have a family. He did his own thing, and he liked that. So why was the carefully structured world he had created crumbling now?

The cabin door shook at a knock. Eric was startled, and that didn't happen often. "What!" he barked.

Joe snapped open the door and closed it behind him, carrying another one of his damn files. He pulled out a chair on the other side of the desk and sank into it. "You look like shit. I heard about Abby. Is she all right? Did the labor stop?"

The sincerity in his voice was enough to take the edge off Eric's irritation. What Eric really wanted at that moment, as he squeezed the tight muscles clenching up the back of his neck, was to lie down and get some sleep for a few hours. A headache was beginning to dig in at the back of his head.

"She's resting now. Her labor seems to have stopped." The words softened somewhat, but he heard the gruffness still in his voice.

"You look tired. Would you rather I came back later?"

Shaking his head, Eric ran his fingers over his raw, overworked eyes as he attempted to refocus. "Nope. Sorry, Joe, I'm just really tired. What is it?"

"I just heard back from Edwin, unofficially of course. It appears that Mister Seyed Hossein, our illustrious captain, is looking for someone or something."

"It's Abby!" Eric shouted, slamming his fist down on the solid desk. "God dammit." His weariness fled as adrenaline pulsed through his veins, pumping him faster than any shot of high-octane caffeine would. Reaching across the desk, he ripped the report from Joe. "This is un-fucking-believable. Can you believe he has the unmitigated gall to be looking for her, that motherfucker?" Eric cursed again, reading the rest of the report. "Is this information for real?"

Joe nodded slowly, eyeing Eric. "Yup, he knows how important this is. You may not like this next little bit: Edwin said the CIA suspects that Abby knows something more than she's saying about this guy. He kind of indicated off the record that the CIA is baffled about her disappearance. They want some answers, and he said they *will* be talking to her. They're aware you're keeping her here on board, by the way." Joe paused, looking directly at Eric before continuing. "Edwin also said this Hossein may be involved with a local terrorist group—you know, boats running into our boats to blow them up—and maybe Abby knows a whole lot more about it. Could even be involved."

That last had his gut sinking as if a boulder had been dumped into it. An icy chill raced up his spine because he knew the CIA were famous for using the innocent, and he was truly afraid of what they'd do to her. "Shit!" Eric pushed out of his chair, feeling as if he had aged ten years. Panic threatened to nip at his heels, so he started pacing around his desk and stopped in front of Joe, then tossed the file he squeezed in his hands back on the desk.

Walking over to the couch, he flopped heavily and sank back into the leather cushion. He sank all ten fingers into his short dark hair and fingered it back until he was positive it standing on its ends.

"You know she needs protection," Joe said. "Have you thought about maybe moving her to the base in Bahrain? They could protect her there."

Eric didn't look up when he said, "No, she's staying here. This is the safest place for her." He waved a hand to stop any further talk on the subject. "I spoke with Doc a while ago. She's too far along to be moved safely today, anyway, and with this little bit of information, there's no way I'm sending her ashore. If I did, you and I know the CIA would be in there like a dirty shirt and grab her, and then what would happen to her? No, for now she's under my protection, and she stays right here until it's safe for her to be moved someplace where the CIA isn't going to swoop in and take her."

Joe slid out of the chair and joined him, taking one of the chairs by the couch and crossing his long legs out in front of him, tapping the arm of the chair. "Eric, I've never known you to have feelings for a girl, especially a girl like this. Are you sure it's not just pity because this situation is so volatile? What she's been through would really mess up a person. What do you think you can do for her? This baby—look at the violence in how it was conceived. Does she even want to keep it? Have you asked her this? What do you really know?"

Eric shut his eyes and leaned his head back. Everything Joe said had already gone through his mind. He also hated the nitpicking and the tough love that Joe sometimes used on him. Sometimes, he was worse than a damn woman. "Shit, Joe, back off. I don't know. I'm tired, and if you'd seen the kind of fear in her eyes that I did, I think you'd be doing the same thing."

Joe said nothing, only narrowed his eyes and glanced away. "Are you going to tell her that Hossein is looking for her?" he asked.

Eric stomped both feet to the ground and stood up so fast he almost knocked the coffee table over. "No! And don't you dare say a word to her. My God, that is the one thing that she is so damn afraid of. She told me he won't stop looking for her, and she's right. That goddamn animal bought her and believes he owns her. He will hunt to the ends of the earth for her." Eric started pacing, his mind racing a mile a minute. "Joe. Does anyone else on this ship know about Hossein looking for her?"

Joe pushed himself up and stood with his hands on his slim hips. "Just Petey, but I'll make sure he doesn't say anything."

"Be sure he doesn't." Eric paused briefly to run his hands over his dark facial hair. He knew he looked rough. Hell, his hair had to be sticking up, too. He really needed to clean up, shave. Sleep would have to wait. "Look, Joe, I'm tired. I need to clean up."

"There's another matter that's just come up. And it's quite serious."

When Eric glanced over, he gestured in irritation. "What?" he snapped. It was the first time Eric had seen Joe have trouble putting two words together. He firmed his lips into a fine white line and gestured with his hand to sit, which Eric ignored.

"A charge has been laid against you for sexual harassment," Joe said. He just stared at Eric, who was having trouble understanding what he had just said. Joe sighed and finally continued, "By Gail Carruthers."

Eric could hear nothing but a buzz that seemed to vibrate up from the floor, shooting through him like a rocket. Time could have ticked by, for all he knew. Then his head started to clear, but he felt dizzy, as if he'd just been blindsided. "Huh" was all he managed to say, because he was stuck in a strange sensation, as though he were in a vacuum. He was waiting for someone to jump out and say it was all a big, sick joke.

"You heard me right. She filed a report of sexual harassment."

Eric leaned back against his desk and crossed his arms. He wanted to hit something, slam a chair against the wall, grab Joe by the shirtfront and shake him and make him say it was a lie. But he did none of it. He crossed his arms and then glanced over at Joe, who appeared to have a ring of fire surrounding the sharp blue of his eyes. Finally, he said, "Are you fucking kidding me? This has to be a joke!"

Joe shook his head, his own eyes mirroring Eric's fury. "Sorry. No joke. She filed the report directly with command. The admiral's assistant sent me a copy. I guess Carruthers figured that if she filed with me, I'd try to bury it."

Eric felt the fire burn in his cheeks. His headache, which had just been a subtle pressure earlier, slowly building, now exploded inside his head to the point that he clamped his hands to his temples. "Why, that conniving, fucking, lying little bitch. I want her off my ship now!"

Joe kept his one hand braced on his hip and held his other out to try to calm and reason with Eric. "You can't touch her right now. She's not going anywhere pending an investigation, and just so you know, she's already asked to have you removed as captain."

Eric absolutely lost it. He couldn't stop the string of curses from rolling off his tongue. As he finished, he winced as sobriety sank in at his own crude reference in comparing Gail to a donkey's ass.

"Look, Eric, calm down. I'm just giving you the heads up right now." Joe added, "They're not going to replace you."

Joe spoke calmly and evenly, but the more Eric thought about the ridiculous accusation, the more a burning hatred sizzled once again, pulsing through his veins until he thought the top of his head would blow off. "Just let them try and replace me!" He flung his hands in the air, then pounded his palms on the desk and winced from the sharp pain that shot up his arms.

"Look, you need to be smart about this. I know this

charge is bullshit, and so will the higher ups, but you know how it is right now. There's so much fucking media spotlight on assault on female personnel in the military that they simply can't ignore it. We need to disprove this quickly and quietly and make it go away."

Eric leaned forward, resting his palms on the desk, dropping his head in defeat. Then he pushed away and started pacing once again. "As soon as I do, I want that fucking bitch off my ship." The words were intentionally sharp so there would be no misunderstanding.

Joe inclined his head. "I'll see to it personally, with pleasure."

"As captain of this ship, I want to see the formal complaint she filed."

Joe pulled the complaint from the file on the desk and handed it to Eric.

"What I really want to know is this: When did this alleged incident happen, and what is it exactly that I supposedly did to her?" Eric scanned the pages of the report.

"She said it happened in sickbay—yesterday, as a matter of fact. Abby was asleep. You brushed up behind her and…" He paused to clear his throat. A telltale blush rose in his cheeks, which was so unlike him. "You cupped her butt, gave her a tight squeeze, and told her to go into the bathroom so she could, and I quote, 'Let you fuck her.' She said she refused and you threatened her with reassignment, along with putting her on report for some incident you would create if she didn't cooperate." Joe cleared his throat again and then rubbed his chin, looking damn awkward and a bit sheepish for having to relay the details.

Eric's dark eyebrows raised—he felt the tightening in his forehead. He looked over Joe's shoulder at the closed door, blinking as he tried to absorb such a tale. Jabbing a forceful finger at the papers he held, he said, "This whole thing is a bunch of crap. Who the fuck would want to fuck her? You've seen her. Shit, anybody in their right mind… shit. I can't believe—" Unable to form a complete sentence, he began to laugh at the incredulity of the situation. The woman, he'd swear, was barely one step up from a homely mutt. He dropped the report on top of the file and walked away.

"You know," he said, "I am so damn angry right now for having any woman on this ship. You know how I feel about women in the Navy, period: They don't belong. Even when I fought so hard to keep them out, some of my superiors, you know, the ones who agree with me but won't back me, they told me to stand down. I wouldn't win that fight and needed to use caution when expressing my opinion. But to me that is just bullshit. I'm also aware of all the senior officers on this ship, how you've seen to it that they keep all the women billeted under their direct command well away from me."

"Well, it didn't stop you from shoving your foot in your mouth, though," Joe said. "Remember that one petty officer—what did you say? 'You have no business being in the Navy. You should be home looking after your husband and being a mother to your kids. Try being a good role model for them.' Oh, yeah, and then my favorite: You said to that young lieutenant, 'You have no business traipsing all over the world with a bunch of guys, trying to pretend you've grown a pair of man's balls when what you are is just a woman.' " Joe leaned against the door and shook his head. "I'm afraid you may have pissed off the wrong one."

He knew his reputation of being a chauvinistic bastard. The exact wording used by the women serving under him had most of them running the other way, but there had been one or two who'd seen it as a challenge, a fun challenge. One in particular had done her best to find any way she could to get him into bed with her, and she had been the one to cross the rigid military regulations of fraternization. He had put her in her place, and not in a nice way. Hell, Eric didn't coddle anyone. Especially women.

"Eric, you've always had issues with women. They're not all like your mother or those that fostered you, you know. There are good, decent women out there. Don't let this incident have you tarring and feathering all women again." Joe cleared his throat as Eric tried to take in what he was saying. Right now, hearing any woman's name left him with a bad taste in his mouth, except when he thought of Abby.

"So what really happened with Gail?" Joe asked.

"I dismissed that stupid twit as soon as I got there. I didn't want her to wake up Abby."

"Was Abby awake?" Joe asked.

Jamming his fingers in his hair again, he tugged and then closed his eyes. "No, I think she woke up shortly after."

"So then it comes down to your word against hers."

The reality hit Eric like a freight train plowing over him. Any situation without a witness became a he-said she-said, and for assault on a woman in the military, it could go either way. Looking over to meet Joe's pensive gaze, Eric was very aware of his friend's efforts to lighten the mood with a smile that seemed so pasted on it almost appeared painful. All the light had gone out of his eyes. Crap, this was really bad.

"Does the crew know?" Eric asked.

Joe shook his head and waved his hand toward the door. "Some of the officers do, but they know it's bullshit. The crew doesn't know yet, but I'm sure they will by day's end. You know I can't stop news like this. It's impossible.

You can be sure Gail is making sure everyone knows. You know, tell everyone, build allies, and do her damnedest to destroy you."

"God fucking damn her. Why now, when morale is low enough with news of the extension in our deployment? You can bet the crew will be taking sides and cause problems, all right."

"Eric, I want to talk to Abby to see if she remembers anything. Maybe she wasn't asleep and she can clear up this whole thing before it goes any further."

Shaking his head, not willing to budge, Eric gave a clear warning. "No, Joe, leave her out of this. She was asleep, and she is so upset that she's barely holding it together. After last night's close call, just leave her be. I don't want her to know about this, anyway. My God, she'd probably hate me. I'm going to put a call in to the admiral and see what help I can get from him."

Joe appeared to want to argue but then held both hands up in a show of surrender, grabbed the file, and rapped it against his leg. "Eric, I know you're angry. You have every right to be, but I need to warn you again: Be smart and avoid Gail. You are never to be alone with her anywhere on this ship. Don't give her that kind of power. Okay?"

Eric was beyond furious and gave only a dismissive wave in response. Joe opened his mouth, and Eric knew he probably had a whole lecture and a list of rules set out for Eric, but he was grateful when he spun on his heel and left, pulling the door closed behind him. He didn't need to say one more word about where this was going. This was a serious charge that might not just mean the end of his career, which was his entire reason to live. He could be facing years in hell: Leavenworth.

Chapter Thirteen

Eric made half a dozen calls to the admiral and finally spoke with the young woman who served as the admiral's assistant, stressing the urgency of speaking with the admiral right away. Eric had hesitated because he was well aware that the assistant had been the one to send over the report, but, to the woman's credit, she wasn't rude or abrupt. She was kind, and she even told him that she'd track the admiral down and see to it that he called back right away.

That had left a lump in his throat and clouded his black and white lines where women were concerned. He knew there wasn't a chance in hell that he'd be able to get any sleep right now, short of keeling over from exhaustion. He also knew that when he was on such a short fuse, he'd most likely do and say something stupid. Eric couldn't shake this feeling of helplessness, and he'd already worn a path in his carpet from pacing back and forth.

He grabbed the phone on his desk again. "Petey, I'm going down to the gym. Track me down if the admiral calls."

Then Eric was out the door. By the time he was dressed in a pair of shorts and facing the eighty-pound black bag, he set a pattern of right, right, then left jab, pounding away at the bag. He allowed the force of the blows to rock the bag, chained and hooked to the pipe above. What was he going to do? If these charges stuck, it would mean the end of his career in the Navy. He had enough put away financially that he would be okay, but his life would be worth shit if he couldn't spend it at sea. What would he be able to do in the private sector? Who would hire him? What about Abby? How could he protect her now? He didn't want to think about this or make plans, but he had to. This type of charge was a black mark that would haunt him for life, always there. People would always judge him. Even if he were cleared, everyone would always wonder if he had really done it.

Out of breath, he stopped and leaned heavily against the bag, sweat dripping from his forehead. His hair was soaked. For a moment, he felt as though his muscles, his bones, had aged far past his thirty-five years. He could not help the direction his thoughts were taking as they drifted back to Abby. God, what would she think of him if she ever found out about this? Would she feel hatred, maybe disgust? He couldn't bear that thought. He cared for her more than he expected, more than he had any right to, and he realized it mattered what she thought of him. Concerned, he felt a desperate need to check on her for his own peace of mind, just to see how she was doing.

Pushing away from the bag, he used his teeth to rip the Velcro encircling his wrists on the well-aged faded gloves he donned. Dumping them in his bag, he grabbed a towel to wipe away the dampness on his face. He tilted back his head, sucking down the water from the bottle he had packed with his gear. He emptied it, then gasped for breath as he wiped his mouth with his forearm. Done and drained, Eric gathered his gear and dressed in just his shorts. He pulled on a t-shirt and yanked open the door.

Petey stood on the other side with a guilty flush staining his cheeks. Sighing, Eric anchored his hand over the top of the door to lean on it, his bag slung over his shoulder. "Are you watching me? Did Joe send you to stand guard?" he snapped.

Petey suddenly swallowed. The color drained from his face, and his eyes widened as if he'd just been caught with his hand stuck in the cookie jar.

Eric sighed. "I'm going to grab a shower, then head to sickbay —since I presume the admiral hasn't called."

As he turned away to pass Petey, the young man cleared his throat roughly and said, "I was real sorry to hear about what Gail Carruthers did, accusing you like that. Me and the boys know none of it's true and would like to help if there's anything we can do, sir."

Eric stopped after a few steps and glanced back at Petey. "How well do you know her?"

"Well... not real well, but my friend Ernie Biggs in engineering says she hit on him a few times, only he didn't like her, said she was trouble. He said she likes to recruit others to do her dirty work, makes things up about people. He said she's got a dark cloud she carries over her."

"What did your friend mean by 'trouble'?"

"Ernie said she never does anything without a reason, like she thinks everyone has it in for her. He says she's a real screwball."

Eric wondered as he listened if maybe there was more to her background. It certainly wouldn't hurt to dig. Quite often, women like this had skeletons stashed a mile back in their closets. Maybe she'd done this before and was now just getting good at it. That thought alone spiked the hairs on the back of his neck, bringing an icy wariness of how truly dangerous she could be. He knew he hadn't done this, and everything about how she filed the report, her false accusation, it was as if she had planned it.... He stared at Petey hard and then glanced away, shuddering to think of what would happen to his career if he didn't get this cleared up. Everything he treasured—his ship, his crew, his status in the Navy—everything about it had shaped him into who he was, and this bitch had taken him by the balls and would, if given the opportunity, shake him til they rattled. The more he thought about it, the stronger his heated feelings of resentment for Gail became.

"I want you to go talk to the XO and tell him what you told me," Eric said. "Also, make sure you mention to him that I want him to speak to your friend Ernie, too." He started down the passageway, his sneakers squeaking, and then stopped and turned completely around. "Thanks, Petey, for all your support."

The young man gleamed, puffed out his chest, and offered a proud salute. This time, Eric saw how deeply this man worshipped him, and that took some of the sting from the awful ache and loneliness that he'd been feeling.

Chapter Fourteen

Abby was sitting up in bed with her thick blonde hair neat and shiny, reading a book. When Eric shut the door, she was watching him with something deep and soft and loving, and it reached across the room, right into his heart, and squeezed until he thought he'd go mad if he couldn't see her. It was beautiful, just like she was, and his throat thickened. He almost choked at how much it would hurt for her never to look at him that way again. That was exactly what would happen if she ever learned of Gail's dirty, cruel accusation.

Something caught his eye over by the lockers. Larry was watching Eric with such awkwardness that Eric wanted to race over there and throttle the man. The way his eyes widened and looked away, well, he just hated that shit. Abby was watching him, and then she glanced over at the doctor and back to him. Her eyebrows rose, and he knew she picked up something. He just hoped she wouldn't ask.

"Larry, don't go anywhere, I need to have a word with you," Eric said. Then he headed straight for Abby, feeling as if the floor would give out on him until he stood right beside her and she looked up at him with something that had him choking up: absolute trust. God, no woman had ever looked at him that way.

"Is everything all right?" she asked.

He couldn't help but touch her. He slid his hand over her shoulder and his calloused thumb across her jaw, and she leaned into it. "Fine, Abby. I just wanted to check and see how you are this morning." He tried to smile, but he also knew it didn't reach his eyes. Not even close.

"I'm fine, and no more contractions." She pointed a finger over to Larry. "The doctor said everything's okay this morning and told me to take it easy today." She was too intuitive for her own good, because she squinted those dynamic blue eyes at him as though he were a puzzle she was determined to solve. "You look tired. I'm so sorry I kept you up."

He grinned. "I'll survive, and you didn't keep me up. I wanted to be here. I need to talk to the doc for a minute. Don't go anywhere."

"As if I could," she answered in her soft voice. Eric left, with Larry behind him.

THE LAST THING Eric wanted to do was speak with Larry in the passageway, where every crew member could chance to pick up on what they were saying, especially in light of what Gail Carruthers had set in motion. So he led Larry straight to his cabin and shut the door.

"Captain, I am so sorry about Gail. If I'd known what she was going to pull, I would have put a stop to it." Larry shook his head, clenching and unclenching his fists in front of him. "I spoke with her in the mess hall, and she never even gave mention to this, this…" Larry gestured wildly with his hands as his face glowed a faded pink. Then he stopped and said nothing further. He stared like a helpless man at Eric, as if he somehow felt responsible. "I'm sorry."

Eric reached out and slapped him on the arm. "Larry, stop beating yourself up. I know you would have stopped her. Did you get a copy of the report?"

"Yes. Joe was down earlier and brought it to me. He questioned me, but I'm afraid I wasn't much help." Agitated, Larry began pacing the length of the office, clenching and unclenching his fists.

Eric watched him for a while until his own unease and anxiety, and anger, threatened to get the best of him. He stopped Larry, saying, "Frankly, I don't understand. Why the hell would she pull this?" He didn't wait for Larry to reply, because his mind was spinning a mile a minute. "What do you know about her past? I mean, when she transferred in under your department, were there any problems she had at other postings?"

Larry finally stopped pacing and approached the desk. He shook his head, his eyes blank. "I read her files and made a few inquiries, but nothing I could see.… And no, she has never spoken of anything." Larry shrugged. "But she wouldn't talk to me, anyway. But she *might've* talked to some of the women."

"Is there anyone you know she's close to?"

"I don't think there are many. I'll check around, but she is pretty isolated, keeps to herself. Does her work, though, so I've had nothing to complain about." Checking his watch, he winced at the captain. "She hasn't reported for duty yet, but I expect her in about twenty minutes. When I spoke to Joe, I told him I wanted her out of my department. What really pisses me off is that right now, he said I can't move her. If I start reassigning her or posting her to shit jobs, she could yell and scream that you're trying to get back at her."

"He's right, but let me be clear: I don't want her around Abby right now."

"Captain, do you think she would physically hurt her? Is that what you're worried about, because I can assure you —"

Cutting him off with a wave of his hand, Eric said, "No, no, it's not that. I don't want her to say something that would upset her. I don't want Abby to know of these charges, and I definitely don't want Gail telling her this fictitious story she created. How safe is it right now to move Abby?"

"Move her off the ship?"

Eric didn't miss the surprise that registered in Larry's voice. "No, not off the ship, but to one of the cabins reserved for the visiting officers and guests."

"Not right now. Maybe in a day or two. If we do, she can't be left alone. She's too close to delivering."

Eric sighed, hearing an edginess creep in the man's voice.

Larry continued. "I'll find a way to keep Gail out of sickbay and away from her as much as possible."

"One more thing, Doc. I don't want any word of this getting back to Abby. She doesn't need any more stress."

"As her doctor, I agree. She's just stabilized. The contractions have stopped, but any stress right now could bring labor back on. I doubt we'd be able to stop it a second time. I'd be happy if the baby held off for another week, and we could get her into Bahrain."

"No, she won't be going to Bahrain. Not yet."

The doctor looked rattled for a moment, but he didn't say a word.

Eric squeezed his neck, trying to work out the tight

knots that burned like hooks up the back of his neck. "I'm going back to talk to Abby," he said.

"Listen, before all the stuff with Gail happened this morning, I was going to talk to you about the nightmare Abby had, the one that brought on her early labor. The fear she had in her eyes, it's something I don't think I've ever seen before," Larry said.

"Shit, I was going to talk to her. I know some of her fears, and maybe I can talk to her and reassure her again."

"Yeah, well, I'm no shrink, but if it happens again next time, her labor probably won't stop. I can give her a sedative to help her sleep. That will probably keep the nightmares quiet, but I don't want to keep doing that. It's just not safe."

Wincing and then lowering his voice, Eric said, "I'll talk to her right after we're finished here."

Larry gestured to the door. "I'll make sure you're not disturbed, and as for Miss Carruthers, I'll make sure she's occupied elsewhere for the day."

ERIC WAS JUST behind Larry as he opened the door to sick bay. The guard outside flushed a deep red when he glanced nervously at the captain and then at the doorway. He started to say something when Eric spied Gail holding a chart and speaking with Abby, and in that instant he felt a red tide hamper his vision. It was the first time in his life that he thought he could kill someone.

He didn't realize he had even made it through the door until he saw Abby's wide eyes fix on him, then over to Carruthers and then Larry. Of course she knew something was going on.

Larry stepped in front of the captain. "Carruthers!"

Gail dropped the clipboard. It thunked on the floor as her head snapped toward Larry.

"I need to speak with you, now!" He pointed stiff fingers at the door. When she refused to move, opening her mouth as if to protest, Larry snapped, "I said now, Carruthers."

Slowly, so slowly, she stooped and picked up the clipboard, then dropped it without care on a side table. She appeared to thrust her stubby nose in the air and paced unhurriedly past the captain. Eric had to dig deep inside himself to not look at her, because all he wanted to do was give her a good kick in the rear to send her flying just as she walked past. He didn't, but he did count until he heard the door close and then looked over at Abby, who was watching him with a questioning look filled with such worry that he thought she'd leap out of bed and come over to him.

"What was that all about?" Her voice sounded breathy, and she pointed a finger towards the closed door.

With an edgy sigh, he turned a brief, heated look at the solid door before sliding a chair up to the bed and straddling it, resting his arms over the back. "Forget it. Just a little trouble that will be resolved shortly." The weariness crackled in his voice. Then he reached forward and squeezed her arm before allowing his hand to fall away. "Abby, I'm more concerned about what happened last night. Your nightmare scared you enough to put you into early labor. I want to talk to you about it —"

The buzz of the phone interrupted Eric.

"Just a minute, I need to get this." Jumping up, he reached the phone in two long strides. "Hamilton." He gazed back at Abby, realizing his talk would have to wait, as the admiral was on the line, waiting to talk to him. "I'll be right there," he said, hanging up the phone. He hesitated. "I have an important call coming in. I have to take it." He paused briefly while his eyes softened. "I'll be back to talk to you in a while. See if you can't get some rest in the meantime. Okay?"

She just nodded. "I'll try."

Eric hurried to the door and glanced back at a woman who would *not* sit quietly by and do nothing. She was quiet, honest, but she had a fighting spirit that he'd swear would go to the death. She was one woman he prayed he'd never disappoint.

Chapter Fifteen

"Admiral James, thanks for returning my call." The pounding headache Eric had struggled with earlier returned, pulsing viciously, as the tentacles tightened at the back of his neck. He leaned back in his chair and reached around, grasping his neck, squeezing, trying to relieve the building pressure.

"Sorry I couldn't get back to you earlier. Listen, I was going to call you anyway about this report I received via a Petty Officer Jennifer Hampton, filed by an HM3 Gail Carruthers. When I read the accusation, my first response was 'What the hell?' Frankly, I'm speechless. Tell me, is any of this true?"

Eric realized he would be questioned by so many as to whether he had done such a dirty, dark thing. However, having a man he had looked up to for years question his morals and whether he could even consider assaulting a woman had him wanting to throw the phone against the wall. "Admiral, I hope you know me better than that. Yes, it's bullshit! I would never do anything like that."

He could hear something in the admiral's voice on the

other end of the line, and he wasn't sure what it was, but he also knew he was so tired that he could read anything into a situation that wasn't there.

"I'm sorry, Eric, but I had to ask," he replied. Eric could hear tapping on the other end. "I've been questioning this, though. Why didn't you call me before I got it?"

"Actually, Admiral, believe it or not, none of us knew. This blindsided me. Since that scheming bitch fabricated the entire accusation…" Eric had to bite his tongue before he continued, because he was headed off track. "She didn't follow proper channels in filing the report. Joe was the first to get it, and he got it from your assistant."

The deep voice growled on the other end. "Are you telling me she did an end run around her commanding officer, sending it directly to the top?"

"I'm afraid so, Admiral."

"Why, that fucking little bitch! And this Petty Officer Jennifer Hampton who filed it for her, what's that all about?"

"I can't believe any of this, Admiral, so it makes no sense why Hampton would do that. Admiral, what do you know about her past postings? Any trouble there with former commanding officers or other sailors? I mean, something like this —"

"Eric, you're grasping. And there will be an investigation. Don't go poking your head into her past and do something that will blow up in your face. I don't think I need to tell you that there is more focus right now on women's rights in the military. The media are all over any perceived abuse, especially assault on women." The Admiral paused before continuing, his tone sympathetic. "Eric, I'll do what I can to help, but I gotta tell you, if the media gets a hold of this, shit's going to hit the fan. You, of all males, have been quite vocal in your low opinion of women, saying they've no place in the Navy. The rest of us have learned to find a way to deal with them, checking our mouths before we say something really stupid or what we're really thinking. You haven't, and I've warned you on more than one occasion to find a way to deal with it, to stop getting in every female sailor's face and telling them they should be bed warmers for their husbands."

"Are you saying I asked for this?" Eric fumbled in the top drawer and grabbed the bottle of Tylenol. He popped off the lid with his thumb and dumped a couple pills in his mouth straight from the bottle.

"Oh, don't be an ass, Eric. That's not what I'm saying. What she's done is reprehensible. But you *have* to wise up. What you've done with your mouth has made you an easy bullseye. What I want to know from you is what really happened."

Eric dug his fingers into his scalp. "She disregarded protocol, refused to acknowledge me as her commanding officer. I dismissed her abruptly. I believe I was too easy on her. I realized I can be quite abrupt, but, having said that, the attitude and the situation in sickbay at the time warranted the dismissal. With all due respect, Admiral, I am concerned more by her complete disregard for my authority as captain of this ship. Look where we are, for God's sake. I mean, how did she get it to you…?" Eric stopped cold mid-sentence as it hit him, the security breach. How had she been able to get it off this ship without anyone knowing? God, what the hell was happening on his ship?

"Eric, you have a ship to run, and when your people are sending information off your ship without anyone knowing, I'd say that you have a major security breach. All those involved need to be taken to task."

"You're absolutely right, Admiral. I'll lock it up tight."

"Listen, is there any way to disprove this claim of hers quickly and easily? Any witnesses? Or were you truly alone with her, like she said? Because I got to tell you, that's about as bad as it gets."

Sighing heavily, he rubbed his eyes with his thumb and forefinger. "There were no witnesses, no one. There was someone there, but they were asleep at the time."

"You know, Eric, unofficially, I'll do everything to block this thing, but between you and me, it's going to be real tough to squelch an official investigation. It's already gone too far. I'll find out who else has it. If she sent a copy here, where else did she send it? Unfortunately, you and I both know what that means."

He answered for the admiral, the pain lingering in his voice. "Yeah, I know, suspension of duties." Eric felt as if he had swallowed his heart, finally admitting aloud what he'd already known could happen.

"Is Joe investigating on your end?"

Eric nodded. As he did, his throat was so thick he couldn't speak for a moment. "Yeah, he's already begun speaking with the crew."

"Okay. Well, I want to talk to him. In the meantime, make sure you're never alone with the girl, got it?"

Just hearing the admiral have to tell him to stay away from her, as if he was already guilty, scraped away at the ache, which was so much like a festering scab that he almost flinched. "Don't worry. I have no desire to be alone with her."

Eric set the phone back in its cradle and then leaned back into his chair, feeling as if all the starch had gone out of his limbs. It was defeat that was nipping at his backside, and he didn't like it one bit. He was damn tired, and his head ached, so he leaned back, propping his feet up on his desk and closing his eyes for just a minute, just until the unrelenting pounding went away.

The pounding on the door startled him. Jerking his feet off the desk, he slammed them on the floor and had to blink a couple times to shake off the cobwebs in his head. Glancing at his watch, he was shocked to realize he'd fallen asleep for nearly three hours. He swiped his hand over his rough, whiskered face, which he still hadn't shaved, and called out, "Come in."

The door popped open, and Joe stepped in. Eric knew he looked a mess, but Joe confirmed it as his open gaze showed his concern.

"You look like shit. Seriously, did I wake you?"

He rubbed the corners of his eyes, which scraped as if sand had blown into them. "What do you want? Sorry, Joe, I didn't mean to snap."

The Tylenol had done nothing to ease the pounding in the back of his head, so he grabbed the bottle and swallowed a couple more pills. He jumped when Joe appeared beside him, handing him a glass of water. He gestured his thanks and downed it, wiping his mouth with the back of his hand. "What's up?" he asked, pressing his fingers firmly to his temples while trying to massage away the vicious pounding in his head.

"I spoke with Petey, and he filled me in on your conversation this morning. I followed up with Ernie Biggs and some of the other enlisted men. Well, none of them like her. That pretty much sums it all up, even before this incident. A few even mentioned to me that they would want to teach her a lesson."

A lesson? Eric rolled his eyes but said nothing. He couldn't condemn any of them, because the same thought had drifted through his own mind.

"I spoke with the admiral a short time ago. I wanted to

let you know he agrees with me that Gail needs to be watched closely—you know, for her protection, of course," Joe said.

Eric didn't miss the sarcasm dripping from his voice. He turned his chair around to face him.

"Of course, she'll be given the option of reassignment to headquarters by Vice Admiral James. If she refuses, she'll be assigned a female guard who will shadow her. Again, this'll be for her own protection."

"Jesus, Joe, how do you come up with this stuff? You're one sly bastard. Remind me never to piss you off." He felt better as he watched the devilish spark in Joe's boyish, charming gaze. You couldn't help but take him seriously if you didn't know him well.

"I wanted to let you know first before I talk to her. As you're probably aware, she's going to lose it, maybe. She'll definitely raise shit, but it'll only backfire on her. You know how it is. We're doing our best to make sure that she's kept safe and protected, and that's exactly how I'll make sure it's viewed."

Eric noted the smugness in his tone. "Holy shit, Joe. I'm so glad you're on my side."

"Eric, go get some sleep. You really do look like shit. I'll get Petey to defer anything dicey to me for a few hours. I need you to be well rested so we can fight this with a level head and not with your temper."

Eric said nothing because it irritated the hell out of him that everyone had to remind him over and over to watch his step, as if he were a reckless loose cannon.

"We'll beat this." Joe signaled to the door, and his grin faded to the concern that Eric was tired of seeing on everyone's face. "I'll see you're not disturbed."

Eric just watched as his friend left, shutting the door behind him. He realized then that he had friends and they cared about him enough to go to bat for him, to do the damnedest creative things, and Joe would always have his back. That kind of trust and loyalty was something Eric would live and die for. But Joe was right: Eric needed sleep, and he was tired. If he could get his head to stop spinning and working overtime, creating problems and picturing all the what ifs and should haves, then he might be able to sleep for a bit. It was that constant droning in his head that had made him into who he was, though, and right now, as he groaned like an old man making his way to his bed, he collapsed, boots and all, and closed his eyes, but it was Abby's kind, soft blue eyes—the color of some of the cleanest water down south—that followed him into his dreams.

Chapter Sixteen

Larry escorted Gail to the wardroom. He could feel the fury pulse through him as he ground out his steps in a hurried pace, and he hoped she was finding it difficult to keep up. He pushed open the door and shot a look at one light-haired officer lingering over coffee. The officer took one look at Larry and who was behind him, and, with a sharp incline of his head, he left, keeping an obvious distance from Gail.

When Larry faced Gail, looking down on the short, stubby woman who was far from a prized beauty, she stuck her stubborn chin up and crossed her arms, staring right back at him.

"I want to know right now why you would file a false accusation against the captain. What you did and how you went about it are absolutely reprehensible. Explain to me what happened, because you obviously misread something somewhere."

"No, sir, everything that happened is in the report." She said it in such a calm manner that he was, for a moment, stunned.

"Ah, yes, the report you filed and sent directly to the admiral. By the way, that was quite the end run. Who in the hell do you think you are pulling this? There are protocols, and you know quite clearly the chain of command. That report should have come to *me*. You were to come to *me*. How dare you forward the report directly to headquarters?" Clasping his hands behind his back, he studied her and the hardness that transformed her face. Her hazy brown eyes stilling, she looked straight at him until a frosty sheen had her blinking.

"I felt it was necessary. Sorry to disappoint you, sir, but the charges are true, and everything that happened is in the report." Her voice shook when she spoke.

Larry stepped closer and put his face inches from hers. Intimidation wasn't something he did, but this woman was taking his emotions and the balance of right and wrong and tossing them right out the window. Maybe he could scare her into confessing. He considered it. "You and I both know that report was bullshit! Just what the hell are you trying to pull?"

She didn't move a muscle; her control was amazing. Instead, she looked straight ahead at something over his shoulder, now refusing to meet his eyes. "My report stands, sir, and I will not be bullied or intimidated by you or any other officer on this ship into recanting my story. It's the truth, and it really happened." A smug righteousness, as if she'd managed to gain the upper hand, snuck into her voice.

It was so sudden that Larry actually took a step back. Her chin began to tremble and tears popped into her eyes, streaming down both her cheeks. The woman was absolutely appalling, as if she truly believed it. An amazing actor could pull this off, but so could an accomplished liar, a sociopath. He was reaching, studying her, trying to figure her out. Then he glanced around at the long table with the line of black chairs on both sides for the officers. The fact was that he was very much alone with her, and he shouldn't have been.

"Until further notice, you will confine yourself to the supply room to complete a full inventory. You will not step foot into sickbay. Do I make myself clear?"

"You can't do that, sir. You're just getting back at me! I know this is a boy's club, and you all lie and stick together."

Larry felt his face heat and could feel the pulse of his blood pressure soaring. "You heard me, Carruthers. I gave you an order." He let out a low sigh of frustration. "No more games. I want you to go report to the personnel office for reassignment pending the outcome of this investigation."

As her mouth fell open, he waited, expecting her refusal. He hoped she would, because right now, his common sense and sound reasoning had taken a hike, and he was left with a fury that demanded he act and would only be satisfied if he could physically drag her down, consequences be dammed.

"I'll be filing a grievance," she threw back at him as she turned on her heel and stormed to the door.

He shouted after her. "Go right ahead, Carruthers, but heed me: You will not get away with this. I'll see to it you're roasted alive." Larry was breathing hard as he stepped into the doorway, watching as she stormed down the hallway, shouldering several crewmen out of the way. His sound reasoning crashed in on him when two of the sailors in the passageway stared at him as if they'd just been caught doing something they shouldn't have.

Larry rubbed his hand roughly over his face and then fixed them with a look that said they'd better find their way quickly back to their stations.

"Sir," one of them said as they hurried the other way.

Larry was so distracted he almost stumbled when he came around the corner and saw Abby in the passageway with Gail. The guard was standing there, looking as though he wished he was anywhere but there.

"What are you doing out of bed?" Larry said. Abby jumped, and her hand immediately went to her heart. Larry put his hands around Abby's shoulders and guided her back through the open door.

"I didn't know she was supposed to stay in there. I was just told to keep the other crew out. I didn't know what to do when she said she was just going for a walk," the guard said defensively as he followed the doctor and Abby through the open door. Larry glanced over his shoulder to where Gail stood in her tan uniform, her face pink. A few other members of the crew were hurrying past, everyone peeking in to get a look at Abby. "You heard my orders," Larry snapped. He could feel Abby cringe from the bite of his words, and Gail just shrugged and continued on down the passageway.

Larry settled Abby back on the bed.

"Really, Doc, I'm sorry. She just opened the door...." The guard was behind him, and Larry could just imagine that the possibility of making the captain angry was what had him so upset.

Cutting him off before he could finish rattling on, Larry said, "It's okay. I know you weren't told, but Miss Abby is to stay in bed, and she knows that." He dismissed the guard with a simple gesture of his head.

Larry didn't turn around. He just grabbed his stethoscope and blood pressure cuff from the secured drawer. "What were you thinking? You had no business getting out of bed. You were just in early labor, Abby, and did I not make it clear for you to take it easy? Are you trying to have this baby early?" He was abrupt, which was unlike him.

"What's going on with Gail Carruthers? I mean what I saw earlier and now out in the passageway…" She gestured with a hand to the door as if Gail was just on the other side.

Larry cut her off as he approached the bed. "Abby, that's just some on-board conflict that will soon be resolved. It's nothing for you to worry about."

She automatically held out her arm to him as he wrapped the blood pressure cuff around it. He pumped up the cuff and listened through the stethoscope, watching her watching him. He had to shut his eyes and take her blood pressure again, he was so distracted, and then she yelped when he pumped the cuff too tight.

He ripped off the cuff. "Abby, I'm so sorry."

She rubbed her upper arm where a red welt now appeared. "I know there's something going on. I'm not stupid, you know. Look how distracted you are. Why won't you tell me what's going on?"

He did his damnedest to get his head together as he folded up the cuff. "It doesn't concern you, so please stop worrying. You're looking good despite your little adventure. Have you had any more contractions? Is the baby active?"

"No and yes," she said. "Please… where is the captain? Is he all right?"

Maybe if he sent the captain down to deal with her, she'd let it go, but when he glanced at the worry and determination that filled her amazing blue eyes, he could see the attachment she had to the captain.

"The captain is fine. He'll be here soon. I believe he's getting some well-deserved shut eye. Abby, listen, I know you care. There are some problems, but…" He straightened and frowned at her, trying his best to give her a stern doctor look "You need to focus on you, young lady. Please don't take on the problems of the ship. Conflicts happen. This is my responsibility and the captain's to handle, and after last night, we need to get you safely through the end of the week without you going into labor again. That's the most important thing." Larry tried to focus and pulled out her chart, scribbling down her vitals.

Abby cleared her throat. "I'm sorry for being so pushy. I didn't mean to cause you any worry. Is Gail Carruthers in some way related to the unsettled conditions around here?"

Larry hesitated a second, then another, before turning around and studying the tiny battered woman they'd pulled from the sea a few days ago. She wasn't backing down. She just kept coming at it from a different angle. "Shit," he muttered under his breath. Sighing deeply, he dropped the pen and turned back to her with his hands on his hips. "You're just not going to let this drop, are you?"

She shook her head with determination.

"Abby, you're going to have to talk to the captain," Larry began. They were interrupted by the captain's voice in the corridor. "Thank you, God," Larry muttered as Eric strode in, looking much more rested.

"Captain," Larry said as he approached Eric by the door and gestured his head toward Abby. "I found her out of bed in the passageway. She told the guard she wanted to take a walk, but Gail was there, too. I ordered Carruthers to personnel for reassignment. Abby knows something's wrong. She keeps asking, and she's figured out it has to do with Carruthers." Larry shot Abby a glance over his shoulder, and he could tell she was doing her best to hear what he was saying, but she couldn't from that distance.

"You found her where? Out there?" Eric pointed firmly while maintaining a close, steady distance with the doctor.

He glanced over the doctor's shoulder at Abby, unmoving. "Okay, did they talk?"

"I'm not sure what was said before I arrived, but she doesn't know anything about…" He waved his hand as if to continue in place of the words.

Nodding, Eric said, "I understand, Doc. Is she okay otherwise? Any more labor?"

"No, she's fine. She is concerned and is questioning the situation with Gail and the on-board conflict. She picked up on something." Larry glanced down at his watch. "I'm going to go and get her dinner."

Eric let the doctor pass. He didn't move, keeping his arms crossed as he tried to figure out what he was going to say. Was she mad at him? She'd be furious and would look at him like a monster, the same look she carried in her eyes for Seyed, and if she knew what Gail was accusing him of, well, he just couldn't stand that.

"Captain, I hope you got some rest?" she asked.

He inclined his head and took a step toward her. Every time he was around her, she did something to him that made him want to be a better man, but he also wanted to protect her so that nothing bad could ever touch her again. He wanted to smooth away those worry lines that creased her brows, and he wanted to be the one who put that easy, carefree smile on her face and had it lighting up every time he walked in. "I did."

"Has Gail Carruthers done something to cause discord or trouble on this ship, to you or to the doctor?"

Eric could not help smiling at the fire that was in those deep blue eyes, which saw far more than he had first realized. Bending down, he ruffled her blond mass of hair before ignoring the chair and sitting on the bed beside her. Her scent—my God, the way she smelled from plain old soap and water—was a perfume of her own, as if it was just for him. He wanted to sit beside her, to touch her, but he didn't. He set his hands in his lap and then linked them together so he wouldn't be tempted to reach out and take hers. "Abby, there's nothing for you to worry about. I'll handle it. I didn't get to where I am, commanding my own ship, without encountering a few problems here and there." Softening his tone, he leaned forward, meeting her steady gaze. "I'm touched by your concern, but it's nothing, really."

She watched him, and he could see she was thinking, but for the life of him he didn't know of what. Then she offered a subtle tilt of her head. "Understood," she said.

The door jerked open and Larry stepped in, carrying a blue plastic tray with several covered dishes. He gave only a passing glance at Eric sitting so close to Abby. "Here's your dinner, Abby."

Eric slid off the bed, and Larry slid the tray on the bedside table, the utensils clanking as he slid the table in front of Abby.

"I'll make sure she eats," Eric said.

"Well, I have things to check, so I'll leave you and be back later to check on you. Lieutenant Lynn will be in in about an hour to check your vitals again."

After the door closed, Eric started pacing while she lifted the metal warmers off the plates.

"Are you hungry? I could share," she said.

He just shook his head "No, I'll eat later." He watched her while she picked up the glass of apple juice and pried off the plastic lid. Sometimes she looked so childlike that he wanted to hide her in a closet so nothing would ever again hurt her.

Abby dug into the roast chicken and vegetables on the plate, cutting a bite and putting it in her mouth. She didn't eat fast but took her time, tasting each bite and enjoying it in a way he hadn't seen before.

"This is really good." She pointed with her fork to the plate. "I had no idea how much I missed simple food."

"Glad to hear, because I wanted to talk to you about something."

She laid her fork down on the side of her plate and picked up her napkin, wiping her mouth. "Oh?"

"No, keep eating." He motioned with his hand.

She picked up her fork, cut another piece of chicken, and put the tiny morsel in her mouth, flicking her tongue over her lower lip. Eric found himself staring at the spot, and for a moment he wanted to put his own tongue there.

"You will be staying on this ship. We can't risk moving you right now," he said. She nodded, such trust in her eyes. "I also wanted to talk to you about your nightmare last night."

She gripped her fork quite hard and then set it down, lowering her gaze to her plate.

"Abby, one of my concerns is your fear that Seyed will get you back, and I'm worried that brought on your nightmare. I want you to know that you're safe here. He can't get you."

"I dreamed of when I was taken. I could smell the sandalwood burning. I could feel the rope burns. I wore a blindfold, and it was knotted so tightly that it pulled into the back of my head. I couldn't get it off. I wasn't the only one; there were others. I couldn't see, and the sound of metal doors closing shot through me a fear I have never felt before. There were rough hands that grabbed me, dragged, stuck me in a room, barefoot and chained up like an animal. There were other girl's whimpering, crying. I remember when the door opened, the chill I felt wasn't from cold but an icy dread. I didn't know the hell I was in or what would happen to me, if they would hurt me, kill me. It was a fear of the unknown. Then this man grabbed me by the hair and pulled me up, and I remember him saying—I thought at first his accent was English, but then I realized, no, it was Australian, and I could smell the tobacco on his breath as he pressed his lips to my cheek and ran his tongue over my ear. And he said what a pretty price I would fetch and how much they liked the towheads." When she glanced up, her eyes were red rimmed and filled with sadness. She refused to shed one tear, though. "I didn't know then what would happen to me. I got away, but what about the other girls? There were so many."

Eric swallowed, but the lump that jammed his throat felt so much like dry gravel that he couldn't speak.

"I am so ashamed of what happened," she said.

He started to jump in, to try to make her believe she had nothing to be ashamed of, but she held up her hand. It was trembling, and he could see the strength in her as she fought to steady it.

"I know I did nothing wrong. But you're not a woman. To have someone own you, tell you when to eat, when to sleep, what to wear, when to speak, to be beaten and taken violently, to be chained like an animal…" She touched her belly, and Eric wondered then if she'd want to get rid of the baby, if it would be an ugly reminder of what she'd survived.

"If I could make it all not have happened to you, I would." He wasn't sure if he should sit beside her, but the way she watched him was as if there was a cord pulling him down beside her, so he sat with her on the bed and slid the table over.

"I know you would." She stared at him so intently that for a minute, he wondered what she'd do if he leaned down and touched her lips. Then he reminded himself of what she'd been through. The last thing she needed was some man, any man, pawing at her. He rested his hand on her belly and smoothed it over the swell. She raised her hand as if welcoming his touch.

"Are you okay with the baby and whose it is?"

She furrowed her brows, and her eyes snapped with something resembling fire. "Whose it is?" she repeated. "This baby's *mine*, and no one will take it from me. When I was floating on the dinghy before you found me, I was so afraid he'd find me. It was just a matter of time. I wondered if I'd have the strength to drown myself and the baby, because it would be better than any life with that monster. A boy would have everything, but a girl… she would have no future."

"He won't get you. You'll stay here. I'll protect you and your baby. This is my ship, and nobody comes on board without my knowing."

She stared at him and then frowned as if she had just realized something. "Is Seyed trying to get me back? Is that it? He could find a way to get on board. You can't put anything past him."

"Abby, we don't know anything about him, really. My ship is so secure that an army couldn't get on if it wanted to. As soon as the doctor says you can get up and move around, I'll take you around the ship and show you how secure you really are."

"You never really answered me. Is there some reason I should be worried about Seyed?" she asked again, and she stared at him with such big, imploring eyes that he couldn't lie to her, but he didn't want to scare her, either.

"Our sources have confirmed that someone fitting his description returned to Kish Island a few days ago." Eric watched her face pale, and she let out a gasp as she turned away. He cupped her chin in one hand and looked down into the distress in her face. "I will protect you. He will never get his hands on you again."

Her eyes were swimming with tears when she looked up at him. "I want to believe you. And I do trust you… it's just —"

"I know, Abby." Eric slid his arm around her shoulder, and this time she leaned into him. He rested his chin on top of her head, realizing how much this woman needed him. For the first time ever, a fragile woman had somehow found a way in a tiny corner of his heart. For the life of him, he didn't know how she had managed to sneak in and hold parts of him he never believed could feel anything in her tiny hand, and he needed her, too.

Eric didn't know how long he held her, but she relaxed so much that he could feel her breathing even out. When he looked down, he realized she'd fallen asleep. Just as he eased her head down on the pillow, he took in her image, which was so much that of an angel.

He'd just reached for the phone to call Petey when the door flew open, and Gail Carruthers stepped in and closed the door behind her. Eric just held the phone and flicked a wary glance at Abby, who was breathing deeply, her eyes closed. He did not want her disturbed or to witness whatever this unstable woman was about to unleash on him. Where the hell was the guard? He was supposed to be standing right outside the door. How had Gail gotten past him?

Gail gave him an expression as if she was goading him. At any other time, he would have lost it on her and yelled and watched her cower, but he could feel Abby's peaceful energy behind him, and it was only that which got him to the door.

He yanked it open, startling the guard who was

standing post. "Kaskin, why did you allow her in here? I personally heard the doctor order you to keep her out."

"Sir, she said—"

"I want you to escort Carruthers out of sickbay, and until further notice, she stays out."

"Yes, Captain." The guard stepped inside the room, in front of the captain, and extended his arm, gesturing for Gail to precede him through the door. They both nearly tripped over the doctor, who now stood in the passageway.

"This way, please." Seaman Kaskin gestured again when Gail wouldn't move any further. When he grabbed her elbow to move her, she yanked it away and moved down the passageway with the doctor and captain following.

"Carruthers, you'll take yourself and report to the XO. You will be put on report. This conduct is unacceptable, and it will not be tolerated." The captain gritted his teeth, doing his damnedest not to lose it on Kaskin. "See that she gets there and doesn't get lost along the way. Then return to your post. Tomorrow, I'll deal with you for disobeying orders."

"Yes, sir, Captain."

Eric dismissed Kaskin and turned to Larry. "What was she doing here? I thought you assured me—"

"I ordered her to the personnel office this morning and told her sickbay was off limits." Larry was quite defensive.

Eric narrowed his eyes on Gail Carruthers' retreating backside, wanting nothing more than to toss her overboard. "Well, it seems that Miss Carruthers has decided to balk at all authority. Just so you know, Joe has just ordered a female guard to be with her at all times. Why she is not with her now, I will find out. I will personally see to it that these orders are followed through. No more disregard for authority on this ship by anyone. I don't understand what the hell's going on. It's as if everyone has lost their minds." Never in his experience of commanding a ship had his authority ever been questioned or orders so flagrantly disregarded. Why weren't orders being followed? He needed to have a serious discussion with Joe. This would be addressed first thing in the daily department head meeting; he would clamp down on everyone and bring a firm reign to this ship, seeing to it that every sailor knew their role and who was in charge.

Eric let out a groan that sounded more like a growl. "Just so you know, the guard will be dogging her every move from now on." He offered a conspiratorial wink, his lips twitching in amusement all the while. "You know, for her protection, of course."

"Leave it to Joe to come up with something like that. Just don't underestimate her. I think that was my first mistake," Larry said.

Chapter Seventeen

Eric met Joe in the wardroom for a late dinner. When the last officer left, Eric threw down his napkin and pushed the plate away. "So, did Gail find her way to you?"

Joe was across from him, and he choked and coughed before leaning back and chuckling. "Oh, yeah, she found her way, escorted by the good Seaman Kaskin, who looked as if he'd have just as soon tossed her in the brig. From the glare she gave him, it appeared that he may have had to drag her along at some point." Joe wiped his mouth with his napkin. "She's a piece of work, that's for sure. I spoke with her and gave her a choice between reassignment to headquarters or a female guard. She refused both, of course, so I assigned Chief Petty Officer Cindy Hawkins to her. I made her wait while I sent for Cindy." Joe shoved his plate away with a flick of his fingers. "Don't worry. I had a chat with Cindy, and she'll stick to her like glue."

"Joe, what took so long to talk to Gail? I understood when we spoke in my cabin she was your next stop."

"Sorry, Eric. She was off duty and asleep last night after we finished speaking. She was first on my list this morning to deal with, but an emergency from home came up for one of the new recruits. It's been handled, but it took longer than expected. Some of them are having a hard time adjusting with the extension in deployment."

Eric could tell by the frown on Joe's face that the deployment was more of a problem with the crew than he was letting on. He knew that taking care of the sailors was such a vital part of Joe, something he lived and breathed, because he really cared for these sailors. Life at sea wasn't easy, especially for new recruits, and Joe was always pushing his way into whatever personal conflicts popped up.

"We're a team here, Joe. We bond together or we all die. I know you're the one to keep the peace here. This is no place for dissension and petty conflicts, so you look after everyone. Just make sure you look after you, too, my friend."

Joe laughed and then wiped his hand roughly over his face.

"Larry lost it on her, you know," Eric said. "He confronted her about her accusation and tried to get her to confess. Then he sent her off for reassignment, banning her from sickbay. Joe, from now on, I want a daily report of her actions. Keep it unofficial, though, so it can't be used against me."

Joe pushed away from the table and walked across the room to the coffee urn. "You want one?" he asked as he poured a cup and stirred in some powdered cream.

"Sure."

Joe poured a second cup into a large white mug and set it on the table in front of Eric. Joe took a swallow as he walked around the table. "I checked, and Gail never arrived in the personnel office when Larry ordered her there." Joe continued, "I did make sure her behavior and misconduct has been written up, and she's been put on report." Taking another sip of coffee, he appeared lost in thought as he frowned. "You know, Eric, there's one thing I've wondered about. I did a little checking this morning. Gail had help getting that report off this ship without anyone finding out."

"I forgot to tell you, and it slipped my mind, too. When I spoke with the admiral, he told me it was filed by Petty Officer Jennifer Hampton. Isn't she in the administration department?"

"She is, a nice girl. Quiet, never been any problem. I'm stunned." Joe gestured with both his hands.

"Why the hell did she do it? Did you talk with her?"

Joe winced and glanced at the door and back to Eric. "You may not like hearing this, but your barbaric views on women have earned you somewhat of a negative reputation. She said Gail convinced her that you would block this if she went through regular channels. She begged her for help."

Leaning his head back over the plush high back of the leather chair, Eric gazed up at the mottled gray pipes, shaking his head in disbelief.

"After Master Chief Bud Hansen was through with her, I kind of felt sorry for the girl," Joe said. "It was a bad decision on her part. You could tell she sincerely regrets what she did. She's been put on report for her actions. Even though she has no previous record, Bud said he would like to bring charges if possible against her for misconduct, to use her as an example."

Eric winced. "Wasn't she due for promotion?"

Joe took on a hard look Eric had only seen a time or two before. "Yes, spotless service record, too. Stupid move on her part. Could be a career ender."

Eric didn't know why he did it, but he said, "I want to

talk to her. Set up a meeting for tomorrow. Tell Bud to be there, too, and tell him to hold off possible charges until after the meeting."

Joe appeared surprised but then downed his coffee and left the table. "I'll let you know what time we're meeting tomorrow." Joe let go of the handle and pressed his hand against the door as he turned to face Eric. "I realized I forgot to ask: How's Abby doing?"

"She's doing fine, but she picked up on the problem with Gail. And she's…" He almost told Joe about her nightmare, what she had shared with him, but it was too personal. It would feel like a betrayal of her if he shared it.

"And what?"

Eric just shrugged. "Nothing, she's good. I'll see you tomorrow."

He watched the back of the steel door and allowed the ship's rumble to soothe his anxiety. Eric realized this was the first time he'd ever kept anything from Joe.

Chapter Eighteen

All the commanding officers from each department were present in the wardroom for breakfast. Although everyone was well aware of the unsavory accusation filed by Gail Carruthers, almost every man present was uncomfortable. Maybe it was the fear, so much like a poison, that it could happen to them. Eric was no fool—he sensed deep down that some of them needed to keep their distance for their own peace of mind. This was the deepest, darkest worry of every man in the military, that it could happen to them, too. It took something really bad to see who stuck by you and who'd let you get pulled down and swallowed in the quicksand.

A few of the officers had been barely able to control their outrage. They'd yelled curses, and he'd seen in each of their eyes that Gail Carruthers would forever be burned. One day, she'd be brought down.

"Everyone knows the charges are false. I know some of you are scared shitless that it could happen to you. Let me be clear: The woman lied."

"Yeah, she's got the face of a toad. Fat chance she'd have of getting some guy to fuck her in the back room."

Another of the officers barked out, "Only in her dreams."

Everyone else laughed. Eric gestured to Joe to rein the guys in.

Joe stood up. "Okay, everyone, listen up. I'll be meeting with all relevant crew members to investigate this incident and to question Gail's credibility. As many of you may not be aware, I've assigned a guard to shadow Gail until further notice, for her own safety, of course."

A resounding boom of laughter shook the walls of the wardroom.

When the laughter died down, Eric spoke over their shouts. "Listen up. Everyone is to give full cooperation and to send anyone with firsthand knowledge directly to Joe. Follow protocol to the letter on this one, boys. That'll be all."

Each of the officers either patted Eric's shoulder or offered some words of support as they passed. It was very much an old boys' club. Most would help him beat this, he was sure of that, but even in a boys' club, there were those who lived and breathed survival of the fittest, and if it wasn't in their best interest to support Eric, they'd throw him to the wolves. As each officer left, he started putting each one of them into categories: those who would hang him out to dry or those who would stand by him for whatever it took. Unfortunately, the latter category was less than half of the officers.

"Bud, stay behind. Joe?" He gestured to his XO, who shut the door after the last officer left. Bud was a large, stocky man in his early forties. He had worn his hair in the same crew-cut style in all the years Eric had known him. His large arms and chest resembled a barrel, and he walked around with a perpetual scowl on his face, which always made any new sailor wary of him. When he was angry, he had a terrible temper, and Eric could almost visualize the upbraiding that Jennifer had received. With his set of lungs, when he yelled, you would swear you felt the walls shake. He had a propensity to get right in someone's face when he was angry, within inches, noses almost touching, just waiting for the other person to flinch.

"So, Bud, I understand you want to bring Jennifer up on charges," Eric said.

Without blinking, Bud nodded firmly. "You bet I do. She pulled quite a stunt, considering where we are. What she did could have serious consequences for everyone on this ship. There's no room for any crew member to start picking and choosing what rules or procedures he or she wants to follow. If she wants to do that, she can get out of the fucking Navy and go work for some poor schmuck and ruin his life."

Eric swung around in his leather chair and faced Joe across from him, then Bud at the end of the table. "Let's reserve that decision until after we meet with her, but let me make myself clear: I agree with you, Bud. What these women did could have compromised everyone on this ship." Turning in his chair to look at Joe, he indicated to the door. "Where is she?" Looking down at his watch, he noted the time, 0711.

"Should be here. Told her to be here at seven hundred, no excuses." Joe stood up and strode to the door on long legs. His head disappeared around the corner of the door, then his arm. Soon, she appeared. He held the door open for her to pass.

Her long dark hair was neatly pinned up. Small and pretty, the girl next door was how Eric would describe her. Standing, she reached just below Joe's shoulder, and she was trembling so hard that Eric wondered if she was about to break down in tears. Dread filled her china-like face when she glanced warily at the captain, and he noticed how completely devoid of color she was. Her eyes were red rimmed, with gray circles underneath. Visibly shaking, she came to attention and waited for her superiors to acknowledge her presence.

"Petty Officer Jennifer Hampton, sir."

Waving her to an empty chair at the head of the table, Eric remained at the center, watching her every move. "Sit down," he said sternly. "Petty Officer Hampton, your recent conduct of events is clearly a dereliction of duty. I want to make it clear to you that charges are being considered against you."

Looking straight ahead, stone-faced, she nodded. "Yes, sir, Captain."

"First, I want you to explain yourself. I want to know everything that happened in detail, along with whatever possessed you to flagrantly disobey regulations."

Her eyes darted to Eric's. She licked her lips, her anxiety clear in the way the lump in her throat flinched when she swallowed. "Um… permission to sp-speak…" She cleared her throat. "To speak freely, sir?" Her voice cracked.

Feeling somewhat sorry for the girl, he leaned forward, pushing a pitcher of water and a glass across the table. "Go ahead."

Jennifer nodded and poured herself a glass. She took a sip and then set the glass within easy reach. She clasped her hands together on the table. Her fingers were trembling. She took a breath. "Two days ago, Gail approached me, telling of an incident that happened in sickbay. She told me you had it in for her, and since you were friends with her commanding officer, her allegations would never see the light of day." She paused briefly and met Eric's eyes, her expression reflecting true remorse. "I'm sorry, sir, but at the time, um… Well, sir, you've made it no secret that you don't like women and have voiced your objection to having us women in the service. Gail suggested that retaliation by peers was common and a criminal investigation would most likely be blocked by you, sir, Lieutenant Saunders, and Commander Reed. You, too, sir." She looked over at Joe respectfully with what appeared to be regret. "Sir, there have been many reports of abuse in the service. I have met some of these women who suffered harm. Sir, what was worse for them was the retribution from their commanding officers."

Eric remained silent but crossed his arms.

"Anyway, I just wanted to help her. I thought I was doing the right thing at the time, but I do regret my decision now."

Bud jumped in, the growl in his voice practically rattling the walls. "You damn well should regret that decision; it was a fucking stupid thing to do. If I had my way, you would be bounced right off this ship and out of the Navy right this second."

Eric held up his hand to Bud. "Let's all calm down here." Looking over, he could not help but notice Joe's calm demeanor. It was a character trait Eric coveted.

Joe stopped making notes on the corner of a manila file folder and looked up. "Did Gail Carruthers at any time indicate to you any of the details of this incident?"

Jennifer cringed. Her pallor turned ashen as she squeezed her puffy red eyes shut. She stuttered. "A-actually." Her eyes flitted to the captain and then over to Joe, sitting across from him. Scrunching her eyes closed, she swallowed before continuing. "It was Saturday night in our bunkroom. Gail, well…" She paused with a nervous glance at each of the three men. Her face began to color a light pink. "She was really pissed off with you, sir. She said she wanted to knock you off your high horse."

All three men glanced at each other. "Go on. What else did she say?" Eric harnessed his budding anger with all the control he could muster.

"She said she had a plan to get back at you. I frankly wasn't interested and left right after Mary-Jo, I mean, Petty Officer Johnson."

Joe twirled a pen in his fingers. "A '*plan*'? Petty Officer, just who exactly was there?"

She hesitated.

"Petty Officer, I must remind you that you are in serious trouble, and I doubt very much you would want filing a false report, among other charges, added to it. For a young thing like you, you could be looking at confinement, and I somehow think you might be smarter than that. As it stands right now, we are prepared to be lenient, depending on how helpful and cooperative you are."

The red-rimmed eyes seemed to grow bigger with the realization that she might be able to alleviate some of the trouble she was in, but then she pulled back, as if thinking of the ethics of tattling on her fellow crew members. "I don't want to say, sir."

She looked down, and Joe slid a piece of paper across the table, along with a pen. "Don't say their names. Just write them down, and while you're writing them, think about passing them to me. For now, it will stay between you and me."

She glanced at Joe sharply and then took the pen, pushing it to the paper and then stopping.

Just watching her, Eric wondered if she really would walk out without writing their names down. Then, all of a sudden, she started scribbling names, one under the other.

Then she folded the paper over and slipped it across the table to Joe. "I'm not a snitch, sir." She licked her lips again. "At the time, I believed Gail when she came to me for help to get her report filed."

Eric leaned forward, deliberately showing her no compassion. "Did it ever occur to you that the report might be false? I mean, for Christ's sake, have I ever acted inappropriately with you or any other female members of the crew?"

Her face colored a deep mottled red as she sheepishly shook her head. "No, sir, you haven't. Not in that way."

Shaking his head in disgust, he turned to Joe, allowing him to assume control of the meeting.

"Petty Officer Jennifer Hampton, what you did may have been done with the best of intentions. Your actions, however, showed a total neglect of Navy rules and regulations. Gail Carruthers was required to report to her commanding officer. There are procedures to follow when filing a report. I would also like to point out that dozens of servicewomen in the Persian Gulf are saying they were sexually assaulted, and they are all investigated. A few have turned out to be unfounded. Do you have any idea what happens to a man's career, even if charges are unfounded?" Joe asked.

Numb, with tears in her eyes, she shook her head.

"The damage is done the moment the accusation is made, and it is damn hard, if not impossible, for a good man to rebuild the dignity and respect he has commanded over the years." Sucking in a breath, Joe expanded his chest, maintaining a steady calm in his voice. "I'm recommending an investigation into your conduct. Until further notice, you are relieved of your duties and you'll be confined to your quarters. Dismissed."

Standing and saluting, Jennifer, with her shoulders sunk

forward, left. Joe unfolded the paper Jennifer had slid back to him, and he frowned as he read the names.

"Joe, who are they?" Eric asked, but a wary glance from Joe had Eric pausing.

Joe cleared his throat. "Three names on here. I'll talk to them first, and I'll get back to you, Captain. Also, the JAG investigator will be here tonight. I'll be working with him on the investigation." Joe's eyes were focused on something on the table in front of Eric.

He let his eyes follow Joe's gaze… to his hands, clenched into fists on the table before him. He unclasped them and lay them flat on the table, feeling the cool wood on his palms. Once the investigator arrived, the charges would be an in-his-face reminder of how bad and serious this was. Worse, suspension of duties was creeping up faster than he liked. There was so much to this, including the tainted mark on his career, even if they were able to prove the falseness of the charges against him.

Clearing his throat, Bud pursed his lips as his face softened in sympathy. "Captain, I'm truly sorry for my petty officer's actions. Please accept my sincerest apologies. I feel like I dropped the ball."

"Bud, it's not your fault. What's done is done. I just want to see this thing resolved. I have a ship to run. I don't have time to challenge a schoolyard bully who can't fight clean."

Bud stood awkwardly. "You have my full support. Anything I can do to help, please, Captain, let me know."

"Thanks, Bud."

He watched as Bud left, slamming the door behind himself. Everything about the man was large and loud.

He didn't like any of this, because any investigation would probe into his deeply private life, where no one had a right to go. It would be made public. Everyone would know his secrets, what a lowlife scum he'd been growing up. And Abby—his heart ached just thinking of her. He had promised to protect her, and she looked at him now with such softness and caring that it had his heart jackhammering all over the place. When this investigation started and when she found out everything dirty and ugly about him, she wouldn't look at him that way again. He didn't think he could survive when her look of love and trust quickly turned into hate and disgust. That was enough to make him feel physically ill. Eric sighed aloud, realizing his fists were once again clenched in front of him.

"What is it?" Joe asked.

"Abby. There's no way to keep this from her."

Joe nodded. "Did you get a chance to talk to her yesterday? You know, about her nightmare?"

Eric felt his mood softening. "Yeah, I did." He plucked a paper clip from the folder on the table and turned it over and over. "I'm a little worried. What she's been through is nothing short of incredible. You know, not just surviving each day, but how she escaped. I'm no shrink, but I think she's handling it pretty damn good. She's definitely one strong young lady."

"You know, Eric, it makes my blood run cold, trying to imagine what she's been through." Joe shook his head and firmed his lips in a fine white line. "We know what happens out here. Trafficking of women is such a low priority. Governments would rather fight a war."

Eric didn't know what to say in response to that, because he'd never thought of it that way.

Joe sighed. "So what has the doc said about her? How's she doing?"

Eric stretched up his arms, trying to work out the kinks. "He wants her to have a week of peace and quiet. He feels it's imperative she get through to the end of the week. After that, if she delivers the baby…"

Joe was normally calm in the most stressful of circumstances, but this time he tensed as he sat up straight. "Eric, you're not planning on having her stay here to have the baby, are you?"

"I haven't planned that far, but in order for her to go to the base in Bahrain, I'd have to be guaranteed of her safety."

"Are you still worried the CIA will grab her or Seyed will get her?"

"Aren't you?"

"Eric, she can't stay here forever."

Eric pushed away from the table. "Come on. Let's get on with things. I've got a ship to run, and don't you have some women to interview?" Eric held the door open and waited while Joe picked up his file and followed. "You're right, though. I need to be prepared for this JAG guy when he shows up tonight."

Eric left feeling guilty for not answering Joe's last question. It was the real reason he had no idea what he was going to do.

Chapter Nineteen

Eric didn't linger in the wardroom after Joe left. Lately, he'd been doing a lot of soul searching, which was something he had never done. He'd heard others speak of how'd they sit up all night under the stars or with a cup of coffee right at dawn, watching the sun make its way over the horizon as the birds chirped and the sounds of morning came alive around them, and they listened and were still. But Eric had always brushed that off as a waste of time, choosing instead to throw himself into whatever he did with both hands: doing, not thinking things to death.

Now, at the oddest times, he'd find himself just watching something and wondering if he could have made better choices. What should he do to make things better for him, but first for Abby? If she was happy and safe, he'd be happy, too. He just knew it.

Eric paced the width of the bridge, clasping his hands behind his back, studying the open sea but not seeing one thing. Even with the radio static, the voices of the crew, the buzz and hum of activity, everything reminded him of Abby.

"Captain, did you hear me?" Deputy Intelligence Chief Monroe called out from the other side of the bridge.

When Eric glanced over, he didn't miss the way the crew were watching him, and there was that odd look, or frown, or worried expression, as if each wondered if maybe he was a ticking time bomb who'd snap on any one of them.

"Sorry, Chief, can you repeat that?"

"Sir, a British destroyer was spotted miles offshore, navigating toward a naval gunfire support position."

"Did you notify the Vincent?"

"Yes, sir."

"Okay, update me when you find out what they're doing there." Eric didn't wait around. He was starting to feel damn awkward on his ship, a ship that was the only home he had ever known, and he didn't like that feeling at all. He didn't have a clue where he was going, which was unlike him, but he walked and kept going, crew members jumping off to the side in the passageway as he hurried past.

He went the one place where his heart ached a little less, to see Abby. When he popped open the door, she was leaning against a mound of pillows on her bed, reading a book. Her eyes immediately darted to him, and she dropped the book in her lap. His heart zinged right to her, and he didn't know how he made his feet move, because just standing there watching her had turned his feet to lead. Then he was beside her, looking down on her and the bruises on her face that were beginning to fade.

"How are you feeling?"

A slight blush colored her rounded cheeks as she looked up and put a protective hand over her swollen belly. "We're fine." Then she licked her lips as if gathering courage to say something, and his heart flipped again. "I asked the doctor if I could get up and told him you'd show me around the ship. He said I could as long as I take it easy, but that's if you're still able to show me around?"

Eric crossed his arms, and her eyes immediately skimmed over the eagle tattoo on his tight bicep. Many women had said he had the arms and abs of a fighter, and he was proud of the shape he was in. The eagle was his symbol, one he'd never commented on, but the tattoo had been the first thing he did for himself after he enlisted.

"That is beautiful." She gestured to it. "I've always loved eagles, loved their call. Do you know when they choose a mate, it's for life?" She said it and then lowered her gaze as if worried she was saying too much.

Eric sat on the bed, the springs squeaking. He pushed up his sleeve. Abby didn't move away, but she did tuck her hair nervously behind her ears.

"I had this done in Thailand, my first deployment when I was still a kid. This eagle feels so much like my totem."

Her eyes flew up to his, and she smiled and nodded. "I knew that when I saw it. It suits you."

Eric didn't know how he could keep his hand from her, from touching her, because all he wanted to do was run his hands through her thick blond hair, to run his fingers over her jaw line. What he did instead was move away and try to kick start his brain before he went any further down this road, because everything right now made it impossible.

"Let me call the doc and find out if he *really* said it would be okay to take you," Eric said.

She flung her feet over the edge and winced when her bare feet hit the cold floor. Eric grabbed the phone and called admin, because he knew this was when Larry would be filing all his reports.

"Larry, it's the captain."

"Yes, Captain?"

"I'm with Abby in sickbay. She says you've given the okay for me to take her around the ship. I want to make sure we're not getting our wires crossed."

He watched her from the corner of his eye. A light pink tinged her cheeks as she smoothed her hand over the borrowed blue shirt and pants. She was a vision of loveliness, with the sleeves of the large shirt rolled up, and the shirttails bunched about her on the mattress when she sat back down. He stifled a grin as she bent her leg up around her tummy to put on the borrowed sneakers that sat on the bed beside her. He didn't know where she'd gotten them, but they were better for walking than the thongs she'd worn the other day.

"As long as she doesn't try to run a marathon, she's good. Just a nice, comfortable walk. Don't do lots of standing around, though," Larry said.

"Thanks, Doc," Eric said before hanging up. "Well, good news and bad, Abby. Doc said an easy walk without lots of standing, so I won't show you the whole ship."

"It'll be nice to just get past these four walls. I miss the fresh air. Could we go outside? I'd really like that."

How could he deny her that? Eric himself loved this life for the openness of the sea, and whenever he was able, he found his way on deck. "Okay, let's go," he said. With a secure hold on the back of her elbow, he helped her stand and escorted her to the door, holding it open and then guiding her out.

"Thank you" was all she said as she gazed up at him with a joyful look that lit up her entire face.

Eric was in charge, and he led her down the

passageway and then through the hatch that opened out onto the deck. "Watch your step, Abby. Hang on to me."

The first few steps on deck, he felt her hesitation as they stopped. It was through her eyes that he remembered his first time on deck: the powerful sense of awe that had pumped through his blood and left him lightheaded, feeling the power beneath his feet, the steel of the ship that was larger than anything he'd ever expected, with miles and miles of bright blue ocean in the backdrop. He still got chills, and he realized, watching her watching all of this with her mouth gaping in awe, that he'd forgotten to say thank you.

It wasn't until he noticed movement beside him that he realized there were others on deck. Sailors jumped to attention, and one of them seemed to stumble over his own feet when he saw Abby. Of course, just the sight of her had many of them sprouting peacock feathers, eager to get her attention. What Eric did though was shoot them a warning glare, each of them, except Jamieson, who seemed to be ignoring him.

"Good to see you again, ma'am...." Jamieson said.

"You got nothing to do, Jamieson? Find the XO and get him to assign you some work," Eric said, cutting the young crewman off before he could prattle on.

"Yes, sir," he said and hurried off through the hatch.

"Watch your feet, and don't trip."

Abby's foot caught on the armor plate around the hatch. It happened so fast that one minute, she was stumbling, and the next, he was lifting her in his arms. Her own arms flew up and wrapped around his neck. My God, having her arms so intimately around him, holding on, had his heart thumping. His thin rein was about ready to snap, and he wanted to start stamping his mark like a caveman, proclaiming "This is my woman" to everyone, including

Abby. She was really testing him. What he really wanted to do was tuck her in bed with him, lock the door, and not let anyone in. But he couldn't, and as much as he hated doing it, he set her down. His body mourned the loss of all her curves against him. Reluctantly, he dropped his arms from around her and pumped his hands, which now felt so empty.

"You need to be more careful and watch where you step," he snapped.

"I'm sorry, I just… well, I have a hard time seeing over the baby. I haven't been able to see my feet for a while." The wind was whipping her hair in her face, across a wan smile, and she looked up at him. "Please don't be angry with me."

Angry, she thought he was angry. If she only knew. "Abby, I'm not mad at you. I just want you to be safe."

She looked so serious, and he was stunned when her finger reached up and touched just below his eye. "You have a scar there. What happened?"

He didn't want her to take her hand away. He wanted her to put her hands everywhere, all over him. "Fighting a drunk."

She ran her finger over the scar. "I feel so safe with you. How do you do that?"

"I want you to feel safe. That's why I brought you out here. As long as you're here, with me, you're safe."

"But at some point I have to leave. Then what?" She blinked hard, and he could tell she was fighting back tears and worry. It was the same feeling he had, the hounds nipping at the gates. It would be time soon, and she'd have to leave. He had to start making plans for her.

"Abby, you're right. Soon you will have to leave, but I plan on keeping you here until I know you'll be safe." He placed both his hands on her shoulders and studied her face, every inch of it, as if burning the memory of her in his mind so he'd never forget this moment. "Do you trust me?"

She inclined her head, and her expression turned serious. "Yes."

Time seemed infinite in that moment, as if there were no here and now. It was just them.

"Let me take care of seeing to it that you're safe, because I will. I don't know where or how, but I'll figure it out."

She nodded and then gazed out at the sea. She took a deep breath that he felt pulling from his own lungs. He knew what being out at sea did for him— her power filled every part of him, as if he could overcome anything and nothing could touch him. Until he stepped inside.

She smiled up at him, and he slid his arm around her shoulder. She leaned into him automatically, as if she were his. He wanted so much just to enjoy being with her and this moment, but at a flicker of movement off to his right —a female crewman saw him, started, and hurried the other way—everything came crashing in. He remembered Gail and her ugly charge that would rip his entire life apart, taking his hope for a chance for something good and loving.

He looked down on Abby with deep longing, because he wondered what would happen to her if he was convicted. Where would she go back in the US? Would she meet a young man who could make her happy, who would love her and her baby, who would touch her at night while they lay side by side, whispering their dreams to each other long into the night? His eyes burned, and for a moment he wanted to hit something as he struggled not to lose it. The thought of another man touching her hurt so much that he thought it would be kinder to feed his heart through a meat grinder.

"Are you all right?" She reached up and placed her slender hand flat on his chest. She was watching him with such concern that he knew he needed to pull it together or she'd be poking around, asking and questioning until someone finally broke down and told her the ugly truth of what Eric was facing. The idea shamed him even though he hadn't done it.

She shivered and leaned in closer.

"You're cold." He rubbed her trembling shoulder, down her arm. "It's time to go back. I promised the doc I wouldn't keep you out here long. You need to go back in and rest before dinner." He surprised himself by what came out next. "Would you like to join me for dinner tonight? We'll eat with the officers in the wardroom." He blurted it out because he didn't want his time with her to end.

"Yes, I would love to have dinner with you tonight."

As he guided her back toward the hatch, he stopped as they faced aft and gestured with his hand. "I know I didn't give you the promised tour, but just being on deck, feeling her power, really tells you a lot about a ship. She's a powerful warship, able to hit targets deep inland if needed, with pinpoint accuracy, at any time, anywhere, under any conditions." His voice softened.

"She is you," Abby said, and when he looked at her expression, he knew she meant it. The words were spoken with so much respect and pride that his heart expanded with more love than he thought was ever possible.

Chapter Twenty

Eric had neglected so many of his duties that he was amazed the ship hadn't fallen apart. "God, get it together, man," he barked at himself as he did up his last shirt button on a clean uniform shirt while dressing for dinner. He checked his image in the mirror: He had a tanned complexion, eyes the color of golden whiskey, but he couldn't hide the sadness lurking in him like shadows. It made his eyes duller, his face harder, but there was nothing he could do about it. He'd love to give himself a hard kick in the ass to make himself focus, get on with things.

He yanked open his door and realized his hands were damp. He wanted to laugh at how pathetic he was. When was the last time he'd been this nervous over a woman? He slammed the door behind him, and one of the crewmen coming his way paled and moved aside.

"Captain," he said.

Eric kept walking, looking away, his eyes forward, nodding at the passing crewmen. The guard at sickbay opened the door for him, and there she was, looking so fresh and pretty, sitting there waiting. Her whole face lit up when he stepped in.

"Are you ready for dinner?" he asked.

"Yes," she said eagerly while easing herself off the bed. "I think all that fresh air earlier made me really hungry."

He was absolutely powerless at the sight before him. All swollen with child, she was lovely, even in the sailor's cast-offs. He was sure at that moment that she would make a grain sack look good. It was instinct for Eric to take her arm and guide her out the door, up to the wardroom where all the officers gathered for dinner. When he stepped into the lush, dark wood room, with Abby's fingers digging into his arm, a hush fell as all eyes turned and looked at Abby. Eric sensed her tensing up as her grip tightened on his arm. She must have felt as though she was on display, because she stepped closer and darted a worried glance at him.

Eric searched out Joe, who cleared his throat and said, "The captain's now here, everyone. Abby's his guest tonight. You all remember Abby? Let's not embarrass her to death."

Eric pulled out a chair in the middle of the table for Abby and slid her chair in. He sat beside her. A seaman appeared at his side with two plates, placing one in front of Abby, the other in front of the captain.

"Sir, your dinner's pre-ordered. Is there anything else I can get you?"

"No, that will be all."

"Sorry, Captain. We didn't wait for you," Joe said from across the table.

Eric leaned down to Abby, as she was looking confused. "It's customary for the officers to wait until I've arrived before eating, but we were late." He watched her staring at the plate filled with a huge portion of roast beef, potatoes, and broccoli. To him, it smelled so good his mouth was watering. "Do you like roast beef?"

Her eyes widened when she glanced at him again. "I haven't had roast beef in so long. I think I'm in heaven, it smells so good." She picked up her fork and knife, cut off a piece, and shoved it in her mouth. She chewed and thought for a moment, and she groaned in pleasure. When he glanced around the table, he noticed the other officers were carrying on their own conversations, with the occasional odd glance at Abby.

"This is a lovely room. I didn't realize Navy ships were furnished so nicely," Abby said.

Eric took in what she was seeing: the mahogany table, the sofa and chairs surrounding the flat-screen TV, everything dark wood and first class. She was right. "This is a newer ship. The officers are looked after quite nicely on board. The enlisted, well… nowhere near as nice."

They ate silently, side by side, and he watched her shy glances across the table to Joe and the other officers. They too looked up from the captain to Abby, but it was when Eric heard someone say something—"That Carruthers broad, which one of us will she try to take down next?"—that his blood ran cold. He stared so hard at Joe that he felt every one of his muscles knot up with icy dread. He knew what they were talking about, but how could he get that idiot at the end of the table to shut the fuck up without ripping him out of his chair and ramming his fist down his throat?

"Taylor, did you get those reports on all the activity in the Gulf today done for the captain yet?" Joe said.

Taylor was the idiot mouthing off about Carruthers, and he blinked as if confused. "Well, no, XO. It's never done after twenty-three hundred hours." He looked from Joe to the captain, and he should have realized, if he was on the ball, what he'd done. But then, Eric had never told any of them *not* to talk about what Gail had done, and none of them were ever around Abby. The only person Eric could blame was himself, but he was still pissed.

"Well, tonight the orders have changed. The captain needs it on his desk in an hour," Joe said.

Taylor did the only thing he could: He wiped his mouth and pushed away from his seat, leaving his dinner half eaten. It wasn't until Eric took another bite that he could feel Abby staring at him. Her plate was almost empty, and she was holding her fork and knife as though she was waiting for him to say something to her. Her expression was… dark, worried. He was right, which was the worst thing ever. She had heard enough that she'd needle him to death now to find out what was going on, but instead of asking right now, she offered him a smile, took another bite, and gestured with her hands that she was done. She then leaned back into the soft butter leather and waited for Eric to finish.

Chapter Twenty-One

"Captain Hamilton, I've heard great things about you." The young JAG officer assigned to investigate the accusation stood before him with a vivid smile and a beautiful set of white teeth, and she saluted him.

Eric felt as though the solid steel floor had crumbled beneath him and the water was about to swallow them up. Not one intelligent word would solidify in his brain as he stared at the dark-haired beauty who had gripped his hand and given it a hard shake. For some unknown reason, he had expected a man, and Eric could honestly say the fact that they had sent a woman to investigate Gail's alleged charge against him bothered him more than he could put into words.

"Commander Joan Foxworth from Langley, Virginia."

"You don't look old enough to be a commander."

Joe rolled his eyes at Eric's inappropriate remark, and Eric wondered by the flinch in his arm whether he was going to reach out and nudge him.

To Joan's credit, she didn't react and fly off the handle. She smiled brightly and said, "Thank you, sir. I'll choose to take that as a compliment, but I assure you I am old enough and more than qualified."

Her reply had Joe stifling a grunt beside him, and Eric was unable to match her smile. "Have a seat." With a motion of his hand, he indicated the empty chair across the desk, beside the chair Joe usually occupied.

Joan was dressed in a white uniform shirt and pants. She did have a very nice figure, and she walked with a grace he hadn't seen in a long time. "Thank you, sir." She settled in the chair, her briefcase on the floor beside her.

"Enough with the formality. I presume Joe has filled you in on what he's come up with?" Eric took his leather chair behind the desk.

Looking over at Joe, Joan nodded with a chaste smile still pasted to her face. "Yes, but I would like to get your official statement, sir, if you don't mind." She was professional, a plus in her favor. She didn't sound as if she'd formed any opinion. She pulled a file out of the black leather briefcase and dropped it on her lap, rifling through the pages. "I have reviewed Gail Carruthers' statement, along with the statements of the three women: Petty Officer Jennifer Hampton, Seaman Apprentice Brandy Sanford, and Seaman Cassie Hodges. I've also read your statement, sir, and I have to say that there does appear to be malice on the part of Gail Carruthers. Can you tell me, sir, why you believe she would accuse you of such a thing?"

For the first time, he found himself at a loss for words, as he scratched his head and gestured blankly in the air. "I don't know. Maybe you could tell me why a woman would do something like that."

"I have no idea, Captain. I'm asking you on your best guess: Why do you think she did it?" Joan gestured with a pen toward the captain.

"Commander, she is disrespectful, flagrantly disobeys

orders, and I haven't hesitated to take her to task. But I can tell you, I've never behaved inappropriately with her or any of the female crew on my ship. Let me be candid with you, Commander. My feelings on women in the military are simple. They don't belong, especially on a navy ship, and this incident with Carruthers only convinces me further. Mixing men and women in close surroundings... you're asking for trouble."

Joe openly groaned at Eric's blatantly politically incorrect words. He shot him a "What the fuck are you doing?" look as he shook his head.

Joan didn't seem offended in the least, and she offered a polite smile. "Captain, I understand your feelings, and I can assure you I will be conducting a thorough and fair investigation. I would actually like to get settled, and if it's possible, I'd like to speak to Carruthers tonight." She stood up and lifted her briefcase, tucking the file back in the side. "Captain, it is truly a pleasure to meet you."

Eric frowned and watched the woman with curiosity, because she truly sounded as if she were happy to meet him. Joe joined her and opened the door, holding it for her while she left and then giving Eric another one of those looks that said he'd put both his feet in it.

"You are unbelievable," Joe said, and he left, directing Joan down the passageway.

Eric wasn't about to apologize to anyone for who he was, even though Joe wanted to plant his foot in his backside right about now. But, hell, he was thrown. A woman, they sent a woman to investigate him?

"Oh, sir, I almost forgot." Joan popped her head in the door. Joe was right behind her, glaring at Eric with sparks shooting out of his eyes, as if warning him not to say anything else stupid. "I know this is very difficult, but I will keep you informed, sir." Her reply was courteous and professional, betraying no resentment to the captain.

Joe then said, "I'll take you to see Gail Carruthers and then see that you get settled, Commander."

"That would be great. Thank you so much." She grinned at first the captain and then at Joe, and she once again headed down the passageway. Joe let out a sigh and followed.

Chapter Twenty-Two

Joan sat on the dark green sofa in the guest cabin, which had a double bed and separate bath. She flipped through the piles of paper and notes, rereading the scribbled statements from each of the women. She placed them side by side along with her notes from her meeting with Gail last night. Gail had been downright defensive from the moment Joan had walked into her private cabin, which she'd been assigned after filing her grievance.

She told Joan she had been treated unfairly, but she had also paced and snapped about the guard she was assigned, as if she were the criminal. She said that the guard even refused to leave her alone when she had to use the bathroom, saying it was for her own protection.

Then she had snapped at Joan and said, "You're protecting the captain, that man who hates women. Ah, the good ol' Navy, such a boys' club. So how long did it take you to find your way in?"

"Excuse me?" was all Joan could say.

"Well, I'm a lowly corpsman, an interloper who dared

to accuse the renowned Eric Hamilton. I'm just refusing to let him get away with what he did, so now I'm being punished." She'd paced the small boxlike room like a caged animal.

"You're not being punished, and I'd like to hear from you what happened," Joan asked, digging really deep, trying to find a way to listen.

"Why? It's not as if this is really going to see the inside of a courtroom."

"Gail, I need to hear from you. Start from the beginning," Joan directed her.

Gail refused to look at her and gestured with her hand in the air. "Oh, well, when I walked in —"

"Wait. I thought you were already in the room and he came in."

Gail squeezed her eyes shut. "Yes, yes, what I meant was that I was there when he walked in. He came right up to me, and I was over by the lockers. He leaned back and crossed his arms. He stared down at me and said that if I expected a promotion, I needed to go into the bathroom and let him fuck me."

Joan had stared at the girl because she thought that at one point, she sounded awfully calm, and not once would she look Joan in the eye. When she finished, she gave a nervous smile. Joan had scribbled down what she said but had been more interested in how she was reacting.

Now, this morning, as she compared the filed report from Gail, she noticed some inconsistencies. In her filed allegation, Gail had said the captain had threatened to put her on report. Last night, she had mentioned a promotion. The problem was that this whole thing was far from neat and tidy. The girl could just be overstressed. Being dogged day and night by a guard and isolated on a ship like this would make anyone a little unsteady.

But there was just something about her. She was by no means good looking: plain, ordinary, with small eyes, a pudgy nose, and thin lips, definitely not the type of girl guys went nuts over. However, when it came to sexual harassment no one was immune. But the captain, he was distinguished. Hell, Joan had been shell shocked when she met him. He was tall, by far one of the handsomest and most well-muscled men she had met. She might have compared him to a Greek god, and she just couldn't see why he would go for Carruthers. It made no sense. Did the man have some hidden perversion?

But if this was fabricated, why would the girl do it? No, she needed to talk to all the crew, get a feel about the captain and Carruthers, and she needed to talk to the guard who was tailing Gail. Joan glanced at the big black watch on her wrist, which her father had given her when she joined the JAG corps.

She had treasured it since he died a year later, one week before she won her first case. "Oops," she muttered and scooted off the bed. Nine hundred hours, and she had a meeting with Joe and the captain.

She packed up her files, including her notes. She had grabbed a quick bite with the enlisted first thing this morning in the mess hall, joining a table with mixed crew and listening. She hadn't needed to ask too many questions because all the talk was focused on the captain, how long he'd get in Leavenworth, and when he'd be stripped of his command. One of the men actually spit on his plate when Gail's name was mentioned, and another called her a skank. Everyone respected the captain, though. The women said he was opinionated, and the men all said there was no chance in hell that he would do something like this.

One of the files Joan had ordered before she arrived on board slid on the floor as she packed up. She lifted it and quickly fingered through the papers. It was from Gail's prior postings. What had troubled Joan were the three other accusations of sexual misconduct against Gail's commanding officers. All of them had been buried, hidden, and never shared with her next posting.

As she closed up the file and slid it in her briefcase, she realized that if this was another false report, it was going to hurt all the innocent violated women in the military, women who had been abused by their commanding officers. Any good lawyer could say the women in the military were filing these false charges to retaliate for a promotion they did not receive, or for being reprimanded in a way that made them feel slighted. "Not good, not good at all," she said to herself while shaking her head.

She clicked the lock on her briefcase and glanced in the mirror one last time. Her dark hair was neatly pinned up. Her blue eyes had a ring of violet around them, and the dark mole on her cheek that had once bothered her growing up now looked like a mere imperfection. Even her dimples, which the men seemed to love, she would trade in a second to be a Cindy Crawford lookalike.

Joan grabbed her briefcase and headed out the door, her heavy shoes clicking down the passageway as she mentally planned her day. First, she had to meet with the captain and Joe, the good-looking XO—she smiled at that. Then she had to meet Petty Officer Johnson. She remembered an Abby who had been mentioned in the mess hall. Several of the crew whispered that she had been in sickbay when it happened. Joan smiled, because with all the gossip she could still pick up from the crew, they were worse than a bunch of women at a tea party. This always made investigations that much easier.

She almost bumped into the captain when she rounded the corner to the wardroom. "Excuse me, sir." Then she noticed the tall, dark, and extremely handsome XO behind him. He had the most amazing deep eyes, filled with a passion for life that had her heart tripping over itself. She didn't bother glancing at his ring finger, because sailors never wore rings.

"Good morning, Commander. I trust you have everything you need," the captain said.

"Yes, thank you, Captain."

"We missed you at breakfast." Joe indicated the wardroom they'd just come out of.

"Ah, yes, well, I thought it would be more productive to breakfast with the enlisted and really get a feel for the ship and the crew. It helps with my investigation."

"Ah, yes, your investigation. Well, let's go to my cabin, then, shall we?" Eric led the way, listening to Joe and the commander chat behind him. She had one of those pleasant voices that he didn't mind listening to, and she didn't prattle on and on like some women.

Up ahead in the passageway, there were two enlisted persons scrubbing a side of the passage that had been clearly marked off. As he stepped closer, he didn't miss the sway of long blond hair tied in a ponytail and the presence of a protruding belly on one of them. He had to blink a couple times before it sank in. He was standing right beside her, and Abby was scrubbing his floors. He was speechless. She looked up with widened eyes as she wiped a lock of blond hair that had escaped from the elastic holding her hair back. Eric knew no one was talking. He could feel Joe behind him, and he heard the commander gasp.

"Commander, let's continue on to the captain's cabin," Joe said.

Eric glanced at Joan's wide eyes and Joe's flushed face. Joe gave him another look of "What the fuck?" and gestured with his head at Abby.

Eric crossed his arms and blew out a couple breaths, then stared back at Abby, who held a scrub brush in one hand and was massaging her lower back with the other. He could feel a twitch in one cheek. It didn't happen very often, only when his temper was pushed to the point where he was about to lose it.

It was then that the young man with her leaped up. Seaman Recruit Jeff Taylor stood ramrod straight, his face pasty. Eric ignored the young seaman and let him stand there. He extended his hand to Abby, and she, being the very smart young lady he thought she was, put her hand in his and let him help her up.

Without releasing her hand, he shot a warning glance at the seaman. "Report to my office in one hour. And you, come with me," he growled while grasping Abby's hand, tucking it under his arm and locking it there securely. Abby did not say a word as he took her into the now vacant wardroom and closed the door behind them. He put her in one of the big, comfortable leather chairs and then stood in front of her in a stance he used on deck. Then he leaned over, placing his hands on the chair arms, locking her in the chair. He brought his face within inches of hers.

"Just what the hell do you think you were doing?" He didn't yell but ground out each word as if he was chewing on bullets. He didn't give her a chance to reply. He continued ranting. "For God's sake, Abby, you're about to have a baby. What are you doing scrubbing the floor, of all places, on my ship? Every time there is no guard at your door, you sneak out." His voice became louder and louder, and he was unable to suppress his rage. "Well, what do you have to say for yourself?"

Crossing her arms, glaring, she appeared far from afraid. She watched with a toughness and stubbornness he hadn't seen before, but he had known it was buried somewhere under all that hurt and subservient brainwashing that had been hammered into her. She said, "I was trying to help you."

Pushing up and away from the chair, he ran frustrated fingers through his hair, trying to comprehend what she was saying. "You were trying to help me? How?"

Taking a deep breath and then smiling weakly, she explained, "I was trying to find out what's going on, what you weren't telling me, and I did." Ungracefully, she managed to get up and out of the chair, then waddled over to him as a gray shadow fell over her face, betraying her frayed emotions. "Why didn't you tell me that Gail filed charges against you for sexual harassment?"

Closing his eyes tight, he turned away, shaking his head and feeling his heart rip open, as if a hundred bees had rammed their stingers into his heart. This was it, and he couldn't bear to see the hate, the disgust that she'd have for him now. For a minute, he wondered what it would be like to slit his wrists and allow all the warm blood to drain out.

"Eric," she said softly as she touched the eagle tattoo and then ran her hand up to his shoulder. He slowly turned around and faced her, but he couldn't look at her because he couldn't bear to see it. "You don't honestly believe that I'd think you even capable of something like that. God, how could I? You're not a monster."

"Abby, how do you know I didn't do it? You don't know me that well." His voice sounded odd, even to his own ears.

"We haven't known each other long, but I feel it right here." She motioned with a hand to her heart. "And I'm not blind —I just don't believe you're capable of it. You have more honor in you than any man has a right to. You're honest, maybe a little arrogant, but I've never met a man so secure in who he is. I know what a monster is, Eric, and I do know the type of man that could do something like that. And it's not you. Gail's not a very nice woman, and she hasn't behaved honestly."

He was touching her face, running both his hands over her cheeks and just holding her so he could look into those heavenly blue eyes that had lassoed him and dumped him right over the side of a cliff. He was a goner. "Oh, Abby, what am I going to do with you?"

Smiling, she whispered, "I just want to help. I won't let her hurt you."

He couldn't help it: He leaned down and pressed a tender kiss to her forehead and then rested his forehead against hers. She didn't flinch but slid her hand up over his shoulder and held him to her.

HE WAS ABSOLUTELY HOOKED to her. She was his. After a few moments, he let out a heavy sigh. "You surprise me, but for now I want you to get some rest. No more wandering my halls and scrubbing my floors." He walked her back to sickbay, helped her onto the bed, and pulled a blanket over her. "I may not get a chance to come back until later. If the doc says it's okay I'll take you up to the bridge and on deck tomorrow."

"I would love to see your bridge, where you command everything," she said. Then she winced, and her hand flew to her back.

"What's wrong?" Eric touched her back in the spot where she was digging in with her hand. He used his thumb to massage in circles.

"Sometimes I think this baby is going to kick its way out of me. Don't worry, I'm getting used to this."

"Let me call the doc and have him check you out."

"No! I'm fine, really. It was just a twinge. I have a lot of those lately. Besides, the doctor already told me this is normal at this stage of my pregnancy. I'll be fine, really. I guess I shouldn't have scrubbed the floor."

Eric shook his head. "Promise me you will stay here."

Abby laughed. "I promise. Besides, I'm tired. You're right; I think I'd like to rest a bit."

Eric couldn't help himself. He leaned down and kissed her cheek, then brushed his thumb over her cheek before he finally he stepped away. "Get some rest, my girl. I'm going to get the doc to come and see you." With that, he left and closed the door behind him.

Eric sat behind his desk, reviewing the reports of the day, trying to catch up on the endless paperwork. He couldn't help smiling as he remembered Abby earlier in the day, on her knees scrubbing the passageway, and the expression on both the commander's and Joe's face when he finally joined them in his office. He'd sat back in his chair for a couple minutes and just listened to the two of them banter back and forth. They worked well together, and he'd been impressed by Joan's work ethic. He'd damn near fallen off his chair when she slid two pieces of paper across his desk and used the end of her ballpoint pen to point out the inconsistencies in Gail's statement. He'd been speechless. Joe had smiled, and when the two of them left, the poor seaman who had let Abby help him in the passageway had been standing out in the hall shaking. Joe had leaned in and mouthed, "Go easy."

Eric just waved him away. The poor kid stood ramrod straight, trembling, in front of Eric's desk. For a moment, Eric worried he was being too hard on the kid, but then someone needed to teach the kid some values when it came to women. He listened when the seaman tried to explain how Abby had just appeared, offering to help. He had refused, of course, but she would not take no for an answer. Instead, she had picked up a scrub brush and just started to clean, and that was when the captain had come along.

Eric didn't yell. Standing up, he walked behind the kid and paced behind him. "Son, when you are a man, there are several things you do and don't do. One of the things you never do is allow a *pregnant* woman, who's not even in the Navy, help you scrub the floor," he said. Then he had dismissed him. For a minute, he had thought the kid was going to burst into tears.

He knew Abby wouldn't have taken no for an answer and the poor kid didn't stand a chance. He just shook his head, smiling. He wondered if he was starting to go soft.

Stretching, he felt a weariness sink in, then decided he would turn in for the night. Gathering the papers together, he heard a soft knock on the cabin door. Taking a quick glance at his watch, he was shocked to realize it was just after midnight. Annoyed at the late hour, he wondered who would be disturbing him at this time of night. "What?" he barked, clearly annoyed.

Eric looked up as the door opened, then stopped halfway. Walking around his desk to the door, he could not believe his eyes as he saw Abby clutching the door, hunched over and grasping her belly in obvious pain. Reaching her in a few quick strides, he didn't need any doctor to tell him she was in active labor. As she struggled for breath, he scooped her up, knocking the door closed with the heel of his boot.

"Abby…" He hurried across the room and juggled her in his arms as he opened his bedroom door and laid her on the bed. "Shh, I know it hurts," he said. He put his hands over hers and waited for her to stop struggling, and then she looked at him and took a deep breath.

"I think I'm in labor," she said, a little out of breath.

Eric flicked her hair back and tucked the strands behind her ear. "Oh, I think you're right. Do you know how far apart the contractions are, Abby?"

Shaking her head, sounding a little breathless, she replied with a little panic. "I don't know.... Maybe two or three minutes. I don't know. I'm just guessing." Her voice shook, then began to rise as panic set in. "I was alone and I didn't know what to do. I needed to come to you." Her face scrunched and she let out a groan, and her eyes took on a wild, panicked look. She held her breath and curled on her side, fighting against the pain.

Eric cupped her chin with one hand and held it. "Look at me, Abby. Open your eyes now. Don't hold your breath —it just makes the pain worse. Come on. That's it. Take a deep breath in.... Let it out. That's it, breathe. Breathe through it." He knew his tone was loud and stern, but it was what she needed right now, no kind words. They would be no help to her at this moment.

She grabbed at him, her wild eyes locked on to him. He placed his hand on her belly and could feel it tightening. The contraction seemed to go on and on repeatedly. "That's it, look at me. Breathe in and out.... You've got it, good girl."

Just then, there was a gush of water, soaking her pants and the blankets on the bed. "Oh, Eric, I am so sorry." She started to cry.

"What for? C'mon, no tears. Sit up. I need to get you undressed." Eric helped her sit up. He helped her out of the damp clothes. Grabbing one of his shirts from the drawer by the bed, he slid it over her naked skin, her large breasts, and started buttoning it up. She grabbed his wrists, holding on and moaning as another contraction ripped through her.

"Come on, breathe through it. That's a girl." He talked

her through it until he felt her relax a bit, and then he lifted her to the chair by the bed and ripped off the wet blankets, tossing them in a corner. He grabbed a blanket from his locker and spread it over the bare mattress, lifting Abby back on the bed when she doubled over again and cried out.

"Abby, let me call the doc. I'll be right back."

Grabbing hold, she began to cry. "Please don't leave me. I'm scared."

Holding her soft, rosy cheeks between his hands, he said, "Abby, look at me now. I'm not leaving you. I'm going to the other room to phone the doc. I'll be right back, in less than a minute, okay?"

He wasn't sure she understood, as she was having another contraction, so he pulled away and hurried to the phone, snatching the handset. When a groggy Petey answered, he shouted as Abby moaned in pain, "Find the doc! Abby's in my cabin in labor. Get him here now. She's going to have this baby now."

He hung up the phone and raced back to Abby. She was in absolute agony as she lay on her side, sweat glistening her forehead. She was gripping the mattress so hard he could see her knuckles whiten. He could hear the door and footsteps and voices behind him, and then Abby grabbed his arm.

"Oh, no, I have to go to the bathroom. Please help me," she said.

Eric slid an arm around her back to help her up. "Okay, I'll carry you."

"No, put her down," interrupted Larry. "Lie down, Abby. That's probably the baby pushing." The doctor dropped a bag on the chair. His hair was sticking up and his eyes were bloodshot. Obviously, he had just woken up. "Abby, I need you to lie on your back. Come on, knees up,

Abby," he said. Then he spread her legs and pulled on gloves, and Eric, for a moment, was struck by her near nakedness as the doc examined her. The intensity of her pain was increasing, and the doc shouted at her, "Don't you dare push yet! Breathe out. Pant like a dog, like this." Larry glanced up with look of worry, "Grab some towels. I can feel the baby now. She's fully dilated."

Eric grabbed all the towels from the bathroom and dumped them on the bed beside Larry, who lifted her bottom, sliding the towels underneath. Eric could see a fair bit of blood now. He knew having a baby was nothing easy, but he'd never seen a woman give birth. He had no idea what they went through.

"Okay, Abby, on the next contraction, I want you to push," Larry said. Her legs were trembling as he pushed them wide. "Eric, get behind her."

Eric lifted her shoulders and sat on the bed with her, leaning her against his chest. He took her hand, and she yelled and screeched, moaning over the strength of the contraction.

"I need to push," she shouted.

"Push, Abby, on the next contraction," Larry said, and then she strained against the captain, pushing and screaming while she did. "The baby's head is crowning. You're doing great. It's almost over, Abby."

Her body took over, and she gasped and panted for breath. Then she screeched again, pushing, and her hand squeezed Eric's so strongly he almost winced.

The doctor yelled, "Stop! No more pushing. The head's out. Pant like a dog, that's it. Blow out.... You're doing good, girl."

She groaned, and her expression was filled with so much pain. "Oh, Eric, it hurts."

"I know it does. You're almost there. Just hold on to

me." He rested his cheek against her head as the doctor eased the baby's shoulders out.

"Okay, Abby, a little push. We're almost there.... That's it."

The baby cried as Larry placed her on her tummy, the cord still attached. Eric was absolutely shocked by how tiny she was, with dark hair and covered in blood. The doc wiped her with a towel.

"It's a girl, Abby. A beautiful girl." Larry tied and cut the cord while carefully wrapping the baby in a towel. Eric slid out from behind Abby and shoved a couple pillows behind her, and the doctor slipped the baby in the crook of her arms.

Eric sat on the edge of the bed, and Abby gazed at her baby with a look of awe. Eric touched the baby's head. He'd never felt this sense of fullness in his heart. It was bursting, and he felt his eyes mist. "She's her mother's image, a beautiful girl," he said.

Abby's entire face took on a surreal look as she gazed at him with such an abundance of emotion. It called to him, and he couldn't help but lean down and kiss her forehead.

"Abby, we're not quite done. I need you to give a little push to deliver the placenta, that's it," Larry said. Abby was clutching the baby, and she winced. "I know it hurts, but we're almost done. There's a small tear, but it doesn't look like you need any stitches."

After the doctor delivered the placenta, he got her cleaned up. That was when Abby started trembling, her teeth chattering away.

"Just her body cooling. Perfectly normal, Abby," the doc said.

"I'm so cold," she said. She held her baby, and Eric strode over to the locker against the wall in the small bedroom and grabbed the last brown blanket from the shelf. He flicked it open and covered her.

"How's that?" he asked, tucking the blanket around Abby and the baby.

"Abby, I just need to check her out. I'll give her right back." Larry reached down and lifted the baby. Abby tried to sit up and winced. "Let me finish with your girl, and then I'll get you something for the pain."

Eric sat beside her again on the bed and pulled the blanket up around her. "Just lie there and rest. I think you've done enough work for now." He smoothed back her hair, and they exchanged a look. There was no way either wanted to be anyplace else.

"Have you got a name for this girl yet?" the doctor asked from where he listened.

"Rachel. I've always loved that name."

Eric looked over at Abby, smiling. "That's a beautiful name, just like her mother's."

The doctor handed Rachel to the captain while he reached into the bag for some ibuprofen. He strode into the bathroom and filled a glass with water, and he gave the pills to Abby along with the glass. She swallowed and wiped her mouth.

"It'll help relieve some of the ache," Larry said. Abby nodded and pulled the blanket up over her shoulders. She was still shaking. "I'm going to get you another blanket," the doctor said as Eric stood beside the bed, holding the tiny miracle in his arms. He stared at the round face and tiny mouth, the pink lips and tiny little hands that waved around. Abby's eyes were starting to droop, and Larry reached down and touched her arm.

"Okay, we should probably get them moved back to sickbay right about now, get them settled before Abby falls asleep."

Eric shook his head. "No, Larry, just leave them here for the night. Please, just make sure we get some dry bedding up here and something to put the baby in to sleep."

Larry grinned and gestured to the baby in his arms. "I didn't know you liked kids, or babies. You look quite comfortable."

Eric wasn't sure how to respond, and he couldn't look at Larry because he was starting to wonder what he saw to make him jump to that conclusion. The fact was that Eric knew nothing about kids. Other than the time he spent with Joe and his family when in port, which wasn't often, he didn't think he was a natural at all. Eric glanced up at the doc, doing everything he could to keep his expression blank, but it was next to impossible, holding such a precious bundle, a new life who looked to him to protect her.

Thankfully, Larry said nothing further and left the bedroom. Eric could hear him on the phone, though. A few minutes later, there were voices, and Larry carried in a couple more blankets and some bedding. Eric glanced out and glimpsed Petey.

"Abby, let's get you up, and we'll get some bedding on this bed and you back in it," Larry said. Abby sat in the chair while he made the bed, quickly tucking in the sheet and flicking a couple blankets over it, then helping her scoot back over. "We need the baby to nurse now, Abby. It's really important that you try. I'll be right back," Larry said as Eric set Rachel in her mother's arms. He then set a couple more pillows behind her back so she could sit up.

"I think she's hungry," whispered Eric as Rachel turned her tiny head into Abby's breast.

Abby glanced at him with an expression of sheer panic. "I don't know how to do this."

"I can't help you there, but it's the most natural thing in the world, Abby. You were born for this. Your breasts were meant to feed and nurture a child." He reached down and unbuttoned the shirt she was wearing, exposing her breast. It was so natural to be helping her, sitting with her while she struggled to figure it out, to awkwardly set the baby to her breast. When the baby latched on, she jumped, and her vibrant blue eyes seemed to dance with color at this new feeling they were both experiencing.

Eric was content to sit there on the edge of the bed beside her and just watch mother and child. For a moment, he imagined this was his child, his woman, and it felt so right. The cabin door clicked open and closed, and footsteps and whispers had him shooting a glance over his shoulder at Petey and the doc. Petey carried in an armful of bedding, and the doc carried a steel drawer.

Eric met them just outside the bedroom door. "What's that for?"

"It's a drawer and will be perfect for a cradle." The doc carried it into the bedroom and stopped beside the bed. He said something to Abby as he watched her nurse, and Abby smiled up at him and then at the drawer beside the bed.

Petey cleared his throat. "Sir, is there anything else I can do?"

Eric glanced at his young ensign, who'd been dragged from bed in the middle of the night. His hair was sticking up, and he looked very tired. "Thanks, Petey. That'll be all." Eric headed into the bedroom and heard his cabin door close, and he knew Petey had left.

"It looks like you got the hang of it," the doc said. Then he faced Eric. "I'll be back in the morning to check on them. Call me if you need me before that."

"Will do, Doc."

Eric watched as Larry left. Rachel soon fell asleep, slipping off her mother's breast. Eric was mesmerized, watching Abby snuggling as her own eyes drooped. Then she blushed and pulled at the open shirt to hide her breast. She was so innocent in some ways.

"I'll get her settled in," Eric said. He slipped the baby into his arms and settled her in the padded drawer, tucking another blanket around her and moving the nightstand over so the drawer was secured by the bed in case of any sudden movements by the ship.

After he settled Rachel, he leaned over Abby, who was watching him as if she had just handed him her heart on a platter. With his large, calloused fingers, he slid back her hair and traced his hand down the side of her face. He pulled a second blanket over her and watched as she closed her eyes and relaxed in a way he hadn't seen before, as if she felt so safe that she could drop her guard and sleep soundly.

Eric closed the door behind him and strode over the carpet to his desk, glancing over the papers and files covering the desktop where he had been working and reading just a few hours before. He left everything where it was, a disorderly mess, as he sat in his black leather chair, settled his hands behind his head, his feet on the desk, and rested, dreaming of how lucky he'd be if this truly were his life, his wife and his child, with no nightmare hanging over his head.

Chapter Twenty-Three
___

The sharp knock rattled the door, and Eric opened his eyes and blinked a couple times as he struggled to orient himself. When everything slowly came back to him —Abby, the baby—he leaped from his chair, glancing at the closed bedroom door as he yanked open his cabin door. Petey stood on the other side with a boyish smile and a tray with Eric's breakfast and coffee.

"Good morning, sir!"

"Abby's sleeping. Keep it down." Eric gestured to his desk. "Just set it there. Listen, can you get another tray for Abby? I'm sure she'll be hungry when she wakes up."

"Yes, Captain," he replied, as if having Abby there was the most normal thing in the world. He hurried out while closing the door with a soft click behind him.

Eric realized then that the whole ship probably knew that Abby had had the baby, and here she was, occupying his cabin, because no one on this ship could even sneeze without everyone knowing.

There was a tiny cry from the other room, and a

rustling. Opening the door, Eric walked in as Abby struggled to get up.

"What time is it?" she muttered, groggy.

"It's six thirty." Bending over, he lifted Rachel, whose tiny mouth was open. She was crying and waving her tiny fists. He couldn't help but breathe in the newborn scent of this innocent bundle before setting her in her mother's arms.

Abby allowed her long, mussed hair to fall over her shoulder, peering down as she awkwardly pulled the gray blanket up to protect what she could of her modesty. Her cheeks glittered a hint of pink, but all he could think of was the natural essence from the plump rounded breasts that still appeared over the top of the baby's head.

"Breakfast is on its way. I hope you're hungry," he said.

Abby offered a shy smile. "You know, I don't remember ever being so hungry."

Enchanted, he reached over and put his hand on Rachel's head, touching the soft dark hair that lightly covered it. "Well, I'm not surprised. You had a busy night." He watched her as she looked hesitant at first, then looked around the room, eyes wide as if seeing it now for the first time. He looked to see what she saw from the double bed that took up half the room. There was a nightstand beside the bed and a private bathroom across the room. The walls were bare; the room was impersonal, with no pictures or anything displayed.

"I'm sorry to put you out of your bed," she said. "Where did you sleep? Did you get any sleep?"

"It's okay, Abby. Don't worry about me. I've spent more nights sleeping in my chair than I can count."

A knock shook his cabin door.

"Enter," Eric called out as he got up, striding through

the bedroom door to his office. Petey opened it, juggling a tray.

"Thanks, Petey. Just set it on the desk."

"Will there be anything else, Captain?"

"No, that'll be all. I'll let you know if we need anything."

Eric didn't wait for Petey to leave. He carried the breakfast tray in to Abby, and she looked up with an expression that lit the entire room. If he had concerns before about how she'd feel about this baby, just watching her with Rachel erased all doubts. He'd never seen such love, which seemed as if it magically connected her, in an invisible cloud, to this baby.

Eric set her tray on the nightstand and waited for Rachel to finish nursing. "I'll hold her while you eat," he said. He cradled the tiny baby in his arm and he sat in the chair. He couldn't get over how she wasn't even the length of his wrist to his elbow. He glanced up as Abby lifted the tray to her lap and dug into the plate of eggs. She consumed her breakfast like a starving man, shoving the eggs in her mouth as if she hadn't eaten in a week.

A knock on his door again had him call out, "It's open."

Larry strode in with Joe, who had a smug expression and was carrying something in his arms. Eric carried the baby out in his main cabin, and Joe stepped up and pulled back the towel to peek at her face.

"Ah, she's beautiful," he said.

"How is she this morning?" Larry asked as he walked past the captain.

"She's awake and fine, eating right now."

"I need to examine her, so I'll be a minute." Larry closed the door behind him.

"What did you bring?" Eric gestured to the bundle Joe had set in one of the chairs.

"Diapers Abby can use for the baby, until we can get some supplies." Joe held up a cloth square resembling a dishtowel. Then he flashed a smile. "My wife always used cloth. Thankfully, I didn't have to change too many diapers."

Eric was still holding the baby, feeling so much like a proud papa. He realized it was impossible not to bond with something so innocent and trusting. This was where it all began, and he wanted to protect her in a way that he had never been protected. He cleared his throat when he felt himself swimming into a mood that was too melancholy. "So, how's the investigation coming?"

"Well, Joan, I mean the commander, has been doing some checking into Gail's past allegations. Actually, it's quite interesting. It seems she filed similar charges against three former commanding officers."

"Really, why wouldn't I know about that before she came aboard my ship?"

Joe frowned and crossed his arms, his face showing his annoyance. "Well, when Joan spoke with them, none of the three were too happy about hearing her name. From what Joan said, no formal charges were ever laid at all, but the damage was done to these officers by the implied implication. She apparently made a lot of noise, telling everyone who would listen, you know, like the squeaky wheel, to the point that it appears everything was made to go away. But what did she get out of it?"

Joe gestured helplessly and continued. "We know she was given a transfer with a slight promotion after each incident, mainly to appease her and shut her up." Joe leaned forward, then lowered his voice. "It does appear she was questioned quite thoroughly. Although there were no witnesses to support any of her allegations, she refused to go away or be bullied by anyone."

Eric faced the closed bedroom door and breathed in the news, wondering why this bitch was trying to destroy him. "She's really fucking with my career and my good name. She's going to get away with it, isn't she?"

Joe paused for a moment, his hands loosely on his hips. "We'll beat this. She has created so many lies that this time, we're going to trip her up. She won't get away with it. Remember what Petty Officer Hampton said about her planning something, only she left the room before hearing it?"

Eric looked up from where he watched Rachel and stared into something that shone in Joe's face. His expression was hard, and he was trying to figure out a puzzle. "That's right, and weren't there two others who stayed in there with her?" Eric asked.

"Actually, there were three women. Mary-Jo Johnson left before Jennifer did, and from what I understand, she gave Gail quite the upbraiding. There was a Cassie Hodges and a Brandy Sanford who also stayed. Those were the names Jennifer wrote on the paper she slipped to me. Joan has spoken with both Hodges and Sanford and reviewed their statements. She's meeting with Mary-Jo this morning."

Eric shut his eyes as he rocked Rachel in his arms. Did he dare hope for this whole mess to be cleared up? Bracing his elbows on the desk, he leaned forward to support himself. "That's good news."

Joe smiled at his friend's relief. He leaned back and crossed his arms. "You know, Eric, I'm watching your back. Anything you need to know, I'll tell you."

"I know. But I also know your back is to the wall, too. There is a fine line. As captain and the accused, I'm under investigation, and I know you haven't told me all the details. But I also know you will keep me in the loop so I'm not blindsided."

Their eyes met, and they shared a mutual understanding they'd developed over the years like two brothers. At times, Eric swore they could read each other's thoughts.

Joe cleared his throat. "Joan wants to talk to Abby."

Eric felt the something almost blind him, and Rachel started squirming in his arms. "No," he said through gritted teeth. "Keep her away from Abby. She just had a baby, and I don't want anyone questioning her right now, understand?"

"No one's going to upset her," Joe said softly. "I understand what you're saying, but Joan needs to talk to her. I'll be there to make sure no lines are crossed and that Abby's not upset."

Sighing, Eric leaned forward again. He couldn't explain it, but he didn't want the details discussed with Abby, even though she knew. It was so dirty, and he didn't want any part of this sordid nightmare to touch her.

Joe shook his head, standing his ground. "Eric, this is going to happen whether you want it to or not. Joan has an investigation to conduct. She's been given free rein by the admiral to talk to everyone and anyone."

Eric let out a long breath from his lungs and glanced down at the tiny fragile Rachel. He couldn't explain why, but he wanted to wrap both Abby and Rachel in a cocoon and protect them. He didn't want anyone but himself to talk to Abby. After everything she'd been through, he couldn't trust anyone not to get curious and start asking her about Seyed, which might start her nightmares and fears up again.

"Nobody talks to her for a couple of days. The end of the week is soon enough, and I want to be there to make sure no one goes off topic and gets curious about where Abby's been." Eric shook his head when Joe opened his mouth to argue his point. "I won't budge on this. Those are my terms, so work with them. I'm not flexible on this point at all."

"Okay, I'll talk to Joan. We'll speak with Abby on Saturday," Joe said. Even though they had compromised, neither was happy about the outcome. "So how is she?"

"She's good. Abby named this little girl Rachel, and she's beautiful."

Joe inclined his head and took another glance at the baby. "Hmmm. I don't remember you ever holding *my* kids."

At that moment, the bedroom door opened. "Captain, can I see the baby? I want to take a quick look at her, as well," Larry said.

Eric walked over and slipped the baby in Larry's arms, and he didn't miss Abby watching him from where she was nestled in the middle of his bed. "Everything okay with Abby?"

Larry set the baby on the end of the bed, and she started crying when he pressed a stethoscope to her heart and lungs. He rubbed the metal again. "Oh, I know it's cold. Sorry, baby." He rubbed it in his hand and listened again. "She sounds good. Abby's doing fine, too. We should get them moved back to sickbay, though."

Eric leaned in the doorway, watching Abby and her odd expression as she gazed down at Rachel and something hardened in her face. "No, leave them both here for now," he said. Something subtly relaxed in her. Her shoulders drooped, and her face softened. "The end of the week is soon enough. Leave them be for now… unless there's a medical reason they need to be down there," Eric continued.

"No, they're fine. I'll come back later to check on them. Actually, it would be best to leave them here for now." Larry settled a cleaned-up Rachel in Abby's arms, then packed up his medical gear and slung the bag over his shoulder. "Call me if you need me," he said, and he left.

"I'll be right back," Eric said to Abby, and he pulled the bedroom door closed as he strode across the room to where Joe lingered, waiting to talk to him. "Spit it out, whatever it is."

"So what about Abby?" Joe said. "When are you going to move her off the ship? And do you know where to move her yet?"

Eric let out a heavy sigh. "Yeah, I know I need to move her soon, but not until I get some things figured out first. Do you think Mary-Margaret would be willing to help get her set up? I need to get her someplace secure where she and the baby will be safe."

"I think you know my wife well enough to know that if you didn't ask, she'd have your hide. Just give me the word, and I'll put a call through to her. She'll have Abby and the baby under her wing quicker than you can say 'jackrabbit.' You know my wife has a soft spot for you, but she is going to wonder about Abby. What am I supposed to tell her? Who is she to you?"

"Joe…" Eric shook his head. "I got a lot hanging over my head. I need to do this for Abby so she feels safe. I promised her. That's all you can say."

Joe didn't say a word as he started to turn away. "Oh, I meant to tell you that Joan's meeting with Mary-Jo in an hour."

"Let me know how it goes."

"Listen, Eric, for what it's worth, this is a great thing you're doing for Abby."

Long after he left, Eric watched the bedroom door, looking in to where Abby and Rachel were sheltered, protected. It was the safest place for them to be, under his care, his watch, and where no one could get to them.

Chapter Twenty-Four

"So, what time are you meeting with Mary-Jo?" Joe asked.

Joan lowered her coffee back to the table in the wardroom with a soft thud. She watched as Joe walked over to the thermos of coffee and poured himself one, turning to her with a careful, concealed expectation in his eyes. She was aware of a lot of things about Joe. First, there was the fact that he was the sexiest man—next to the captain, that is—that she'd ever seen. He was well-muscled, tall, and ruggedly handsome, with a boyish mischievous grin and smile that knocked her on her ass and did all kinds of fluttery things in her heart. She loved talking to him, being around him, and she enjoyed the banter that went back and forth between them.

"Soon. I presume you'd like to be present?" Joan asked, smiling as she took another sip of coffee.

Grinning, he lifted his coffee to take a quick sip, swallowing. "Yeah, if you don't mind, I know this is your investigation, but I'd kind of like to be there."

"Sure, that's fine. Just let me lead the questions, and please don't interrupt," she muttered, unable to contain the smile that pulled at the corner of her mouth.

Quirking his brows, he winked, and she wondered if he was flirting with her. "Okay, thanks." He sat right across from her.

Pushing away from the table, Joan walked over to the thermos to refill her own coffee. With her back to him, she struggled to suppress the way her body seemed to have a mind of its own, with the physical attraction she felt toward him. From the moment they met, the attraction, the chemistry had been there. He was handsome in a softer way, with a charm and charisma surrounding him, though not ruggedly, like the captain.

Her hand was shaking when she picked up her mug, took a sip, and then walked around the other side, catching a whiff of his scent. Damn, the man didn't even have to wear cologne to drive her half wild. She felt her cheeks heat, and then she glanced over at him as he appeared lost in thought, scribbling notes on a piece of paper. Then he slid his chair back and picked up the phone behind him. She didn't have a clue who he was calling.

"Listen, I need to get a call out to my wife. Can you set it up, Chief?" he asked.

Joan's heart plummeted right down to her toes, and her stomach felt as if it was full of lead. So Joe was married after all. She wondered now if she had imagined the whole thing. Maybe he was just being nice to pathetic old Joan, rather than flirting. Hell, the last time she'd had a date was a few years ago, so she was definitely rusty. She sat like an old lady in the chair across from him and lowered her head, staring down at the page of notes, but she couldn't read a damn thing.

"That would be great. I'm down in the wardroom right now. Great, thanks, Chief." He hung up the phone and scooted his chair back over.

Married, he was married. It kept running through her mind, and she couldn't look at him because she'd almost done something stupid, and she wasn't ever going down *that* road again, chasing a married man.

"We didn't have a chance to talk about the statement you got from the other two ladies. Did anything come from them?" Joe leaned on the table, and she could feel him watching her. She didn't look up at him as she shook her head. Instead, she pretended to read. "Commander, is everything okay?" Joe asked, and he really did sound concerned.

Don't let him see you're upset. The warning raced through her mind, so she pasted the best smile she could on her face and looked across the table at his puzzled expression. "Sorry, Joe, just preoccupied with this. You know, one thing is that when I talked to the two ladies, Mary-Jo and Jennifer both said they left before Gail started speaking of a plan to get back at the captain. And, just for the record, they both used the term 'get back at him.' "

Joe had this look about him, as he gave her all of his attention, that had her wondering what it would be like to be married and have someone give all of himself to her.

"She never came right out and said she was filing this accusation against him, but the conversation in their quarters supposedly took place after the incident. Gail brought up the name of a lady commander whom she wanted to replace the captain on this ship." Joan took her pen and tapped the file folder. "According to both their statements, Gail asked for their support if she filed a grievance against him. She even went so far as to ask them to simply agree with what she put in the statement. Now, for the record, both Cassie and Brandy said they told her they would never do anything so malicious. At the time, that had been the end of it."

An abrupt knock at the door startled them both. "Enter," Joe responded, swiveling his chair toward the door.

Mary-Jo appeared unruffled and in control. "Petty Officer Mary-Jo Johnson, sir, ma'am."

"At ease, sailor. Sit down," said Joan as she directed Mary-Jo to a chair at the head of the table, between both her and Joe. As Mary-Jo sat, she remained at attention. "At ease. I presume you know why I summoned you here," Joan said.

It was not a question, but Mary-Jo gave a stern nod and then glanced at Joe, who gestured toward the commander. She faced the commander. "Yes, ma'am."

"I understand that on Friday, June nineteenth, at about twenty-one hundred hours, in your bunkroom, a conversation was initiated by Gail Carruthers."

Nodding to the commander, Mary-Jo retained the annoyance in her composure.

"I would like you to tell me the details of the conversation." Joan kept her voice even and steady. Even a fool could pick up the anger that flickered in Mary-Jo's eyes just at the mention of Gail's name.

"She was mouthing off," Mary-Jo began. "She's trouble, that one. She was pissed off with the captain over something, and she ran off at the mouth about the way he treated her, saying the only reason he did it was because she was a woman."

"Treated what way, Johnson?" Joan reined in her curiosity so as not to lead Mary-Jo in her questioning.

Doing her best to appear neutral, she needed to keep the conversation on track and gather facts.

"I'm not sure of everything. She didn't really say, but something happened that pissed her off. She did say she wanted to knock him off his high horse. Then she reminded us of his hatred of women."

Joan directed a questioning look at Joe. He waved his hand and said, "Later." Mary-Jo's eyes danced with a hint of smile from that remark, Joan noted.

"Can you tell me anything about the plan she was hinting at?" she asked.

"She said she wanted to file a discrimination suit against him and wanted our help. She also spoke of some lady commander she would like to have here on the ship in his place."

Joan nodded as she scribbled notes on a piece of paper under Mary-Jo's name, making note of the date and time of this interview. "What did she mean about a discrimination suit?"

"I don't know. I didn't give her a chance to talk about it. I lit into that girl and told her to drop it. Then I left. I never heard another word until I heard about her charges against the cap'n." Pausing briefly, she licked her lips, leaned forward, and hesitatingly asked, "Ma'am, sir, may I speak freely?"

Both Joe and Joan nodded and gestured with open hands. "Please go ahead," Joan said, and she put down her pen, clasped her hands, and leaned forward on the table, giving the girl her full attention.

"That girl is trouble, and I knew it from the first time we met. I don't know the captain well, just what I heard of him and some sharp remarks he made to me when I first came on board. But from what I do know, there's no way this is true. That girl made the story up as sure as I'm sittin' here. She's a schemer. I know her type. I don't know what else I can say to help, but I hope it's enough to get the cap'n off the hook. She's poison just to have around, and she's good at getting people to do what she wants. She oughtta be, practicin' at it all the time. We all know it. Everyone on board does. We just avoid her—when we can."

The more she spoke, the more pronounced her southern accent became. Joan noticed the accent was something the girl had worked on.

"Thank you for your statement, Mary-Jo. I would appreciate it if you wouldn't discuss it with anyone, and I may want to talk to you again."

She stood up and offered a quick salute, acknowledging both Joe and Joan before taking her leave. After Mary-Jo pulled the door closed behind her, Joan just stared at Joe.

"Well, well, well, it isn't looking too good for Miss Carruthers. If anything, let's just suppose it to say that it appears to be a personal vendetta, which can be motive enough for her to create this story. The statements we have so far corroborate that she was looking to get back at him, from this alone. This goes a long way to poke holes in her story. He's a decorated officer. She has trouble even fitting in. We could probably make this go away, but I think we owe it to the man to try to get his name cleared."

Rising from her chair, Joan shone a broad smile, which widened as she paced the floor, back and forth in front of the table. "I also would like to bring charges against this lady for filing a false report. You know, Lieutenant, it's not okay for any woman or a man to lie and bring a false charge. All this is going to do is hurt a lot of women in the military now who are being brutalized and assaulted. No, she has to be held accountable, but I'll need more concrete evidence before I can do that. I would also like to talk to this Abby today, if possible."

Shaking his head, Joe held up his hand, palm forward, to stop her. "I'm sure you heard Abby just had her baby last night."

Joan leaned against the table and crossed her arms "Actually, no, I didn't. I'm afraid I haven't talked to anyone this morning yet."

"Late last night, she had a baby girl. She's resting in the captain's cabin."

Joan's brows rose, but she said nothing, instead giving Joe her full attention.

He leaned forward on his elbows on the table. "She went into labor late last night with no one around." He shrugged. "I don't know why she didn't call me—the phone was within easy reach. Anyway, she made her way to the captain's cabin, where she delivered her daughter. She'll be moved back to sickbay at the end of the week. We can talk to her then."

Joe pushed himself out of the chair, walked to where she sat, and then crossed his arms in front of him. "You should know the captain insists on being present when you talk to her. She is under his protection right now."

"Protection? Is there something I haven't been told?"

"I'd better let the captain tell you. He knows more about it than me."

"It is totally inappropriate for him to be present, and you know that," she snapped.

His voice softened. "Please, Joan, this is important. I would appreciate it if you would concede on this. He wants to make sure you don't upset her."

She was stumped as to who this woman was. She'd met the captain, heard stories about him, too. Why was he so protective of this woman? "Fine, just make sure he understands that I'll be conducting the interview and I want no interference from him. And, by the way, I'm curious: Who is she? I mean, a pregnant woman here on a US military ship in hostile territory? She's not in the Navy, because there are regulations that pregnant sailors aren't allowed on ships, but now there is a newborn baby here, too? Come on, Joe. A lot of holes need to be filled in here about her and exactly what the captain's relationship is with her."

"Look, Joan, you need to ask the captain these questions." Clasping his hands, he leaned forward. "Eric's a good man. I haven't known you very long, and I would never try to influence this investigation, but you need to understand that he didn't do this. I'd appreciate it if you cut him some slack, especially where Abby's concerned. He cares for her very much and is very protective of her."

With a heavy sigh, she shook her head. "You're trying to tell me he's going to make this interview with Abby difficult, aren't you?" She was hypnotized by his charming smile even though she knew he was married. "Okay, I hear you. I'll cut him some slack." Joan stood up, walked back over to the table, reached down, and picked up the file. She gazed up and fixed Joe with a questioning glance. "I want to ask you something, off the record, of course. What exactly did Mary-Jo mean by 'his reputation'?" She gestured toward the door with her hand.

Flinching, Joe scraped a rough hand over his forehead. He laughed, walked back to his chair, and plopped into it while gesturing for her to do the same. "I'm surprised you didn't already know."

Joan pulled out her chair and sank back into the leather, scooting the chair forward. "Fill me in."

"Eric is old school. Actually, probably not even from this century. He believes women have no place in the military. He's never made it a secret, either. He believes a woman's place is in the home, looking after her husband and family. He has very strong views on men as providers and protectors of their women and children. He doesn't hate women, as you might think, but unfortunately he has gone on the record stating that they break all the gender rules by wanting a career in the military. I believe this may be the reason, or one of them, that Gail Carruthers filed her accusation. The Captain has pissed off a lot of women over the years. I mean, look at your first meeting with him."

Joan snapped the pencil she had picked up in half. She was still stuck on the part where a woman's place was in the home. Joe appeared so serious, and she realized as she watched him that he was serious. So everything the captain had said to her before was the unvarnished truth, about his feelings toward women in the Navy. She couldn't help it when she leaned back and laughed.

It took her a minute to catch her breath. "Well, that tells me a lot. Frankly, I don't think I've ever met any man who shares those beliefs. Actually, let me rephrase that, because it's not true. I've never met anyone who is open enough to voice his opinion like that, and, if I understand you correctly, he has no problem voicing that opinion to anyone, male or female. Correct?"

He shrugged his shoulders. "He's honest, and you should know he doesn't sugarcoat anything. What you see is what you get."

She shook her head, then covered her mouth with the palm of her hand, desperate but unsuccessful in suppressing further laughter. Finally, she finished and wiped at the tears in her eyes with the back of her hand. "Well, you know what? I'm okay with that, and I respect that because it's honest. Well, he must really love *me*, then —a woman conducting the investigation. That certainly fills in a lot of unanswered questions for me. Thanks, Joe." She threw him a mock salute.

Joe gave an awkward smile. "You're welcome, I think."

"What does your wife think about the captain? I mean, you're good friends and all."

"She just smiles when he jams his foot in his mouth about a woman's place, then laughs and walks away."

Chapter Twenty-Five

"Excuse me, Captain. Do you have a minute?" Joan asked as she peered around the corner in the captain's quarters. It was dusk, after the dinner hour, a time Joan knew Eric was less likely to be disturbed. He looked up with tired kindness, then gestured with his hand to one of the chairs in front of his desk.

"Absolutely, Commander. Come on in, please have a seat." He sorted his papers together and shoved them in the bottom drawer of his desk.

Joan was aware that Abby had been moved back to sickbay that day after spending four nights in his quarters. She was thankful for that, because she had a feeling the captain cared very much for this young lady, and this was a conversation she didn't want her to overhear.

"Is there something going on with the investigation, something new you have come up with?" Eric asked.

"Actually, I have a few questions regarding Abby that I am not quite clear on." She watched as he tensed, then locked his whiskey-colored eyes on her. For a moment, she thought he was shooting her a warning.

"Oh, and what questions are those?"

Here it goes, she thought. "I'm curious: Why is Abby under your protection, and who is she? I mean, where did she come from? A pregnant Caucasian woman out here, why?"

Eric sighed heavily as he hefted himself out of the chair and walked around the desk. He shut the door before returning to his seat, resting his hands before him on the desk and then clasping them together. "We found Abby in a dinghy. She had been there for a while, beaten up. She is an American citizen who was kidnapped in Paris. What we have been able to piece together from Intel and Abby is that she was sold at an auction to an Arab man."

Joan felt the bile burn in her stomach. She was aware this happened to women, but she feared what Eric was going to say next. She wondered just how bad it was for her, what she may have had to endure, and for a moment she didn't want to know. She felt tears burn in her eyes, and she fought to hold them back as she listened to his account of what she had survived, and her escape.

Joan closed her eyes, trying to shut out the abused image that appeared in her mind. She knew whatever she was picturing would have been a blessing compared to what Abby had actually withstood. She felt the warm tear drench her cheek. She quickly wiped it away as she roughly cleared her throat. "Thank you for sharing that, Captain. I didn't know." He didn't need to say any more. She understood now why he was so protective of her, and it made her want to help him more than she already was. "So what happens to her now? Will she go home?"

"Eventually. I'm making arrangements for her now," he said. He was ending the conversation. Joan saw the hardness in his jaw as he leaned forward. He said nothing further, and Joan took the cue to leave. Emotionally battered herself, she needed to think and put some perspective on this.

"Thank you, Captain. I appreciate your candor. How is Abby doing emotionally?"

He looked away, and everything about him softened. "She's going to be okay. I'll make sure of it."

Joan just nodded as she moved to the door. "Thank you, Captain. Goodnight."

She leaned against the captain's closed door in the passageway. Alone, she wanted nothing more than to break down and cry. It was a woman's worst nightmare, and she didn't know, if she were in Abby's place, how she'd be able to cope.

"Good evening, Commander."

Startled, she pushed away from the door and nodded at the officer in passing. This wasn't the place to fall apart, she reminded herself as she hurried on back to her cabin and the privacy she needed to get her head together for the meeting with Abby tomorrow.

THE NEXT MORNING, Eric hung up the phone, shaking his head. He turned to look at Joe, who sat across from him, waiting to hear about the conversation with the admiral. Eric leaned his head back, really digging into the chair, and then swore as he slammed his fist against the desk. The strain was beginning to take its toll on him.

"So what did he say?" Joe asked.

"They want her sent to the base in Bahrain. They want to question her about Seyed. It appears that your friend Edwin let it slip that this guy may be connected with the bombing of one of the navy ships last year."

"What? I can't believe Edwin did that. When do they want her there?"

"Now!" Eric hissed through gritted teeth. He flung the pen to the desk in frustration. Then he pushed out of his chair, pacing the room. He dug into each step. His mind was racing. He didn't know what the hell to do. He was feeling helpless and wary, not knowing how to stop it, but he was convinced that if the CIA got hold of Abby, no matter how innocent she was, they would end up hurting her, maybe not physically, but by the emotional damage they would do by hammering at her. Those unscrupulous bastards made people disappear, and they didn't care who those people were. He believed that this time, Abby would never be seen again.

"I did my best to talk the admiral into letting me keep her and the baby here on board for the time being. It's safer here."

"Baby on board? How'd he react to *that*?"

"He was reluctant… but at least I bought some time until I can figure out something else," Eric said. What new problem was going to creep out of the woodwork at him? He felt as though he was being ambushed and it was coming from everywhere, above him, below him, and all around him.

Joe cleared his throat, drawing Eric's sharp attention to him. "Are you sure you want to be there when we talk to Abby? I mean, you're upset. She'll pick up on it—"

"Don't even think about trying to talk me out of being there," he said, cutting Joe off. "When are we meeting? And, by the way, where is the commander?" Eric was guarded now, and frustration pulsed behind his eyes.

"Well, we should head down to sickbay if you want to be there ahead of Joan. I know she's been talking to more of the crew, trying to get some more statements."

Eric was at the door and yanking it open in two strides. Then he stared down at Joe. "Well, let's go. I don't want her talking to Abby without me there."

"I'm right behind you," Joe said.

JOAN ANTICIPATED that Eric was going to be difficult about her interviewing Abby, so she had made a point of telling Joe a time that was an hour later than she planned. The rumors she'd heard about Abby still did not prepare her for this moment.

Her throat jammed up, and she swallowed hard as she stood, watching Abby, knowing the very private, painful details of what she had suffered. It took her a moment to gather her wits as she stood alone in sickbay with this young mother. It was not how she imagined, especially after what she heard last night. After seeing her briefly in the passageway earlier in the week, well, she sensed a protective shroud surrounding her.

One question continued to stick in her mind. Why had the captain, with his reputation, staked her as his territory? It was a very primitive thing to do—something she'd love a man to do for her. There was probably no woman around who didn't want some tiny bit of that kind of protection there for her, when she needed it.

"Abby, we haven't formally met. I'm Commander Joan Foxworth. I'm conducting an investigation and was wondering if I could ask you some questions."

Abby smiled up at her, gently swaying with the baby in her arms. "You're investigating the charges Gail Carruthers made."

Her mouth fell open, because she had understood that the captain was so overly protective that Abby might not have a clue what was going on around her. Pulling up a chair to sit by Abby, Joan was distracted by a subtle longing at the sight of the tiny baby in Abby's arms. She wasn't sure why these maternal feelings were beginning to surface, along with a dawning desire to know what it would be like to have a child of her own.

"Would you like to hold her?" Abby asked.

The moment turned awkward. For Abby to be aware of her feelings caused an uneasy discomfort inside Joan. It prompted her to decline, only the words would not come, so Abby stood up and simply put Rachel in Joan's arms.

As soon as that tiny baby was settled in her arms, she was filled with longing, and a warm peace flooded her senses. The purity and innocence of the child was amazing. She stared at the tiny life that yawned with a small mouth and most perfect lips, and she couldn't help herself when she kissed that amazing hand that reached up. Then, with a deep smile that was more forced than real, she handed the baby back.

"Abby, I'm surprised you know anything about the accusation. I was led to believe that you knew nothing about it."

"Oh, I know about it. Believe me, it wasn't easy finding out. Eric wanted to keep me in the dark, but I knew something was going on by the way everyone was acting, and Gail Carruthers had me wondering and confused for a while."

Joan tried not to stare at Abby, seated on the edge of the bed, rocking the baby. Frowning, she asked, "What did she say to you?"

"Well, actually, a few things happened. She came to see me one night. I think it may have been when you first got here. The guard was no longer at the door, and she came in alone. She seemed so interested in how the baby and I were doing, and then she started to check my blood pressure."

"Okay, before I ask about the guard, which I am quite confused about, tell me what she said to you."

Abby closed her eyes as if picturing the incident. Then her eyes flew open. She appeared confused. Shadows of raw emotion clouded them. "I still don't understand it, but I think she was trying to make me doubt Eric. I mean, she said she was concerned for me and the trauma I had been through. Then she told me I needed to be careful with the captain.

"There were too many other things that happened. One was the morning after I'd been in early labor. Eric thought I was asleep. I heard the door crash open, and then I heard Gail's voice. She refused to acknowledge the captain appropriately, and she spoke to him with such contempt and disrespect. I remember hearing Eric open the door and call in the guard. He ordered him to escort her out. I've never heard him so angry, but it was at that moment that I knew she had done something to him. The way she acted with him was more a woman scorned, which is what I'd been thinking. I mean, my God, the captain saved me."

"How do you know he didn't do anything to her?" Joan was disturbed by what she was hearing. For just a second, doubts filled her. Had Gail been mistreated, or were these all lies?

"He didn't do anything. I know it here." Abby placed her hand over her heart. "He keeps me in the dark, trying to protect me. Someone who truly dislikes women wouldn't do that. Besides, in case you haven't noticed, everyone else respects him. I respect him. I snuck out of this room because I knew the captain was hiding something. He was hurting, and I couldn't stand it. I had to find out, because I wanted to protect him like he protected me. When I briefly spoke with the young seaman washing the floor, one thing I discovered along with the truth of the incident is that the crew love and respect him. Her, they view as a viper."

"Okay, Abby, the supposed incident she reported happened here in sickbay." Joan was careful to keep her tone light as she continued.

Startled, Abby blinked rapidly. Her expression was one of confusion as she stared at Joan. So, Abby wasn't aware of the specific details of the claim.

"I'm sorry," Joan said. "I misunderstood. I thought you knew the details?"

"Obviously not. When did this supposed incident happen?" There was a very distinct bite of anger in Abby's voice.

"Friday." Joan paused to review the specific detail in the notes she held in the file in her lap. "She has noted a time of approximately twelve hundred hours. That's noontime."

Confusion shrouded Abby's face and then knit her brows together. She fixed a concerned gaze on Joan. A faint recollection of something seemed to flicker in her eyes, along with anger in her now-quiet demeanor.

"I do remember Friday, right before the doctor brought me my lunch. I can honestly tell you I do remember when the captain came in. I was just waking up, and I heard him talking to Gail. He asked —"

The door swung open, stopping Abby mid-sentence. All at once, the atmosphere changed inside the room to something thick and dark. Eric loomed in the doorway, and his expression was something Joan had not seen before. His unmistakable gaze connected only with her. A sheepish Joe followed behind.

Joan, for the first time in her life, felt her cheeks burn red. She cleared her throat and said, "Good morning, Captain." She was careful to let her voice betray nothing. A curt nod was all the reply she received as Eric moved to stand right beside Abby, almost blocking her from Joan's view.

"Commander, I see you arrived early. I understood from Joe that we weren't to meet for another twenty minutes yet. Or is it that I was given the wrong time?" It was more a statement than a question, as he shot a murderous glare at Joe.

Joe frowned at the commander, and Abby leaned around the captain to look at Joan. It was quite a pickle, and Joan felt very much on the hot seat.

Abby reached out with a free hand and touched Eric's side, drawing his attention down. As he looked into her eyes, his irritation melted away. God, thought Joan, the man was in love with her!

"Eric, I remember that day and what happened. I was awake when you came in."

He squatted in front of her and then put his hands on each side of her. "What day are you talking about?"

Abby looked anxiously at Joan. "On Friday, when this… supposed incident happened." Abby was blushing furiously.

Reaching out, Eric took Rachel from her and faced Joe. "Here, make yourself useful. Hold Rachel a minute."

Joan received another surprise when Eric passed Rachel to Joe and smiled warmly at the tiny babe before shooting another warning glare at Joan.

"Watch her neck, and for God's sake, be careful with

her." Eric's sharp rebuke surprised Joe, who rolled mocking eyes but did not utter a sound.

Returning to Abby, Eric rested his arms on either side of her and leaned in front of her. He deliberately kept his back to Joan, but she didn't mind. Maybe letting the situation run would produce the answers she needed to close this case.

Eric then stood up and took Abby's hands in his. "What do you remember?"

Abby related the bit of story Joan had heard just before Eric's untimely appearance. She listened more closely as Abby embarked on new territory. "You asked her where the doctor was, and at the time there was one thing that puzzled me: I didn't understand then why you were so abrupt with her, but I do now."

That last comment brought a puzzled look from Joan and Joe both, although Abby didn't appear to notice.

"She didn't acknowledge you as her commanding officer when you came in," Abby said.

Joan felt a twinge of resentment for the magic that seemed to pass between Abby and the captain. It was a rare bond they'd formed, and it was something she could honestly say she'd never witnessed before. How many women were lucky enough to find something that magical, a man so head over heels in love that he would do anything to protect them?

"I remember you said, 'That's all,' dismissing her. I had the idea she just stood there because you had to say it again. Then you told her to go to the mess hall. I remember how surprised I was at her behavior and how quickly she left."

Eric reached out and touched her face, cupping her soft, rounded cheek in the palm of his hand. "I didn't know you were awake."

Joan cleared her throat. Eric pulled back his hand and stood, turning to face Joan, who met his stern gaze with her practiced wide smile.

"Well, I do believe Abby's statement here should finish it," she said. Feeling a little out of sorts at witnessing such an intense moment, Joan gave herself a mental shake and focused her attention to closing up this case. "I think that's all I need." Standing up, she paused in front of Abby. "It was a pleasure to meet you, Abby, and thank you for letting me hold your baby."

The captain frowned at Abby. She in turn smiled lovingly at him.

"It was nice meeting you, Commander," Abby said. "I hope I was able to help clear up any accusations against Eric."

Joan couldn't discuss any details, so she inclined her head and gripped her file, turning to leave.

"Just a minute, Commander. If you don't mind, I'd like to speak with both you and Lieutenant Commander Reed in my quarters now," Eric said.

Joe just rolled his eyes as he gently swayed with the baby in his arms. He winked at Joan, breaking the astonishment she felt at the sharp order.

Eric turned to Abby. "I'll be back right after I meet with these two," he said. "Give her to me." He took Rachel possessively from Joe's arms, stealing a quick sweep of her with his eyes as if examining her for some injury she may have suffered.

Joan was stunned, watching, and Joe muttered under his breath, in a voice low enough so as not to alarm the baby, "I didn't harm her, you know. I do know how to look after one. I own three myself."

Abby choked back a chuckle and shared a moment

with Joan. Their eyes met, and Joan felt the silent thank-you from Abby.

CLOSING THE OFFICE DOOR, Eric walked with arrogant purpose around the desk and then sat in his chair. Without a word, he stretched out a hand, palm up, gesturing to the two chairs. On the walk back to his cabin, all down the passageway, with each step and each nod to the passing crew members, he'd managed to work off some of the annoyances, but his irritation at the betrayal was still there. He refused to allow this incident to pass without addressing it.

Joan directed a cautious look at Joe, who only raised his eyebrows as they both sat down in the proffered chairs. Eric said nothing for the longest time. He flipped through a file on his desk, read for a bit, and slapped the file closed.

Joan held up the flat of her hand in mock surrender. "Captain, I'm sorry. I told the lieutenant commander here a later time. He didn't know I was going there an hour earlier. I needed to be able to talk to her without interruption."

"Let me make something perfectly clear to you, Commander Foxworth." Eric kept his tone steady but added an edge to it, relaying to her that if she wasn't careful, she would find herself bounced right off this ship, regardless of whether the investigation had been completed. Coloring slightly, she realized that in that moment, she had made a dreadful tactical error. "No one pulls that kind of crap on me, no bullshit. To be quite frank, I'm very disappointed in you. I honestly started to believe that I may have misjudged women in the military, but I believe that from your current behavior, you have just proven me correct."

She was obviously stunned by his accusation. Anger colored her cheeks. She opened her mouth to say something but stopped and shut it again. "Captain, I agree that what I did wasn't right. I do regret my earlier actions and would like to apologize."

Eric glanced over at Joe and was startled by the sympathetic look he gave the commander. It was a warning glance to end this now and not say another word. She, being a very smart woman, picked up on the cue and turned back to the Captain, looking properly chagrined.

She spoke to Joe in an apparent attempt to gain his support. "I'd like to talk about the statement from Abby." Opening the file she had been clutching, she referred to her hurried notes. "Abby seems to corroborate your story, and, taking into account the other statements we have, it appears pretty clear that Gail, with malicious intent, created the incident as some sort of revenge or retaliation against you."

Crossing his arms, he scrutinized her. "So what now? I presume you'll be in touch with the admiral."

She gave the captain a curt nod. "I want to meet with Gail again, too. I need to discuss… a lot of things with her, to give her a chance to recant her story."

Eric furrowed his brows. "Why would you want to give her any kind of chance?"

"I plan on having her brought up on charges, filing a false report and malicious mischief, just to name a few, but until I talk to her I won't be able to ascertain all the charges. I need to give her a chance to come clean."

"Keep me informed. Make sure Joe's with you when you talk to her."

Eric was relieved to have this almost cleared up. It had

been like a weight hanging over him with the constant fear of when the ax would fall. He hadn't admitted to anyone, especially himself, just how terrified he really was. Expelling a heavy sigh, he closed his eyes tight and focused on a bigger issue: keeping Abby on this ship and away from the base in Bahrain.

Chapter Twenty-Six

Gail Carruthers had been confined to her quarters. She'd yelled and screamed the minute she was put in there, and she'd even pounded on the door, demanding to be set free. Everyone heard her, and it was obvious she'd go down fighting, taking anyone or anything with her.

Joan stood outside the room with Joe. She gave a nod to the guard and opened the door. The first thing Joan saw was a woman filled with such fury that she appeared to be trembling. She was breathing hard and held her arms so rigidly that Joan wondered for a moment whether she was about to spit on them. She had a wild, rabid, caged-animal look about her. This happened to some people who were locked in four walls, even for a short time.

Joe turned to the guard and said in a low voice, "See to it we're not disturbed."

The bulky guard nodded and pulled the door closed. Joan crossed her arms and stared at Gail, trying to figure out what was going through her head. She appeared to be sweating, her eyes widened, and she jerked her head over to the XO now standing beside Joan. Joan lifted the thick manila folder against her chest, and Gail's eyes flew to it immediately. Of course she was wondering what was in it—who wouldn't?

Joan cleared her throat. "Do you understand why you're being confined to your quarters?"

Gail looked straight at her and shook her head. Joan could see the heavy lump in her throat and that she was having trouble swallowing. Joan let her gaze flicker to Gail's sides, and she realized her fists were clenched.

Joan tapped the folder with her fingers. "We've collected statements from several crew members. First of all, they address your public admission that you wanted to get back at the captain. Second, we have a witness to the day and time in question who corroborates the captain's report of the incident."

Joan watched the shorter woman's eyes widen, and her face tinged pink. Gail leaped at Joan and scraped her fingernails down her cheek, and Joan fell back over the chair beside her to the floor. The file spread everywhere. All Joan could hear was the filth that Gail was shouting at her like some raunchy sailor. It was hurtful, and Joe grabbed Gail and dragged her back right before she tried to hit Joan with her fist.

Joe launched his body between them, giving Joan a moment to rise. Her blouse was open. The top two buttons seemed to be missing. She pulled the cloth closed as the lace of her bra showed, and maybe that was what distracted Joe, as Gail kicked him and wrenched free, grabbing Joan's hair. Joe pulled her off and slammed her into the locker, holding her there. Joan got to her feet and set the chair back up. Then Joe heaved Gail into it and yelled, "Just stay down there if you know what's good for you, and keep quiet!" His voice was controlled, but the warning was clear.

"That is bullshit. I'm being railroaded. Who dreamed up the conspiracy against me? You?" She aimed a finger at Joan, but Joan did nothing but pull her shirtfront closed again. Gail then shouted at Joe, "Or was it you? There was no witness; you know it and I know it. There was just that—"

Joan watched the instant alarm fill her expression, and then she snarled, "There is no way that woman saw anything. She was practically unconscious. Anyway, she would lie and say anything he wanted her to. She's nothing but a terrorist and is probably in cahoots with that guy she says kidnapped her. I bet she made the whole thing up."

Joe's hand shot out and grabbed Gail by the shirtfront. He yanked her from the chair and held her mere inches from his face. "Shut your mouth, you lying piece of trash."

Joan pushed herself between them. "Put her down, please."

He did, and Gail sank to the floor, her knees buckling under her weight. Joe's expression changed, and he stared with such disgust that Joan prayed he'd never look that way at her.

"Damn you, Carruthers. It was *you* who started that rumor that Abby was a terrorist," Joe said. Gail looked away and appeared to clamp her mouth closed.

"Gail, I'm giving you a chance to come clean," Joan said. "A second chance, as it were. We know you filed a false report. The evidence and statements we've gathered —several of them, in case you're interested—support that. What I don't understand is why."

She wouldn't answer, but tears were now swimming in her dirty brown eyes.

"Gail, we will be bringing charges against you, but we're willing to be lenient if you'll confess to what you've done and show true remorse."

Still, Gail didn't speak. Joan looked over to Joe, who was standing much like a fighter does, waiting for his opponent to lunge. Joe offered a slight shrug. With a sigh and shrug of her own, Joan turned back to Gail. She was done. She'd given this girl all the chance she could stomach.

"We'll leave you to think about your choices. You are relieved of duties, confined to quarters. Under no circumstances are you allowed to leave this room."

Joe followed Joan out the door, and before the door closed, a pillow was flung. In the hall, Joan winced and touched a hand to her stinging cheek. When she pulled her hand away, she saw traces of blood. She tossed a sheepish look at a silent Joe beside her.

"Thank you for your help in there. I guess the captain was right about sending you with me, huh?"

"He has generally been right, regardless of his views. There are just some things with him I'd never question."

THE WARDROOM WAS full that night, the mood considerably lighter than it had been since Gail's ugly accusation. There was a steady buzz in the room, as the officers present were all discussing Gail Carruthers, everyone with a different theory on why the woman had filed her complaint and on how many other women in the Navy would do that. The captain had not officially been cleared, as of yet, but every one of the officers remarked that this was a mere formality.

Joan felt awkward and smiled stoically while she received appreciative thanks from many of the officers and made excuses for her wounded face. She took her hat off to this man. He was well respected by his crew, even with his primitive views of women. It still set her teeth on edge that he had evidently read a situation better than she had. Where she should have used better judgment, he had the foresight to recognize a problem situation. Although she was still sporting a bruised pride at the upbraiding she had received from him, she realized it was time to swallow it and congratulate him.

Joan spotted the captain across the room, pouring himself a cup of coffee. He wasn't mixing with his officers. He was thinking, doing, overseeing, and for a moment she found herself a little in awe of the man who towered over her. Why hadn't she noticed before? He was one of the hottest men she'd ever met, and his brown eyes shimmered with something that appeared deep and old, like a survivor who had seen far too much. That deepened the aura of mystery around the man.

She glanced at his full lips and wondered how it would be with him, to be kissed and held in those powerful arms… consuming was the word that came to mind. He had a deep tan, with tiny lines around his eyes, a dark shadow of hair on his cheeks. As he stood there watching her, she could almost feel his power, and she wondered if this was how Abby saw him. God, any woman would be lucky to have him, but it would have to be on his terms, with no compromise. That was so clear. He didn't even have to open his mouth for her to get that. She also realized he was unavailable—he had found his mate, and that was stamped all over him.

She cleared her throat, preparing to speak, and he raised an eyebrow, waiting for her to say something. "Captain, I wanted to thank you for having the foresight to send Lieutenant Commander Reed with me to see Gail Carruthers. I underestimated the situation, and…"

He set his coffee down and touched her elbow, gesturing across the room, where there was more privacy to talk. "Commander, you don't need to thank me, but understand it's my responsibility to see to everyone's safety on this ship. And that does include you. Don't be too hard on yourself for misreading the situation, but when you don't play by the rules, that's when slip-ups happen. Remember that."

Joan stopped for a minute when his meaning set in. He was angry still for what she'd done, slipping in early to see Abby, his Abby. She started to leave but then said, "Oh, and Captain, I understand the admiral will be in touch with you. I have filed all the reports to have the charges dismissed against you."

The Captain inclined his head. "Thank you, Commander, and good luck to you."

"Thank you, Captain, and may I say good luck to you, too, sir." Saluting him, she watched as he strode from the wardroom, stopping only for an instant to accept someone's congratulations before leaving.

Joan smiled and waved at an officer across the room who called her, beckoning her to come over. Joan just gestured to her watch and gave Joe only a passing glance as she too left the wardroom. She had packing to do and would be leaving in the morning along with Gail Carruthers, who was to be transferred to the base in Bahrain before being shipped back home to await trial.

Chapter Twenty-Seven

The call from the admiral was expected, but Eric was unable to control the tension that was biting all the way up his back. It had been over a week since Commander Foxworth had left with Gail Carruthers and two days since he'd been officially cleared of any wrongdoing. He remembered the sense of relief he had felt when he heard she had admitted the lies, if only to help officially clear the other three officers and the allegations she had made against them. Even though there were no charges, there was still that tainted question that lingered as to whether they had done it. When someone created those kind of lies about people, they never really went away.

Over the last week, Eric had spent only a brief visit each day with Abby and Rachel. The admiral, as promised, tried to stall having her brought to the base in Bahrain, but the Admiral confirmed Eric's fears: The CIA wanted Seyed Hossein, and since Abby and the baby were, according to them, the only motive he had to come out of hiding, they were willing to sacrifice her to catch the elusive man. Even Langley had called and said he had to hand her over. They were now sure that Seyed Hossein had played a role in the USS Cole bombing in October, 2000.

When the phone buzzed beside him, he lifted the handset with a heavy heart, because they'd come down to their last fight. "Admiral, I hope you have good news for me," he said. Hearing the sigh on the other end, the bottom fell out of his stomach. Eric shut his eyes.

"They're unwilling to budge. They want her and the baby, and they want them now."

For a minute, a powerful jolt went right through him, because he was facing two things: He could either pull something that would anger a group of people who could be a hornets' nest when denied what they wanted, or he could lose the only woman who'd managed to creep inside his heart and fill the big empty void that had always existed inside him. Either could kill him.

"Admiral, I can't let her go. You and I both know what will happen. She's a US citizen who was abducted." He heard a sharp intake of breath and, before the admiral could send a direct command over the wire and leave him with a choice he didn't want to have to make, he added, "No. I have to stand firm. She's under my protection. I won't turn her over to them. Please, you have to help me out on this."

As he gathered a deep breath, an idea sparked in his head. "I also want to run something past you. If I keep Abby and the baby here, the CIA could let it slip that this is where she is. Of course, this means exposing the ship and crew. Ideally, it would draw Seyed out where they could set a trap for him. It's a win-win for them, Admiral. Let them have all the credit. I just want Abby safe."

"It will be a tough sell," the admiral replied. "Exposing the ship and crew to these dangers may not be an option. I would have to get approval from Washington." There was the sound of a chair squeaking. "You should know I'll have a quick answer from Washington, and then they'll be sending someone for her. They'll order you to turn her over." The Admiral cleared his throat, and Eric could hear someone whispering in the background. "Oh, I meant to tell you that the chaplain is still on the Vincent. He's planning on leaving today, though, to return to Washington. You may want to consider having him aboard before he flies off."

Eric was still holding the phone in his hand when Joe knocked, and Eric watched him shut the door and lean against it. Maybe it was the look on his face that had Joe appear grim.

He gripped the back of the chair and said with concern, "Eric, it didn't go well, did it?"

Eric swallowed the lump in his throat. "No, it didn't, and it doesn't sound like I have much time." Taking a deep breath, he looked at his watch, stood up, and turned toward Joe. "Can you track down the chaplain, Commander Julian Dobson? Find out if he's still on the Vincent. Then get him over here in the helo—" He stopped talking and jammed all ten fingers in his hair. Then he blew out a hard breath. "I need to go talk to Abby." He started for the door. "I'm going to ask her to marry me."

Joe's eyes widened, but he didn't speak.

"I... I've thought about it, Joe. A lot. Never thought it would happen like this, but it's the only way to protect her."

"To keep her on board?" Joe said.

Eric nodded. "Partly, but it's the only way to keep them from using her as a guinea pig."

"Do you think she'll agree?"

Pausing for a second with his hand on the door, Eric lowered his head before pulling it open. "I don't plan on giving her much choice."

Chapter Twenty-Eight

She was wearing the jeans and taupe button-up shirt that Eric had arranged to include in the supplies that arrived the other day. He'd guessed on her size, but just seeing her face light up to have regular clothes to wear was worth the effort and favors he'd had to call in.

Even though she'd just had a baby a few weeks ago, she really looked good. She had the most amazing figure, long blond hair that almost reached her waist, a sharp set of cheekbones, and lips that he wanted to lean down and taste every time he looked at them. He also thought her ass was amazing, with the way she filled out a simple pair of jeans.

He leaned against the door as it clicked closed. Abby watched him from where she lingered in the corner, where she and Rachel had a bed out of the way. The first moment her eyes connected with him, her face lit up. Then she seemed to think about something, and she frowned and wrapped her arms around her middle. He started across the room, heading straight for her, giving a passing glance to the sailor lying on one of the beds. "I need to talk to you," he whispered.

She was searching out his face as if she knew something was wrong, and her expression immediately leaped to fear. "What's wrong? You're scaring me!"

When she touched his arm, he could feel how she struggled to stop the tremble, and the last thing he wanted to do was scare her. He knew all too well the places she'd go in her head, so he guided her to the edge of her bed. "Sit down," he said. Then he covered her mouth with his fingers, feeling the softness against his roughness. "Shh, don't be scared. Please don't. There's not a lot of time. Something's going on, and we need to be married now."

She stared at him, and he'd swear she stopped breathing for a second. "What did you say?"

He set both hands on her cheeks. "Abby, I need you to marry me right now. Don't say no or that you have to think about it. I just need you to trust me and nod once, a simple yes."

"Married. Why would you want to marry me?"

It was the first time that he had seen her doubt herself, and he was shocked. Didn't she know what she did to him? Why, she'd all but wrapped him up in a knot! He couldn't go back to his lonely, isolated life as it had been before. He didn't want to go there, and he wanted her with him, to be his, only his.

"Abby, don't you know the way I feel about you? I want you somewhere safe where I can protect you and Rachel." He didn't let her respond, because he didn't want her to start questioning what and why and who the big bad wolf was who was pounding at the door. He knew that knowledge would tip her right over the edge. He leaned down and pressed his lips to hers, so soft and hesitant, but she didn't flinch, didn't pull away as he feared she would. He didn't push the kiss, although he wanted to trace his tongue over her lips to taste her. He realized he needed to take it slow. "Please, Abby, just trust me. Please say yes." He rested his forehead against hers and took in her warm breath. "Abby, do you trust me?"

"Yes, I trust you. You already know that."

"Then will you marry me right now, no questions, just be my wife?" He held her face and then slid all his fingers into her glorious hair, holding her head still as she looked at him. He didn't know what he saw there, and that worried him.

So slowly, her eyes filled with a shimmer of tears, and she blinked to hold them back and whispered, "Yes."

Eric wasn't about to give her time to change her mind. What he did was scoop up Rachel, snuggled in her makeshift cradle on the floor beside the bed. She was sleeping soundly, and his heart tripped each time he touched that innocent bundle. He loved her scent, how content she was, and how she gazed up at him with those dark eyes, not those of a monster but something so innocent. She was looking for him to keep her safe.

"The way you are with Rachel… you want her, don't you? You'll also keep my daughter safe, raise her as your own?"

When he glanced over at Abby, he saw the question she asked as the uncertainty flickered in her expression. "Abby, how could I not want to protect something so innocent? A child should never have to worry about whether she'll have a parent to protect her, to care for her, where her next meal is coming from. I want to do everything in my power to make sure nothing bad can ever touch her."

"Well then, we should go. Eric, Rachel and I would very much like to marry you."

He slid his other hand behind her neck and pulled her against him. "Let's go."

Abby settled Rachel in the bedroom of Eric's cabin. She used the drawer they'd used during her first few days after giving birth. It had stayed here, and Eric couldn't for the life of him figure out why he hadn't moved it. Maybe it was because he knew deep down that he wanted them back here. While Eric fumbled with something on his dresser, he watched Abby study the room as if it was the first time she was in here.

"Will I share this room with you, or will I still have to stay in sickbay? When I came up to see you a few days ago, Petey told me I was not allowed to wander the ship and had to stay in sickbay, so I need to know."

"Petey was right, and you're not wandering the passageway, although I love seeing you. I'm sorry, but you need to understand you're not in the military. You can't wander around with a baby. You could get knocked over. The ship makes sudden turns."

She nodded, but her expression was hidden, as if she didn't want to share what she was really thinking.

"And yes, you will stay here now," he explained.

This time she did smile, and he knew she was happy because the joy reached her eyes, turning the baby blue a shade lighter.

Voices from the outer cabin drew Eric away from Abby. He spotted Joe and the doc filing in the doorway along with Julian, the chaplain, whom Eric hadn't seen since he'd come aboard for an injured sailor. It seemed that Julian was always summoned for those going through a bad time. Eric could feel Abby's heat as she approached behind him. He said nothing to her but held out his hand and took hers. He led her out to the waiting men.

"Commander Dobson, this is Abby." Eric gestured with his free hand and then slid his arm around her shoulders. She stepped closer, pressed against his side.

Julian was a shorter dark-haired man with a receding hairline, a large nose, and hazel eyes that gave people all his attention. He reached out and took Abby's free hand in one of his, covering it with the other.

"Wow, so you're the one who knocked this guy flat on his backside. I never thought I'd see the day that Captain Eric Hamilton would toss his life as a bachelor into the wind and get married."

Eric felt Abby stiffen beside him, and he wanted to kick Julian. The last thing he wanted to do was terrify Abby. "Well, shall we get on with it? I understand you're heading back to the States today."

"Right after I marry you and have a word with a couple sailors, I'll be flying off to the base to catch the military transport home."

Eric winced. He knew how uncomfortable a long flight on one of the transport planes was.

"Well, enough with formality. Captain, Abby, I'll get you both to stand here. You two can stand on either side of them as witnesses." Julian gestured to Joe and the doc. Then he opened his black book and proceeded to marry Eric and Abby. Eric never took his eyes from Abby, and it was only when Julian said, "You may kiss your bride" that he stared down at the simple gold band that now surrounded her ring finger. It was loose, and when they got to port and back to the US he'd have it sized for her or buy her a diamond ring. She was staring at the ring, and he wondered if the plain thin band Julian had brought with him upset her. Maybe she wanted something fancy?

He slid his hands over her pale cheeks, which filled

with pink when she looked up at him. "I'm sorry it's all I could come up with on short notice. I'll get you something better."

"Eric, it's not the ring. I never expected one. Please, I wouldn't care if it came from a Cracker Jack box. No, you can't change it." She was so hesitant, the way she looked into his eyes, and when he leaned down and touched his lips to hers softly and then moved his mouth over hers, she responded. Then he pulled away just as a hand patted his shoulder.

"Congratulations! How does it feel to join all us married men?" Joe asked as he stepped in beside Eric and then kissed Abby on her cheek. "And you, welcome to the family."

"Are you all right?" Eric asked her, as she didn't reply to Joe.

She smiled up at Eric and stepped closer to him, allowing him to pull her close, as was his right as her husband. "I'm fine."

Julian clapped his hands together. "Okay, one more thing. I need signatures on the marriage certificate, and then I've got to run."

Eric took the pen and scribbled his name. He handed Abby the pen and indicated with his finger where she should sign, and she did so in nice neat loops. Joe and the doc both signed as witnesses. Then Eric was handed the certificate, and the three men left. When he stared back at Abby, he could see the whirlwind he'd just put her through, despite the fact that she was now his. No man would ever have the right to touch her again.

She fiddled with the ring on her finger and acted nervous, as if she didn't know what to do with her hands or where to look.

Eric stepped closer and slid his hands over her shoulders. He held her, and she looked up at him. "Don't be nervous with me," he said. "I know you just had a baby. Nothing will happen here."

She frowned. "What do you mean, nothing will happen? I'm your wife. Don't you want me?"

He couldn't believe she had even thought that. "Abby, of course I do, but you're not ready. Come sit down." He took her hand and led her to the sofa.

"Eric, I know you told me to trust you, and I do, but why do I feel as if you married me out of duty?"

He held both her hands in his as he sat on the edge of the sofa beside her. She was staring at both his hands, and when she met his gaze, he said, "Abby, for the past week, I've been battling with headquarters. The CIA has been trying to track Seyed."

At the mention of the man's name, Abby tensed, and he could swear she was trembling inside, because she was no good at hiding her deep feelings, and the fear always slammed into her at mock speed, so much like it would with a soldier suffering from PTSD. He tried to protect her, and she fought it. He was so proud of her for how strong she was.

"They wanted you and Rachel at the base in Bahrain." When he hesitated, she squeezed his hands and slid closer to him. "The only way for me to prevent that was as your husband. They won't be able to touch you now."

"So this was all business, then, for you. What am I, a cause you've taken up because you saved me? Do you feel you need to chain yourself to me for life? What a fool I am! For a minute, I thought you cared for me, that you wanted to marry me."

"Abby, stop it. Of course I wanted to marry you," he snapped.

"You wanted to marry me to protect me. Am I not right?"

Eric was feeling cornered because she was twisting his good intentions, and he didn't like anyone questioning him. He'd asked her to trust him, and now she wasn't.

"So you married me out of some sense of obligation." Her voice caught.

"Abby, I married you to keep you and Rachel safe." Why couldn't she understand how important it was to keep her safe?

Nodding, she was unable to keep a lone tear from escaping down her cheek. She yanked her hand from his and swiped angrily at it with the back of a hand. "I would like to thank you, then, for Rachel, for wanting to protect her." She refused to look at him; she stared across the room at his desk.

She tried to yank her other hand away, but he wouldn't let it go, so she let it relax limply in his, as if removing herself another way. He finally let her go, and she wrapped her arms around her middle and just stared off.

She sat there unmoving, as if she'd just shut down, until Rachel whimpered. When she got up and walked away to her baby, she shut the door behind her. Eric did the only thing he could do: He got up and left. He wandered the ship the rest of the day, snapping at anyone who tried to congratulate him until everyone started avoiding him. It was almost midnight when he returned to his cabin. Abby was curled up in his bed, fully clothed, cuddling her baby next to her. "My wife, my child," he whispered.

He wanted nothing more than to lie down beside her and pull all that warm softness into his arms, but she was hurt and she hated him. She had misread everything, twisting what he'd done for her as if it meant nothing, and that hurt. Didn't she know how much he cared for her? He couldn't say the words, couldn't go there yet and give her that kind of power over him by admitting that he loved her. He didn't know when it had happened exactly, when he'd fallen in love with Abby. With Rachel, it had been at the moment she was born, as he watched her lying there, so safe and soft. He knew he had fallen in love with Abby the moment he saw her lying on the deck of his ship, battered and bruised, alone, as if she'd been sent to him to save him.

This was his wedding night. They should be wrapped in each other's arms, sharing thoughts, dreams. Sadness tore through him. He quietly covered them with a blanket, stopping to take a last look and somehow resisting the urge to lean down and kiss Abby's round, soft cheek. He didn't want to wake her, to see the hurt reflected in her eyes, so he quietly gathered some clothes and personal items, jamming them in a bag. He tossed it over his shoulder and stole out into the night, passing one sailor in the passageway who gasped but said nothing, and he stomped into Joe's cabin, where he knew there was a pullout couch.

Early the next morning, Eric strode onto the bridge of the ship, feeling the vessel's surge of power beneath his feet. He spoke as little as possible, not that he was ever chatty, but he did only what he needed. He reviewed the report from the intelligence officer from the night watch, received an update from the operations officer, and snapped at anyone who got in his way. He kept reliving last night and Joe's startled face, his "What the fuck are you doing, Eric?" response as he'd bolted straight up in bed.

Eric had dumped his gear in the corner, pulled out the sofa bed, and lay down without saying one word. His friend swore again under his breath and soon went back to sleep, but Eric stared into darkness, his gut twisted and knotted, until finally, at dawn, he showered and left a sleeping Joe.

"Did you sleep at all?" Joe said in a low voice as he appeared beside Eric.

Eric grunted.

"Got time for breakfast, Captain?"

"Grabbed something already." Eric refused to look at him because he knew damn well Joe was doing what he did with every sailor, trying to find out what was wrong and help him fix it. But Eric didn't want anyone, not even Joe, anywhere in his business, so he handed the report to the chief as he came onto the bridge. "Not now" was all Eric said as he strode off.

He didn't know where he was going, but he could hear Joe's heavy footsteps right behind him, and he walked faster, stepping through the hatch on deck as wind flicked his short hair. The spray of the sea washed the deck, and Eric moved straight to the side.

"What happened?" Joe asked again. He was like a pit bull who just wouldn't go away. He hung on; he dug in.

"Fuck, Joe, can't you take the hint?"

"Eric, you just married the woman that knocked you flat on your ass and has had you googly eyed and acting like a fool. Everyone on this ship knows you've fallen hard for her, yet here you are, spending your wedding night with me, your XO. While I should be flattered —"

"You're such an ass." Eric stared out onto the water. "You know, I should have expected it. It did seem almost too good to be true."

"What the hell are you talking about?" Joe leaned his back against the rail.

"I told her the truth, that I married her to protect her

and Rachel. That CIA wanted her, and the only way to keep her from them was for her to be my wife. I asked her to trust me. I thought she did, but it's obvious I was mistaken. I have no idea what's wrong, but she pulled away, turned her back on me."

Joe thrust his hands through his hair. "You told her *what?*"

Eric could do no more than shrug one shoulder.

"You really can be a stupid ass sometimes, Eric. You didn't tell her how you feel about her? Rachel, you protect. Abby, you *love*. You need to go back in there and talk to her."

"No, she doesn't want to hear anything I have to say," Eric said.

OVER THE NEXT FEW WEEKS, Eric managed to keep busy by burying himself in work. High-seas hostilities had been building for months, with heavily armed speedboats darting near the US ships. They were taunting them. Seyed had been always in the back of Eric's mind, an enemy he hated, and he wondered if that cowardly animal was in one of the boats out there. Did he know this was where Abby was, where Rachel was? He knew the CIA still hadn't located him, as the man had all but disappeared. Time ticked like a timer on a bomb as he waited, and he knew that soon, she would have to leave, but right now, while she was here, he could look in on her at night. Although Abby consumed each thought, the only way he could get through each day was by personally taking charge and leading the boarding of a few ships. Joe had nearly lost it the last time, yelling at him that he was the captain, that he was not to be taking these risks, that he had a ship to lead and couldn't get himself killed.

But he wouldn't listen to Joe. Even the danger that spiked his adrenaline and kept him on his toes couldn't distract him from Abby and the realization that she may soon ask to leave just to get away from him. The sooner he came to grips with it, the better off he would be.

Chapter Twenty-Nine

"Captain, the XO sent me to find you. He said the admiral just arrived and he needs to see you right now. He's in your cabin."

Petey stood before Eric, who had been overseeing the replacement of the refrigeration system in the kitchen. His hands were covered in grease, and he quickly scrubbed them in the sink, then buttoned up his shirt and brushed at the black stain on the front. He rolled his sleeves down as he strode down the passageway up the ladder, Petey right behind him.

"What the hell? How in the hell did the admiral even get on board without me knowing? Dammit. Anyway, this whole damn ship is falling apart. Everyone is doing whatever the hell they want, and a helicopter lands just like that. What the fuck is everyone doing, holding up a welcome sign, 'Just show up whenever the hell you feel like it'?" He knew he was ranting, but Petey did what he always did, kept his mouth shut and followed.

Eric flew through his cabin door, prepared to face the admiral, and nearly crapped his pants as a thunderbolt shot right through him. Abby stood beside the round table in a red dress that stopped just above her knees, with thin straps showing a hint of her generous, plump breasts. When Petey poked his head around Eric's arm, Eric turned and shoved him back. "You, out," he said. Then he closed the door behind him.

Eric leaned against the door and drank in Abby's beautiful long blond hair hanging straight down to her waist. She wore nothing on her feet or legs, and then she walked straight toward him, holding out her hand and watching him with baby blue eyes filled with such tenderness. For the life of him, he couldn't get his legs to move, not one step, until she was right in front of him, still holding out her hand. Then something in his brain kick started, and he slid his hand in hers, feeling the ring he gave her. Holding up her hand, he noticed the tape she had added to make it fit.

"Eric, I'm so sorry.... I love you." She seemed to study him and wait, and he could see the worry flicker across her face. Maybe she thought he'd reject her. But how could he? He was still stuck on what she'd said.

"Say it again."

She looked as if she didn't understand. "Say what again?" Then it was as if it clicked, and she knew what he wanted—no, what he needed—to hear. "Eric, I love you more than my next breath, more than the sun that rises each morning. With you not here with me, with Rachel, and this..." She took a breath. "I need you. We need you."

Eric jammed his fingers in her hair and pulled her closer, sliding his mouth over hers. With some reluctance, he pulled away, looking up to see a faint glow coming from behind her. There were two lit candles on the table with what looked like two covered plates.

"I hope this is okay. I wanted to plan something special for you... for us, for tonight."

A blush crept up her face, and he took in the scene before him. Lifting her chin with a finger, he held it until, slowly, she looked up to meet his gaze. Then, lowering his face, he tenderly gave her a deep kiss when the reality of her inexperience hit him. It was nothing they had ever discussed in detail. Women of this generation rarely, if ever, came to a relationship untouched by another man. But after what she'd been through, he wondered if he could even touch her tonight.

"Abby, I want to make love to you tonight, but I don't want to hurt you. Would you let me touch you?"

"I want you, all of you. Yes, please touch me. You could never hurt me," she said. He leaned down to kiss her, but before his lips touched hers, she whispered, "Dinner, how about dinner first?"

He pulled back and stared down, and he wondered if maybe she needed time or if she was nervous. He took her hand and let her lead him to the table.

"I had dinner sent here." She lifted the covers off the plates. Eric couldn't keep his hands off her. He slid his hand down her back where the dress dipped low, and she shivered, and he watched the expression on her face, one of pure need. He pulled his hand away with a smile and slid out her chair. He touched her arm, her elbow, and she sat. Eric took the seat across from her and studied that face, that body. Abby would be all his in every way tonight.

"You've been mighty busy today, haven't you?" he asked. She kept her expression to one of innocence and then smiled subtly as a sparkle lit up her face. "Speaking of which, I was sent down here to meet the admiral, who I was told had mysteriously flown in. I was starting to think I was losing it, being so distracted that I don't even know when someone comes aboard my ship. I'm afraid Petey got the brunt of my rant."

"It's not Petey's fault. As you know, it's not as if I can walk around the ship dressed like this to find you."

Eric groaned as his gaze lingered on her creamy white breasts, her cleavage teasing him from the V of that tantalizing dress. He couldn't wait to peel it off her. "Where's Rachel, or is Petey or someone else babysitting now, too?"

"She's sleeping. I nursed her before you came, and hopefully she'll sleep for several hours."

Eric watched as she picked up her knife and fork, cut into the roast beef, and chewed. He was starving, but it wasn't for food. Although he cleared his plate in no time, swallowing the meal, he wasn't even sure what it was he had eaten.

He just watched her, and when she glanced up and took of sip of water, she set it down and said, "Is something wrong? You've been awfully quiet."

He tossed his napkin on his plate and slid back his chair, pacing the room. "We have a lot to talk about…."

When he faced her, she was holding her chin high and stubborn. Then she rose from the chair and stepped toward him. "Yes, we do, but not now, please."

"I would like nothing more than to take you to bed and make you mine right now, but there are things you don't know about me."

She crossed her arms and gave him a look of irritation. "Well then, tell me."

"I'm an overbearing man, and I can be a real bastard at times. You need to understand what you're in for. I will protect you, I will order you, I will piss you off, and I will demand all your attention. I won't let you go, and if you want to leave, you can't. You're mine."

"But if I'm yours, are you not also mine, and is Rachel not yours? Will you love her and protect us? Will we have all of you? Can I depend on you? I want more children, and a home. Will you grow old with me?"

"I won't let you go, Abby, or Rachel. You're my wife, and you get all of me. She'll be mine, too." He still didn't touch her, but she put her hands on him.

"I think I fell in love with you when I saw you above me after you saved me. You're too hard on yourself. I'll tell you who I see: a man who risked everything for me, for Rachel. You kept me safe, and, dammit, you've made me angry, hiding things to protect me when Gail lied and tried to hurt you. I just wanted to help, to protect you like you protect me.

"You're not as bad as you think you are, and I honestly don't want to have a life without you. The thought of being with you and having your children fills me with such happiness… I can't explain it. I do have a mind of my own, so I won't promise not to argue with you or disagree with you, but I won't go against you. I believe in you, in us, and I want you."

"You don't get to put yourself out there for me," he said, resting his forehead against hers. "But I will always, always protect you, defend you, and fight for you. That is my right."

He took his thumb and gently traced the outline of her lips. Leaning in, he rubbed her nose tenderly and caringly with his, and then, ever so lightly, he brushed her soft lips with his, slow at first, then deepening the kiss while tracing her lower lip with his tongue. He tasted her, and she opened slowly on a gasp, and Eric deepened the kiss until she was clinging to him. Her breasts pressed into his chest as he slid his arm around her back and the other around her bottom and lifted her against him so he could feel every part of her.

A cry from the next room had him loosening his arms, and she pulled away.

"Let me check on her. I'll be right back," said Abby breathlessly.

Eric watched the sway of her shapely hips, outlined in that indecently sexy dress, and he wondered who had given her such an outfit.

Abby walked back in carrying Rachel. "I just need to feed her again, and then she should go right back to sleep." She walked right up to him and then turned around, turning her back to him. "Can you unzip me? I can't seem to do it one handed."

As he reached down to unzip her, he felt the pain of such a gesture, wanting nothing more than to take her now. As the front loosened, she sat on the sofa and put Rachel to her breast. When she moved Rachel to her other side to finish, she glanced up and seemed startled that he was watching her so intently. "Why are you looking at me like that?"

"Like what?" he asked with a teasing tone. Crossing his arms, he winked. "I love watching you."

Her grin was intoxicating, and so was the blush that tinted her cheeks. When Rachel slipped off her breast, asleep, Eric moved her cradle out by his desk, securing it so it wouldn't move and so they would not disturb her. Eric had no plans to be quiet.

Abby carefully settled Rachel in bed. When she stood up, she slid up the front of the dress to cover her breast and reached around to zip it up, but Eric stopped her with his hand.

"Don't touch it," he whispered firmly in her ear as he slid his arm around her waist. Turning her in his arms, then pulling her tightly against him, he whispered softly against her lips, "Where were we?"

Before she could reply, he leaned down and kissed her with his tongue. He licked until she opened and deepened the kiss, pulling her to him. He reached around and pulled her zipper all the way down, hooking his fingers in the straps of her dress and sliding it off her until it pooled at her feet. She was standing there in just her plain white cotton underwear and nothing else.

He lowered his head to run his tongue down her neck, tracing the outline of her collarbone, then in a path down to the indentation between her breasts. Cupping her breasts, he ran his calloused hand over her right breast, twisting the nipple gently between his fingers while watching her reaction closely.

She gasped, and he felt the shudder inside her. Holding her tightly as he bent her back over his arm, he lowered his head, taking a nipple in his mouth and then running his tongue over it.

He couldn't get enough of her mouth, of kissing her, and he touched her lips again in a deep kiss that was all tongue and teeth. He slipped his hand under the elastic of her underwear and slid them off until they pooled at her feet and she stepped out. He didn't know how long he could last as he scooped her in his arms. Hers went around his neck, and he set her on the bed, covering her with his body, pushing her arms above her head.

"Leave them there," he whispered, and then he slowly made his way down, alternating between kisses and tracing his tongue over the smooth skin to her navel, then lower to the triangle of hair at the apex of her thighs.

She felt his hands on the inside of her thighs, caressing them, then moving up slowly to where they joined, then beginning to probe her slickness with his thick fingers, pushing deep inside, gently, while massaging the bud of pleasure with his thumb. Withdrawing his finger, he spread her quivering thighs wide with work-roughened hands, then put her knees over his solid shoulders, leaning in and gently kissing her there.

"Eric... no, you can't. Make love to me. I want you inside me." She reached for him, tried to pull him up.

"I plan to, just not yet." He wanted to make sure she enjoyed every part of this loving, and tonight he would see that she was fully pleasured.

Abby grabbed his hair, and she groaned, saying over and over, "Oh, Eric, I love you."

He didn't think he could take any more. He had to have her now. He pulled away, and she whimpered and then watched him with a look of seduction he'd never before seen in her eyes. He tore off his clothes, boots, and tossed them aside, then climbed back on the bed, and she gasped when her eyes ran over his hardness. She ran her hands down his chest to touch him, but he grabbed her hand because he knew he wouldn't last.

"Not this time. I need you too much."

He spread her legs wide, and he was between them. He braced himself on his arms and gazed into eyes that were filled with such longing for him. "Just so we're clear, Abby, you're now mine," he said. Then he thrust inside her, and she moaned.

"Yes, oh yes" was all she could say. He watched her as he moved inside her.

Eric could feel her building and tightening around his him as he thrust into her. Capturing her mouth once again, he swallowed her screams of pleasure as her nails scraped his back, and he kept going faster and harder. He could feel her begin to convulse around him again, and this time Eric couldn't hold back. He allowed himself to let go, transported by the climax, emptying his seed into her womb.

Collapsing on his side, Eric took Abby with him, both arms surrounding her and holding her tightly as he remained inside her. Waiting for their breathing to return to normal, he traced his hands down her back. He heard her sniff.

He pulled away and lifted her chin, and he was stunned by the tears shimmering in her eyes and the stark realization of how hard he had ridden her. Eric was infuriated with himself as he wiped the lone tear with tender care as it fell down her cheek.

"Oh, Abby, I'm so sorry. Did I hurt you? I just wanted you so bad, and it's been so long." Aghast at what he had done, he pulled her into his arms. Leaning her forehead against his chest, he felt the subtle shake of her head, then pulled back just enough so he could that angelic smile light up as she spoke softly.

"No... no, you didn't hurt me. My God, Eric, it was wonderful. No one has ever made me feel as cherished and protected as you have. No, you didn't hurt me," she repeated again as she reached up and cradled his face in her hands. "Oh, you sweet man. You gave me such pleasure.... You've made me so happy."

Eric propped himself up on his elbow to look down on her naked splendor. Then, tracing a hand over her bottom while pulling her closer, he gently squeezed. "Sometimes, you really amaze me," he said. Lowering his head, he gently kissed that lush mouth, and he deepened the kiss as he moved over her. Nudging her thighs apart, he entered her again, this time slowly, with such gentleness that it touched something deep inside him: a connection, this rightness, as if linking two souls together forever.

Chapter Thirty

The sound of the door opening and then closing in the outer cabin had Eric slip his arm out from under Abby. He looked down to see her sleeping peacefully, hearing the soft murmur under her breath while she stirred slightly and then rolled over on her side.

Sliding out of bed quietly, Eric pulled on his pants and shirt. Opening the door of the bedroom and closing it quietly behind him, he found Petey there, clearing away the dirty dishes that were on the table.

Petey jumped when he saw Eric.

"At ease," Eric ordered him in a lowered voice.

Petey finished clearing the dishes. "Do you need anything, Captain?"

"No, that'll be all. You went to a lot of trouble helping Abby set up this dinner."

He stuttered as a deep blush crept up his face. "C-captain, I-I…"

Putting his hand on the young man's shoulder, Eric said, "Just make sure this doesn't become common knowledge around the ship, Petey."

Petey grabbed up the trays and hurried out the door, almost knocking down the XO as he entered and upsetting the whole tray. "Sorry, sir," he said.

Joe said nothing, just nodded, and his eyes widened at Eric and how he must look, standing there barefoot in his pants and an open shirt. Then his gaze landed on Abby's red dress lying in a heap on the floor. Closing the door behind him, Joe strode around the cabin. "So, where is she?"

Eric gestured with his head toward the bedroom door. "In there, sleeping." Eric stepped around the desk and peeked down at a sleeping Rachel, who looked absolutely peaceful. Then he spied what Joe was staring at in the middle of his cabin floor: Abby's red dress and underwear. He scooped them up and tossed them on the sofa, and he didn't miss the smirk on Joe's face.

"I won't stay long.... I presume everything's okay."

"Just out of curiosity, whose idea was it to tell me the admiral was on board?" Eric asked.

Joe chuckled under his breath and then raised his hand in a teasing sort of way.

"I thought so. That seemed too devious for Petey. I'll be sure to get you back for that one."

"Oh, I think you already have. Don't forget I've shared my cabin with you for the past few weeks. I do hope you won't be returning."

Eric flinched with the last remark, realizing he had been quite the bastard since the day of his wedding. He was surprised the crew had tolerated him so well.

Joe casually walked over to the baby, who was sleeping blissfully in her makeshift bed. Shaking his head, he walked to the door. "I'll make sure you're not disturbed tonight," he said, and he left.

Eric allowed his thoughts to wander to his Abby, well-loved and sleeping in the next room. She was the simplest love he had ever known, with her pure innocence, no games or pretenses. It's almost too good to be true, he thought to himself as he felt a rueful smile shining inside his heart. Looking over at the bedroom door again, he muttered under his breath, "You're mine. By god, I won't let you go."

He watched Rachel sleeping peacefully, her tiny thumb stuck in her mouth now, gently suckling. Bending over, he tucked the blankets around her to make sure she was snug and secure, feeling a rush of pure joy wash over him while he crouched down, just watching. Then, from out of nowhere, he was hit by a fleeting panic when he thought about what kind of father he would be. He didn't know the first thing about it, and he scrubbed his hands down his face and headed back to his room and Abby.

Chapter Thirty-One

Eric looked down at Abby, who was lying, peaceful and content, curled up and well sated in the middle his bed. The sight took his breath away, sucker punched him right in the gut. He left the door ajar so they could hear Rachel in the next room, and he took off his shirt and pants and tossed them onto the chair in the corner. Climbing into bed, he settled up against her, pulling the covers over them and running his hand gently over her stomach while pulling her closer to him.

Hearing her murmur, he lifted her hair, kissing the back of her neck, holding her tightly in his embrace. He stopped her when she tried to roll over and face him. "Don't move," he whispered. Running his hand slowly down between her legs, he nudged them open, lifting her leg as he slipped a finger inside and heard a moan escape while she grasped his other arm, which encircled her waist. Slowly, he entered her from behind, anchoring her tightly to him, then lowering his head and taking her earlobe between his teeth, nibbling until he heard the sweet gasp as her breath caught. He slowed his pace, controlled his depth, pulling out and then back in.

"Oh, Eric, please…"

As he felt her begin to lose control, he reached up with one hand to cover her mouth, stifling the screams as he found her hardened nipple with his other hand and rubbed it in a circle. Plunging deep inside of her, he felt his control slipping, then teetering over the edge. He muffled his groan in her blond mass of hair as he buried his seed deep within her.

"My God, I think I need a minute—no, maybe an hour until I can move again," he said to her.

She slid around in his arms and faced him, then reached up with her slender hand, sliding it over his rough cheeks.

"I need to shave," he said, then turned his head. He nipped at her hand and kissed her again. "I didn't hurt you, did I?" he asked while tenderly running a finger over her jaw.

She shook her head. "Is it always so wonderful?"

"Yes, and it always will be. Now, enough talk; we need some sleep."

She snuggled her head against his shoulder. She was a perfect fit. The contentedness that washed over Eric was nothing he had ever experienced before. He listened to her steady, easy breathing as he allowed himself to slowly drift off to sleep.

Chapter Thirty-Two

Eric couldn't keep the silly smile he knew was pasted ear to ear from his face. The last week had been the best week of his life, spending every night in Abby's arms. As they now headed back home to port in Norfolk, he remembered the call from the admiral that had come through the morning after his reconciliation with Abby. He had been having breakfast with her when he received the news: They'd been ordered home.

The crew's adrenaline was pumping, and he could feel the joy come out of every wall and nook of his ship the closer they were to home.

Joe put a call through to Mary-Margaret since Eric had already arranged for housing on base. She volunteered to take care of their basic needs so they'd have a bed, food, everything they needed in their home. When Joe warned Eric to expect everything handled, because Mary-Margaret didn't do anything halfway, Eric hoped Abby would be okay with that.

There was a lot to consider, and as the ship neared the homeport, he wondered about Seyed Hossein. With what he'd done by marrying Abby, well, he knew he'd made enemies, but not knowing and knowing what they were up to were two very different things. That old saying, 'Keep your friends close and your enemies closer'—he'd made an enemy with the CIA, because there was a difference between taking an ordinary US citizen and taking the wife of someone in his position.

Standing on the deck of the ship as it approached the port, Abby cradled Rachel. As they came in, the crew scrambled around her, readying the ship for docking. The crowd that was gathered could be heard as they approached, and it was something that filled every part of Eric with such joy that he couldn't quite put it into words.

Eric leaned down, and, with a subtle brush of his lips, he said, "It's time you went back down. Petey will take you to my cabin. Wait there until I come and get you."

"But I want to watch us dock."

"This isn't the time or place. When I give an order, I expect it to be obeyed," he said. The last thing he wanted was for her to fall over or get bumped by some over-exuberant sailor, and that was a very real possibility. Eric snapped his fingers in the air and got Petey's attention. "Take my wife down, and stay with her until I come down."

"Yes, Captain," Petey said.

Eric could see Abby's disappointment, but, to her credit, she left with Petey.

ERIC LEANED against the frame of the open door to his cabin. He could still hear the roar of the crowd for their loved ones. He knew Mary-Margaret would be out there waiting for Joe in that crowd. He could hear the crew on deck, every one of them shouting and jumping, anxiously waiting to kiss and hug their wives, their girlfriends, anyone who was waiting for them. Eric now had Abby. He took her in with a full sweep of his eyes.

"Thanks, Petey. You're dismissed. Grab your gear."

The young man didn't linger. "Thank you, Captain," he said as he jumped out the door.

"Are you ready to start your new life?" Eric asked as he stepped toward Abby and pulled her into his arms. Rachel was cooing from the cradle by the desk.

Abby didn't pull away but looked up at him with her chin resting on his chest. "Yes, as long as you're with me."

Leaning down, he claimed those luscious lips, soft with passion, cupping her head as he took what was his. He was breathing heavily as he rested his forehead against hers. "My God, woman, what you do to me. Go pick up our girl. Let's go home."

Abby lifted Rachel from her cradle, and Eric lifted the duffel bag packed with all their belongings, tossing it with ease over his shoulder and then leading them out.

Chapter Thirty-Three

Mary-Margaret was waiting for them when they disembarked from the ship. She was bouncing up and down when she saw Joe. She had blue eyes, short brown hair, round cheeks, and a slim figure. After she finished giving her husband a kiss, she looked over to Abby, who glanced at Eric and blushed. Mary-Margaret hit Eric in the arm.

"Hey, what was that for? Joe, your wife just hit me."

Joe just laughed, and Abby wasn't sure what to make of them.

"I cannot believe you got married! Well, introduce me." Mary-Margaret gestured with her hand for Eric to hurry up.

"Abby, this tough broad here —"

Mary-Margaret smacked his arm again. "Hey, be nice," she said, jabbing her finger at him. "Abby, I'm Mary-Margaret." She slid in between them, bumping Eric over with her hip, sliding her arm around Abby. "Now, you come with me. We'll let these two sailors bring up the rear with the kids. Abby, that's Taylor, my oldest. He's ten,

Janey is eight, and Steven is seven. As you see, Joe didn't give me much of a break there for a while." The kids were shouting and hanging off their dad. "Can I hold her?" Mary-Margaret asked, gesturing to Rachel. Abby just nodded, and Eric noticed she was looking a little overwhelmed. Mary-Margaret started fussing over the baby as she walked away with her in her arms.

Eric picked up Abby's hand, smiling at her, and pulled her along with him, following Joe, the kids, and Mary-Margaret. "I think you'll really like Joe's wife. She can be a little out there sometimes, but she's put up with me all these years."

Eric stopped and watched her for a minute. She was taking everything in, and then she stepped closer to him and pulled the sweater she was wearing tightly around her.

"I'm fine," she said. "There's just so many people. And just to be here… I didn't expect all this." When she looked up at him, she tried to smile, but there was something there in her eyes, and she looked away as if trying to hide it.

"Abby, you're safe here. We have a house on base waiting for us. No one gets on or off base without going through security, which is tight. There's an alarm in the house."

She swept her hair back and peeked up at him. "You think I'm being silly?"

"No, but I want you to feel safe." He slid his arm around her and pulled her closer.

Joe whistled and shouted from the purple minivan everyone was piling in, "Hey, you two, come on!"

"Let's go before they leave us behind and take Rachel home with them," Eric said. And this time, when Abby smiled, there was light in her eyes.

Epilogue

TWO YEARS LATER

Abby stood on the pier with the other Navy wives and kids. She felt the familiar butterflies churn in her stomach as she held tight to Rachel, now a rambunctious two-year-old with jet-black hair and dark eyes, like her father.

There were times when she'd catch a glance at Rachel when she was running or reaching for something, just from the side, and she thought of Seyed. She would never, ever say anything to Eric, because the fear that haunted her for so long that he'd find her had returned a few months ago. After Eric left on this deployment, she wondered if she'd ever get used to having him gone for so long at a time, staying at home and pretending everything was fine. He made her feel safe, and while he was here, she slept soundly, peacefully.

She could not see Eric through the flow of sailors disembarking, so she stood on her toes, anxious, searching, when she spotted him in back, almost a head taller than many of the men. She waved frantically to him, wanting nothing more than to run to him and throw herself into his arms.

Making her way through the crowd, she felt the familiar pull to him, which had only intensified over the last two years. Reaching him, she couldn't stop the tears that always came when he left and when he returned. It was a roller coaster of emotions, and her eyes were like a damn faucet.

"There are my girls," he shouted and effortlessly scooped Rachel in his arms while pulling Abby with her, and Rachel screamed with delight, "Daddy, Daddy, my Daddy!" Eric kissed them both and then pulled away as he felt the baby kick.

Reaching down, he laid his hand possessively on Abby's swollen belly. Then he leaned down and kissed her again. "Sooo? How's my boy today?"

Good God, she swore the man was more handsome than when he had left, and he took her breath away. Just hearing his voice made her heart jump, and she felt his hands running over her. She held his hand as she tried to smile through her tears. "Your boy's fine. Your wife is ready to have this baby, though."

Laughing, he bent down and gave her a deep, passionate kiss that still had the power to leave her breathless. He slid his arm around her shoulder, Rachel in his other arm, still carrying the weight of his duffel bag. Eric led them to the car. "Come on, wife of mine. Let's go home," he said.

And Abby knew that tonight, she'd be safe.

Turn the page for a sneak peek of
VANISHED (A 2016 Readers' Favorite Award Winner in Suspense) and the next book in THE SAVED SERIES Available in print, audio & eBook.

She thought her nightmare was over....

—*"I'm an advocate for women in sexual assault, abuse and domestic violence, and I have to give this author two thumbs up for how she writes her stories."*

Reviewer- Jamie

—*"Lorhainne Eckhart is a very prolific and talented writer. Get to know her work, you won't regret it."*

Reviewer - Karen

—*"Loved this book...Five stars don't come from me easily. Tugged at my heart!"*

Kivey

—*"The focus on a woman taken was a very classic ideal because it was set in a military arena. YOU have to read these books, but make sure that you have e box of tissues because you will need them."*

Faybe

In VANISHED, Abby has married the man of her dreams. He rescued her, and he's the father of her child. Everything should be perfect, but she begins to relive her nightmare from when she was taken… and one night she disappears, leaving her children alone in the dead of night, her husband on a military ship halfway around the world.

But when Eric arrives home and the search begins, there are two disturbing questions: Was someone in the house? And how is it possible for Abby to simply vanish?

Vanished

CHAPTER 1

"Push. Come on, baby. You can do this." Eric was behind Abby on the hospital bed so she could lean against him. Her hands gripped his with a strength most men didn't have. She was damp and sweaty, and she was exhausted from being in labor all night, more than twelve hours.

"Almost there, Abby. Just give me one more push." The military doctor, Chase Hargrove, was a young, round-faced man of medium height and build with light curly hair. He glanced at Eric and lifted the baby, setting him on Abby's stomach. "Here he is, your boy." Chase grinned, flashing two dimples, and stood up, glancing at Abby through his round, fashionable glasses. "How are you doing, Abby?"

"I'm okay." She set her hand on the baby's back, trying not to nudge her IV. She watched the baby, and Eric leaned down and kissed her forehead, brushing back the long blond hair that was tangled and stuck to her skin. She gazed up at him with heavenly blue eyes that appeared tired and a little glassy. Exhaustion—it had to be.

"You did good, baby. You okay?" he asked. His arm

was around her, and she leaned against him. Her knees were still up as the doctor finished delivering the placenta. She lifted her hand from the baby and rubbed her forehead, pressing her cheek into Eric's chest.

"I'm just tired. Can you take the baby?" She had lifted her hands as if the baby lying on her was a burden. She sounded off, too, Eric thought, or maybe she was just tired and he was reading too much into it.

The doctor glanced up but didn't seem concerned. A nurse set a blanket over the baby and wiped off most of the blood, and Eric lifted him as another nurse set a white cotton hat on his head. Eric stood up, and Abby lay back down, the head of the bed raised as high as it could go, as a nurse started to check her vitals.

"We're going to get you moved and settled pretty quickly. You should be able to go home at the end of the day," the doctor said.

Eric held his newborn baby, so tiny, in the crook of his arm. He flicked his gaze away from his quiet son, who had yet to make a peep. He had round cheeks and a pink face with a tiny button nose just like his mama's. His eyes were still closed. Eric smiled until he noticed Abby looking away, appearing uninterested in what the doctor was saying. Eric added, "How about some sleep first? With Rachel at home, we risk a very happy two-year-old climbing all over Mommy. I don't think Abby is anxious to get back just yet."

"It's all right, Eric. I just need some sleep," she said from where she lay, turning her head toward him.

It had been ten days since Eric stepped off the destroyer in homeport, met by his very pregnant wife, Abby, and their two-year-old plump little girl, Rachel, whom he had delivered after rescuing Abby in the middle of nowhere in the Persian Gulf. She had escaped her abductor, Seyed Hossein, the man who'd bought her, kept her, and abused her until, one night, she escaped. She had been eight months pregnant. Abby was a human trafficking success story. Of the women who disappeared in Europe, most were never found again, but Eric had found her and saved her, and she was now his wife.

Rachel had dark hair and olive skin, and she didn't resemble Eric at all, with only hints of Abby. She was the only reminder of what Abby had survived, and Eric loved the precious little girl as if she were his very own.

Eric cuddled his son, a light-haired baby who fit in the crook of his arm. He glanced down at Abby, and her eyes were closed. The baby was settled and seemed so comfortable, as if he knew his daddy would always keep him safe. His tiny hand rested over his eyes, and he started to work his lips.

Eric was about to wake Abby when the doctor said, "No, let her sleep. The baby's good. We'll send him into the nursery, and the nurses can give him a supplement of formula if he needs it."

There was a tap on the door, and a nurse poked her head in. "Captain Hamilton, there are people out here to see you."

Eric started to the door because he knew who was out there. "Well, let me go show off my son," he said, heading to meet his old friend Joe, who was his current XO, and his wife, Mary-Margaret.

SHE COULD SMELL THE BLOOD, the antiseptic, and hear voices: deep, low, close whispers. She told herself to pretend to be asleep, to concentrate, to keep breathing in and out, nice and easy. She relaxed her eyelids. She couldn't let them see she was awake. The floor squeaked with footsteps, and the door closed. She heard someone walking away just outside the door, but she also knew someone was still there, waiting quietly in the corner. She felt as if she had suddenly been thrown into the middle of a cat-and-mouse game, and she could feel the room, the locked door, the stiff mattress she lay on. She was so cold, and, try as she might, she couldn't stop the chill that racked her body. She trembled.

A hand touched her, and she jumped. Her eyes flew open, and she gasped at the dark-haired woman standing over her. Who was she? Where was she? She winced as she sat up. The woman's hand was still on her shoulder, and she took in the small, box-like hospital room. It was dim, though the curtains were open.

"Are you okay?" the woman asked. She was wearing a pink scrub top, and Abby stared at the V cut of the neck and wondered why the woman hadn't covered herself. She had pale bare arms, too, and she took Abby's wrist and glanced at her watch. Abby stared at the door—a locked door, or was it?

The door opened, and Eric, her tall, dark-haired husband with vibrant brown eyes, entered and frowned. "Abby, you're awake," he said. "I just showed off our son to Joe and Mary-Margaret. They're here now, and they wanted to come in and see you, but I thought you were sleeping." He glanced down at the tiny baby in his arms. Eric was so happy, as if he was staring at the most precious thing ever. He was so strong, her husband, her man. He was out of uniform, wearing blue jeans and a snug black T-shirt that showed off the finest biceps, triceps, and six-pack abs, as well as the rock-hard chest that had always comforted her.

She watched as he held his son, and her heart pounded

with each step closer he took. She couldn't take her eyes off the blanket and the bundle he was holding. She couldn't see it—she didn't want to see it. She feared the face that would stare back at her. His footsteps became slow and drawn out, and all she could hear was an echo as they came closer. She could feel a pressure on her arm as she stared at the blur in front of her: white, closer now. There was a hand on her face, touching her, warm and strong and familiar, and she grabbed hold.

"Abby! Abby..."

She could hear him, and she stared into a demanding, strong, and a worried expression. Another man appeared, with glasses and light hair. A light flashed in her eyes, and it burned. She pushed his hand away.

"I'm okay," she said to a room that seemed suddenly full of people: nurses, doctors. The lights were on now, bright above her.

"Abby, what happened?" It was Eric. He was beside her on the bed, his arm around her. She leaned against him, just him, no baby. Then she looked up at the dark-haired nurse holding her son. She pulled back the blanket and the wool cap on his head, and Abby sagged in relief at his light red chubby cheeks and the light hair plastered to his head.

About the Author

With flawed strong characters, characters you can relate to, New York Times & USA Today Bestselling Author Lorhainne Eckhart writes the kind of books she wants to read. She is frequently a Top 100 bestselling author in multiple genres, and her second book ever published, The Forgotten Child, is no exception. With close to 900 reviews on Amazon, translated into German and French, this book was such a hit that the long running Friessen Family series was born. Now with over sixty titles and multiple series under her belt her big family romance series are loved by fans worldwide. A recipient of the 2013, 2015 and 2016 Readers' Favorite Award for Suspense and Romance, Lorhainne lives in the sunny west-coast Gulf Island of Salt Spring Island, is the mother of three, her oldest suffers from autism and she is an advocate for never giving up on your dreams.

Lorhainne loves to hear from her readers! You can connect with me at:
www.LorhainneEckhart.com
Lorhainne@LorhainneEckhart.com

Also by Lorhainne Eckhart

The Outsider Series
The Forgotten Child (Brad and Emily)
A Baby and a Wedding *(An Outsider Series Short)*
Fallen Hero (Andy, Jed, and Diana)
The Search *(An Outsider Series Short)*
The Awakening (Andy and Laura)
Secrets (Jed and Diana)
Runaway (Andy and Laura)
Overdue *(An Outsider Series Short)*
The Unexpected Storm (Neil and Candy)
The Wedding (Neil and Candy)

The Friessens: A New Beginning
The Deadline (Andy and Laura)
The Price to Love (Neil and Candy)
A Different Kind of Love (Brad and Emily)
A Vow of Love, A Friessen Family Christmas

The Friessens
The Reunion
The Bloodline (Andy & Laura)
The Promise (Diana & Jed)
The Business Plan (Neil & Candy)
The Decision (Brad & Emily)
First Love (Katy)
Family First
Leave the Light On

The Friessens will return October 2017

The McCabe Brothers
Don't Stop Me (Vic)
Don't Catch Me (Chase)
Don't Run From Me (Aaron)
Don't Hide From Me (Luc)

The Wilde Brothers
The One (Joe and Margaret)
The Honeymoon, A Wilde Brothers Short
Friendly Fire (Logan and Julia)
Not Quite Married, A Wilde Brothers Short
A Matter of Trust (Ben and Carrie)
The Reckoning, A Wilde Brothers Christmas
Traded (Jake)
Unforgiven (Samuel)
The Wilde Brothers: The Complete Collection now available in print!

Married in Montana
His Promise
Love's Promise
A Promise of Forever

The Parker Sisters
Thrill of the Chase
The Dating Game
Play Hard to Get
What We Can't Have
Go Your Own Way

Kate & Walker
One Night
Edge of Night
Last Night

Walk the Right Road Series
The Choice
Lost and Found
Merkaba
Bounty
Blown Away: The Final Chapter

The Saved Series
Saved
Vanished
Captured

Single Titles
He Came Back
Loving Christine

For my German Readers
Die Außenseiter-Reihe
Der Vergessene Junge
Der Gefallene Held

For my French Readers
L'ENFANT OUBLIÉ

Printed in Great Britain
by Amazon